LEAF & SCALE

1

# THE STORMBORNE VINE

## TILLY WALLACE

ebook ISBN: 978-1-0670381-1-3

Print ISBN: 978-1-0670381-3-7

v27012025

Cover design by Malice & Mayhem Book Covers

Editing and proofreading by the team at Kat's Literary Services

To be the first to hear about Tilly's new releases and exclusive offers, sign up at:

https://www.tillywallace.com/newsletter

A MOMENT PLEASE...

**This book is written in British English**, with the odd Kiwi idiom—if I can sneak them in without my wonderful editor noticing!

You cannot offer me enough coffee, or jam & cream scones to prise that extra 'u', 'l' or 's' instead of 'z' from me.

These books are based in England, Scotland, or New Zealand—where we speak British English.

As the old saying goes... *when in Rome....*

# CHAPTER 1



*Nemython House, Drake's Bend. England.*

SOME PEOPLE WALK an easy path through life. One that is paved with marble tiles, fragrant lavender grows at the edges, and fluffy lambs gambol around them while nightingales sing. Then there are others like Fern Oakby. She navigated a shadowy path with treacherous footing. One overgrown with brambles and firethorn as an untuned violin screeched from the trees.

As she pulled a one-inch-long needle-like thorn, belonging to the scarlet *Pyracantha coccinea* from her hand, Fern considered the decisions she had made ten years ago during her debut in London. She had once stood at a fork in the path and decided to strike off down the more adventurous-looking road.

"I could have had a noble husband and gardeners to do the weeding, you know," she told the plant that had stabbed her. Since she had the long thorn between thumb and fore-finger like a needle, she used it to scrape stubborn dirt out from under her nails. Then the barb was tossed into the soil.

Her work brought her a sense of satisfaction and content-ment, even if her path was a difficult and lonely one at times. In truth, Fern loved getting her hands dirty and wouldn't trade her freedom for the suffocation of a gilded cage.

Society expected gently bred women to look decorative, do needlework, and produce heirs. If they fell onto hard times, seeking employment as a companion or governess was deemed acceptable. But Fern, *literally*, dirtied her hands through her work as a plantswoman. She used the botanical knowledge gained at her father's side to support her house-hold by supplying grand estates with rare and exotic plants or figuring out solutions to gardening woes others couldn't solve. She also sold ingredients to alchemists and apothecaries.

After a few months of a season in London all those years ago, Fern had retreated to their home, Nemython House, situated in the south-west corner of the picturesque village of Drake's Bend. The walled garden crammed with trees, shrubs, annuals, and perennials had become her sanctuary. Fern had thrown herself into the study of plants. The high stone walls and surrounding forest kept the world at bay. Or rather, it kept the prying and judgemental eyes of society out.

Fern knelt back on her heels and surveyed her work. She had cleared pesky weeds creeping under the rare lunanavis. The firethorn stood guard beside it. A moment of inattention had seen Fern brush her hand too close to the vicious shrub with its wicked barbs. In many ways, it was like a matron at a ball—lingering at the back, watching, and using her tongue as a weapon to strike down the unwary.

Ten years ago, Fern's father, a renowned botanist, had brought the tiny lunanavis seedling back from one of his many expeditions overseas and planted it in their garden. They had tended it together, watching it grow. A vigil she had taken up alone since his death five years ago.

A shrub with a naturally rounded shape, the lunanavis had taken years to reach its mature size of some three-feet tall and had grey, furry leaves not unlike the lamb's ear, *Stachys byzantina*. At last, after a decade of patience, nine slender flower buds had pushed through the dense mass of leaves.

The plant's habit had a pleasing symmetry. Three flowers would bloom for three nights under a full moon, for the three months of spring. Then the shrub would become dormant until the next year. After blooming just the once, its flowers would shut tight at the first blush of dawn and remain closed, leaving the next three to bloom the following night. The precious pistil, the reproductive organ of the plant, would be highly sought after once fertilised by moon dust.

Satisfied that everything was perfect for the flowers' debut that night, there was little more Fern could do. The plant didn't know it, but it would be the star of a private viewing for her little family. Once night fell, they would gather to watch it greet the moon.

Fern headed back along the paths to the house, imagining her father's ghost walking beside her. Rowan Oakby had passed his love of flora to his daughter—along with a name plucked from nature. He had travelled to the corners of the globe gathering rare and unusual plants. Every leaf and blossom Fern touched was a tiny piece of him that still lingered in the world.

On a bench by the kitchen door sat a bowl of water, a bar of soap, and a towel. Fern scrubbed at her hands and dried them before tipping the water over a nearby moisture-loving lily.

Heading inside, work was underway for the evening meal. Mrs Bentley, the older woman who ran the kitchen, rolled out dough at the long bench that ran under the window. A slight woman with an olive complexion, her once-raven hair was laced with silver, and she had been a fixture of their home for as long as Fern could remember.

"Dinner won't be long. I'm about to add the dumplings. You have time to change out of those filthy clothes." She picked up a long knife, either to ensure Fern complied or to slice the dumplings into even shapes before laying them in the oven to cook.

"I wouldn't dream of sitting down to dinner at your table in dirty trousers, Mrs Bentley." Fern hurried through to the main part of the house before the housekeeper waved the lethal knife at her head.

As she took the stairs two at a time with a long stride, Fern was grateful that she lived far enough away from London that she could wear trousers. In her room, she stripped off her dirt-stained clothes and rubbed at her skin with a damp cloth before dressing once more. This time, she donned a gown of light wool in a pale greyish-green that reminded her of silver foliage. She drew a brush through her short auburn hair and released a twig that had somehow become tangled in there.

Clean, and almost civilised appearing apart from her bare feet, she padded down to the dining room. Breakfast was a casual affair, always taken in the kitchen at the worn oak table. Dinner was held in the room painted a deep green at a polished table that only sat six at most.

Fern paused at the doorway, her two uncles already within. Their bodies angled towards one another as they discussed their day while they waited for her. They were an unconventional household. The spinster of nearly thirty years old, living with two older gentlemen. One uncle by blood on her mother's side, and the other an uncle by bonds of love. Or whom society euphemistically referred to as her uncle's *good chum*.

Of average height and lean, Ambrose had the Reid family red hair (which had faded to a burnished gold as he aged), styled in an elegant fashion, and sparkling hazel eyes. He sat at the head of the table. To his right was George Hawkins. A barrel-chested man with a luxurious beard streaked with silver.

Once the heir to a viscount, George lived a quiet life as a dead man. Thankfully, not actually dead, as Fern loved him dearly, and the Fates had snatched too many loved ones from her grasp. George gave up his wealth and a title for love. His hate-filled family declared him dead, held a modest funeral (closed coffin, since it was weighted with rocks), and his younger brother became the heir and viscount.

"Ah, just in time." Ambrose smiled as Fern took her seat beside him.

"Mrs Bentley had a firm grip on that knife she loves when I came in earlier and she hurried me along." Fern flicked open her napkin and draped it over her lap. She inhaled the aromas wafting from the meal laid out on the table. Butter slid over potatoes sprinkled with rosemary and left a golden trail. Fat, fluffy dumplings were piled on another plate and were begging to be smothered with gravy.

George stood to carve a leg of lamb and picked up the meat fork and knife. "I'm surprised you're not camped out with that plant."

Fern had briefly considered the idea, but there was no point. Nature had decreed it would only bloom by the light of the moon, and prising open the petals to satisfy her curiosity would ruin its delicate beauty. "It won't open until after dark. I can wait."

"Your mother had no patience at all. Once, an aunt wrote to say she had a small gift for Delfie. Unable to wait until our aunt visited, she set off on foot to collect it. Delfie was six years old, and our aunt lived twenty miles away." Ambrose chuckled at the memory of his younger sibling marching off across the countryside.

Fern's mother had rushed through life headlong, eager to experience all she could. A trait Fern had inherited. Although she had learned a small amount of caution over the years. "I have no patience with people. Plants are different."

By the time they had finished dinner, dusk had fallen outside. Before full dark settled over the countryside, George fetched three wooden chairs from the greenhouse. While he had been born into nobility like Fern's father, he also preferred to use his hands. In George's case, he had a natural talent for woodwork and had crafted the outdoor chairs so that Fern could enjoy the garden.

Ambrose fetched cushions covered in canvas from a chest by the back door. He picked a thick one and placed it on the chair where George would sit.

"For all his size, he likes something soft under his bottom," he murmured and winked at Fern.

Fern had gathered woollen blankets from inside to ward off the night chill. While it was spring, the air lost all warmth once the sun disappeared.

Ambrose disappeared into the house and returned carrying a tray. "Hot chocolate for you, beloved niece, and a special coffee for George and I."

Fern settled on her chair and held her mug in two hands. She enjoyed the spicy aroma of the brew before taking a sip. Ambrose made the best hot chocolate with a secret blend of spices that he refused to divulge. While their special coffee had a not-so-secret ingredient—a liberal pour of whiskey.

The three of them sat in companionable silence, lost in their thoughts under a sky scattered with stars. The night deepened around them, and like a diva making her grand entrance, the moon rose from behind the trees. When the silver orb reached its highest point, Fern set her mug down on the ground and got out of her chair to kneel on a cushion before the lunanavis like a worshipper before an icon.

The buds unfurled with a whisper. One by one, the petals peeled wide open until they were nearly horizontal. The dark-grey outer concealed a creamy inner that reflected the moon's radiance. While Fern had studied drawings of the plant in bloom, it paled in comparison to the wonder of seeing it before her eyes.

"It's beautiful," she murmured in a voice tinged with wonder. "The petals are like points on a compass rose."

The flowers were breathtaking. Each one a perfect compass rose, with eight petals pointing to the cardinal and ordinal directions. In the middle of the flower jutted a tall and slender stalk of some three inches that seemed to be made of silver. The stalk was attached to the plant's unseen ovary, hidden in the base of the flower. It had no visible stigma to collect pollen, since it was fertilised in an unusual way—moonlight.

"Lunanavis. Luna for moon. Navis for ship or navigation. The plant's name reflects its compass rose-like appearance and lunar blooming cycle. It is said there is a spell that can be brewed with the needle-like stalk that will point to whatever the seeker desires." Fern recited the passage about the plant contained in one of her botany books.

"It is a wonder. What a shame its blooms are so fleeting and cannot be enjoyed inside," Ambrose said.

"That's why they're so valuable." George leaned forwards in his chair.

"I am a monster, that I must cut down such a marvellous thing to line our pockets." Beside the plant sat a basket and a cloth. The fabric was draped over a pair of secateurs in a similar way to how an executioner would hide their axe behind their back. Once the moonlight had pollinated the flower, Fern would snip the blooms from the shrub. Then she would use a knife to cut away the entire pistil.

"The filthy world of commerce destroys the natural world in order to meet the shallow demands of greedy people.

I shall turn that into an essay for the *Midnight Chronicle*," Ambrose mused from his chair.

"People need to eat and have roofs over their heads. How do you do that without cutting down a few trees or roasting a delicious leg of lamb?" George had a more practical approach to life.

Fern considered how to meet the needs of people without losing the beauty all around them. "We find the balance. While it pains me to pick the blooms, I will leave those from the third night to set seed, so that I can propagate more plants." But she wouldn't make too many plants available. There was another sort of balance. While the plant remained rare and difficult to grow, it ensured a small and highly valuable market for its needle-like stalk. If Fern sold too many seeds or juvenile plants, she would increase the supply of pistils.

As minutes elapsed, accompanied by the hoot of a hunting owl, three blooms fully opened. The petals glowed with the moon's caress, and the stalk reflected a metallic glint. Nature was truly wondrous.

"Father should have been here to witness this. Life's not fair." Tears burned in Fern's eyes. With a corner of the blanket, she wiped them away.

"No. It's not fair. It's like a game of cards. You can only play the ones you are dealt, and sometimes, the Fates stack the deck against you." George reached out to squeeze her shoulder.

"Both your parents should have been here to see this. But I have no doubt that Rowan and Delfie are looking down on us tonight." Ambrose's clear voice carried on the still air.

It comforted Fern to think her parents were reunited in death. But it hurt to navigate life without their love and guiding presence. Why couldn't they have been together on her side of the veil? Why was she deprived of two loving parents, while others who were cold and heartless, lived on?

"None of us know how much time the Fates will gift us. That's why we grab hold of the good we find in this world." George fixed a long stare on the man who had walked beside him for more than three decades.

"I shall remind you of that next time you claim I have hogged all the blankets." Ambrose winked at George, and the large man's shoulders heaved in silent laughter at some private joke.

"I am grateful to have both of you. It eases the loss of Mother and Father a fraction." Fern had an abundance of love for the couple. They were a splendid example of a long-lasting romance that had weathered the many storms life threw at them. The challenges and prejudices they faced could have made them bitter. Instead, they made them stronger.

Ambrose rose from his chair and tugged the blanket closer around his shoulders. "While the flowers are gorgeous to behold, unless they are going to start singing or dancing, I am off to my bed. I need a few hours of beauty sleep before I greet the morning."

George also stood and collected the empty mugs. He paused beside Fern. "Are you going to stand guard all night or go to bed as well?"

"I will stay a little longer before I must cut the flowers."

Fern almost whispered the last three words, worried the plant might hear her and snap its blooms shut and sulk.

"We shall see you at breakfast, then," George said.

They said their goodnights, and the two men returned to the house. Silence draped itself around Fern. On her cushion, she hugged her knees to her chest and stared at the luminous petals. Invisible to her eye, moon dust settled on the stalk and its stigma to pollinate the flower. If she gave the pistil to a magic caster or alchemist to brew her a potion to point to her heart's desire, who or what would she find?

# CHAPTER 2

When a chill settled in Fern's bones and wouldn't budge, and her eyelids grew heavier, she realised the time had come to harvest the rare blooms. She slid one hand under the fabric bundled in the basket and lifted out her secateurs. Still, her hand hesitated, reluctant to pluck what had taken years to form.

"This will keep us in cheese for a month," she reminded herself.

They needed to eat, and the flowers would enable that. Reassuring herself that the plant would have many more flowers in the months and years to come, Fern cut the three open blooms before she changed her mind. Then she placed them in the basket and draped the fabric over them.

"I shall see you tomorrow night," she whispered to the six remaining closed buds.

Back in the house, Fern toed off her boots and made her way to her study with its view of the garden. The shelves were full of leather-bound books, and delicate botanical drawings were pinned to the walls.

She set the basket down on her desk and ensured the curtains remained tightly drawn so that no light would ruin the nocturnal flowers. Then she lit two candelabra and placed them on either side of her desk. The unique scent of the blooms filled the small room. A salty odour, as though they had been drawn from the ocean, but with an underlying tang of lemon.

Before reaching for her sketchbook and pencil, Fern drew a deep breath of the refreshing fragrance that reminded her of a long-ago trip to the ocean with her father. The aroma would go in her notes about the plant. Pulling back the cotton, she placed the flowers before her and drew, capturing every intricate detail of the moon-kissed structures.

She lost herself in her work. First drawing the flowers. Then she preserved one bloom between sheets of parchment in the press. Finally, she drew out a sharp knife and carefully sliced the pistil free from the two remaining flowers. They were laid on a plate to dry in a dark vented cupboard. The flowers were bound with string and hung upside down in the cupboard above the pistils. Every part of the flower would be sold to those who brewed potions with the rare ingredients.

Satisfied with her work, Fern blew out the candles and sought her bed for a few hours' sleep.

THE NEXT MORNING, Fern startled awake as the sun thrust its way between her curtains.

"No! The flowers!" Thinking she had nodded off at her desk, she flung out her arms, ready to defend the nocturnal blooms with her body. Only to discover she was wrestling her blankets.

Having been rudely jolted from sleep, she didn't see much sense in lying in bed. Once dressed, she padded down to the kitchen. She paused on the threshold to the heart of their home. Nobles could have their cold dining rooms with footmen standing sentry. Fern and her uncles preferred to have breakfast in the kitchen, with its row of mullioned windows overlooking the garden that caught the morning sun and the slate floor soaking up the warmth.

George sat at the old oak table in the middle of the kitchen, nursing a large mug of coffee as he read the newspaper.

Mrs Bentley stood at the range. "Take a seat, my dear. Your uncle will serve." She used a wooden spoon like a conductor used a baton and pointed from Fern to table to Ambrose, who stood by the window watching birds splash in the small pond.

"Ready to serve, Mrs B." Ambrose turned and slid his hands under two plates. One was deposited in front of Fern as she took her seat. The other plate was placed before George.

Fern picked up her cutlery and used her knife to lift the slices of bacon aside to reveal a bright-yellow egg perched on a thick slab of toast.

As they ate breakfast, conversation roamed over several

topics. They settled on the one subject where George and Ambrose disagreed and which resulted in gentle argument. George, ever the pragmatist, was a student of science. While Ambrose, with his more romantic soul, championed the cause of alchemy and magic.

"The annual census of dragon numbers has been published, and yet again, there are fewer than last year. Tell me, George, what is responsible if not some malevolent magical force?" Ambrose waved a buttered crumpet at the column on one page of the open newspaper. The list detailed sightings in each district.

George snorted and lowered his cutlery. "Simple. Over-hunting by humans, accidents, loss of habitat, and disease. There's no need for any of your fanciful ideas about curses. The creatures serve no practical purpose whatsoever, and their time on this earth has simply run out."

Fern chewed her toast and couldn't decide if she sided with Ambrose or George. The child within her was fascinated by dragons and found the idea of their very existence magical, just like Ambrose did. The botanist within her agreed that more mundane reasons were probably behind the dwindling numbers. Sometimes, a plant reached the end of its lifespan and sank back into the ground. Like annuals that only enjoyed one summer basking in the sun.

George swallowed a mouthful of bacon before continuing. "If dragons truly were magical like you insist, why don't they just conjure up a solution to their problems?"

Ambrose blew out an exasperated sigh and set down the remains of his crumpet so he could gesture with his hands. "Magic, like all things, has its limits. Perhaps dragons cannot cure whatever ails their species themselves, but need someone else to do it."

"If the three witches can't come up with a cure, then your scaled friends are doomed." George huffed, the sound laced with scepticism.

The *three witches* were a trio of local sisters who could cast magic and who bore an uncanny resemblance to the crones from Macbeth. Fern wondered if anyone in government had sought their advice about the dragon problem. Probably not.

She mulled over the slow disappearance of the majestic creatures, that had first been noticed some years ago. It seemed as though magic and science were two ends of a seesaw. As factories rose with chimney stacks stabbing the air and belching coal smoke, dragons were lost from the sky and returned to the earth.

"Couldn't we find balance in this, like we discussed last night with commerce and nature? There must be a way for science and magic to co-exist. Otherwise, we lose something when one seeks to erase the other," Fern said.

George took a deep drink of his coffee before speaking. "Such is the way of the world. Science pulls back the curtain from things once considered magical or mysterious, and we discover the rational explanation behind it. Like how salt added to pork gives us bacon. As a child, you thought bacon was magic. Now you are older, and you know it is created by a scientific process."

Ambrose shook his head at his partner and tsked under his breath. "And when everything is rational and scientific, what a cold and uninspired world we shall live in. Don't ever let go of magic, Fern, no matter what men like George say. Or how much they try to sway you with bacon."

Fern liked bacon and was thankful that some inventive person discovered that salted pork, once thinly sliced, became the most delicious thing to eat. She also marvelled every time she heard the heavy wing beat of a dragon in the distance. Why couldn't scientific discovery and the wonder of magic *both* have a place in their world like they did in her heart?

That made her think of chocolate-covered bacon. That would be both scientific and wondrous.

After breakfast, Fern headed out to her greenhouse that hunkered along one side of the embracing wall. She collected her leather gloves, a trowel, and a wheelbarrow. With her favourite tool in hand she set to work, kneeling amongst the vibrant flora as though she explored a miniature jungle. The sun warmed her back as she carefully weeded around delicate plants and ensured they had room to grow and flourish. Over-exuberant shrubs were given a light prune so that every plant had its chance to thrive. A camellia with yellowing leaves needed a drink of water mixed with Epsom salts.

As she worked, Fern's thoughts lingered on the breakfast conversation. "Why can't magic and science work together?" she asked an aquilegia with blooms the colour of strong coffee.

Just then a shadow passed overhead, causing her to look up. A dragon flew high above. Its body was the size of a large carriage, and pale-blue scales on its belly blended with the sky and clouds. Only its movement and the slight difference in hue made it visible. Powerful wings carried the creature towards the surrounding forest. Fern paused, transfixed by the sight.

Regardless of what George believed, how could anyone say such a creature was only flesh and blood? There had to be something magical about their very existence. She couldn't recall the last time a dragon had been spotted so close to the village. Possibly not since her father died.

Sadness trickled through her that dragons would soon be lost from their world. Why did no one seem to care? While the annual census noted the decline in numbers, no scientists were investigating the reasons *why*. They were too busy playing with electricity and the new-fangled steam engines.

"Perhaps George is right," she said to the retreating shape. "The time of myth is over, and the era of industry will take your place."

Why did that idea make her eyes mist with tears? She blinked them away. There was nothing else for it. *She* would have to figure out why dragons were disappearing, using the same process she used with a sick shrub. That meant identifying any pests that might be attacking the root or leaves, and finding the ideal spot and conditions to allow it to thrive. Dragons might simply need relocating to a new home that better met their needs, or a bit of fertiliser.

"I will ask Ambrose for books on the topic." Flora was her area of particular interest, but she would branch out into fauna if it meant saving the rare creatures.

As the day wore on and Fern laboured in the extensive garden, sweat and grime trickled over her muscles. When the sun moved past its zenith and nudged into late afternoon, she decided it was time to move indoors.

"I need a bath," she muttered as she sniffed one armpit, then peeled off her gardening gloves to examine dirt-streaked hands. The callouses and roughened skin of her palms were a far cry from the delicate, pampered hands expected of a young woman of her breeding. But they were a testament to the life she had forged for herself.

Fern toed off her dirty boots at the door and entered the kitchen on her stocking-clad feet. Mrs Bentley and her oldest daughter, Alice, were busy preparing dinner. The house-keeper turned and waved the ever-present large knife at Fern's head. "You'll be needing a bath."

Mrs Bentley might be small of stature but no one, not even George, crossed her. Especially when she was wielding the knife.

"That was exactly my plan, Mrs Bentley. I will get the bath down if you'll start heating water, please," Fern said, as she walked towards the narrow door to the laundry attached to the kitchen.

The laundry had the same worn slate floor as the kitchen and one square window set in the middle of the wall. The old glass allowed light to penetrate, but it presented a distorted and bubble-filled view if you tried to peer through it. In one corner of the room stood the enormous wooden barrel with a crank attached that turned paddles to agitate the washing within. It was an ingenious creation devised by George that made the arduous task of laundry slightly less back-breaking. Next to the barrel was the mangle, a piece of equipment that could have been stolen from a torture chamber. The metal rollers squeezed water from clothing and sheets before they were hung on the line to dry in the sun.

A tin bath hung on a hook on the wall beside the door. Since it wasn't heavy, just bulky, Fern stood on an old ladder-back chair to fetch it down. She set the bath under the square window. Next, she found a bar of soap in the cupboard and a clean towel, laying them out on the chair she had positioned next to the tub.

Alice carried hot water from the kitchen and poured it into the tub.

"I'll go upstairs and fetch some clean clothes," Fern called to Mrs Bentley as she headed across the kitchen.

"Oh no you won't. Sit yourself down right there. Alice will fetch you a dressing gown." Mrs Bentley commanded her daughter when she returned the empty pot.

"I shall take over from Alice filling the bath, then." Fern grabbed a hand towel and folded it into quarters, ready to insulate her hands against the hot handles.

"Sit. Down." Mrs Bentley enunciated each word slowly and didn't need the knife to convey she wouldn't be defied.

"I feel useless," Fern complained as she dropped into the closest chair, unwilling to risk the ire of the older woman.

"Your sort are supposed to be useless." The housekeeper chuckled.

"Noble or dirty?" Fern wasn't sure which *sort* she was in her current state.

"Both. I'll not have you dropping dirt on my freshly beaten rugs and swept floors. What would your uncle say if he saw you carting water for a bath?" She set another pot to boil.

Fern's Uncle Ambrose would expect her to help. Therefore, Mrs Bentley must mean her other uncle—her father's older brother...the earl. "Given the earl has declared me *persona non grata*, he wouldn't say a word since I no longer exist to him."

The housekeeper stared at her for a long moment, then she laughed. "Get away with you." She flapped the cloth in her hands, as though Fern was an errant chicken in need of shooing out of the vegetable patch.

Alice soon returned with the robe and carted pots back and forth between the kitchen and washhouse. Fern studied the dragon census and swallowed her guilt at not helping.

"All done," Alice announced some time later.

"Thank you." Fern set aside the newspaper and shut herself in the washroom before shedding her dirty clothes to the floor. She sighed as she stepped into the steaming tub and settled her long frame into the small space. The first thing she did was immerse her head to wash the sweat from her scalp.

Her mother and Ambrose both had flame-red hair. In Fern, the red had been tempered by the dark and earthy colouring of the Oakbys. As a result, her hair was a deep brown shot through with auburn. For convenience, she kept her hair cropped short, and it curled by her nape. Short hair meant she didn't have to manage fancy hairstyles, and it was less annoying when working outside in all sorts of weather.

Once her hair was washed and rinsed, Fern turned her attention to the rest of her. The water had gone tepid and murky with soil by the time she climbed out and dried herself, checking her arms for any sign of sunburn. She had been cursed with the Reid family pale skin that burned easily, and she grew an aloe vera plant to soothe any angry patches she discovered after too long outside. Satisfied that she didn't need to break a leaf today for the healing sap, she slipped into the dressing gown and padded back through the kitchen.

"You look as red as Mr Reid's hair." Mrs Bentley chuckled as she opened the oven door to check on dinner.

"Blasted skin. I wish I had the darker colouring of Father and you, Mrs Bentley. Then I wouldn't burn so easily," Fern grumbled.

"If you didn't burn, you would never come back inside." The older woman winked.

Fern laughed. The housekeeper had a point. She was happiest outside, and only the wrath of the sun drove her inside. "I could always start carrying a parasol like a proper lady?"

Mrs Bentley and Alice both snorted in laughter, and even Fern chuckled at the idea of her behaving *proper*.

# CHAPTER 3

Fᴇʀɴ sᴋɪᴘᴘᴇᴅ through the kitchen into the main part of the house and then headed up the stairs to her bedroom. From the open wardrobe, she selected a fresh dress. One of plain cream muslin, which had no embellishment apart from a row of tiny lavender heads embroidered along the hem. She didn't wear trousers *all* the time but enjoyed the freedom to choose whatever clothing suited her mood and activity.

Returning downstairs, still with bare feet, Fern entered the cosy parlour at the front of the house. Ambrose sat in a chair, catching the last of the fading sun. A large book was open on his lap.

"Ah, my favourite person!" Ambrose greeted her with a theatrical flourish.

"I thought George was your favourite person?" She wondered what it took to remain devoted to someone for over thirty years. How many arguments had erupted and been resolved over the decades? Her only experience had proven love to be a shallow and fleeting thing.

A rare frown crossed Ambrose's handsome face. "Not currently. He used my periodical to squash a spider. Which ruined both the spider's day and my reading material. After your bath you look positively radiant, as though you are ready to attend a ball. Just like Cinderella." He put a bookmark on the page and closed the book to give her his full attention.

"No dance outside of our village would admit me, even if I possessed a magical gown." Fern flopped to the sofa closest to her uncle and tucked her feet up under her in yet another scandalous behaviour of hers—bare feet on the sofa. Once society had painted her as a fallen woman, she decided to lean into the reputation.

Ambrose's eyes sparkled with mischief. "Isn't it freeing though, when you no longer give a fig what a bunch of stuffy old matrons in London think?"

Once, as a wide-eyed debutante, she had thought her world revolved around what those matrons thought of her. Then the illusion of love had shattered that regard.

"I find trousers freeing." Fern circled a patch on the arm of the sofa with a fingertip.

Ambrose chuckled. "Trousers are far more practical, if unseemly, to walk the thorny path you have chosen. But George and I worry that you might be lonely stuck out here in Drake's Bend."

Fern snorted. "I don't have time to be lonely. My occupation keeps both my mind and hands busy. That is more than most noble women can say." Her muscles ached with the weariness of a day's labour in the garden. If she fell into bed exhausted each night, she didn't have time to consider if her life lacked anything else.

"Mind, body, and soul, Fern." He touched his head, torso, and then moved his hand to the left side of his chest. "What of your heart? Do you not wish to find a special someone?"

She had. Once. It did not end well. "I have tasted love and found it a bitter fruit."

Ambrose's keen hazel gaze fixed on her, and he rested his chin on one raised hand. "You loved, but you were not loved in return by that...*cad*. When you find a love such as your father and Delfie had, or George and I..." His voice trailed off, and a faraway look entered his eyes. "Well, you face obstacles together. You do not use the other person in such a cruel fashion."

"What is done is done, Uncle, and I can't regret it. What sort of life would I have led as a noble wife, anyway? My sole occupation would be embroidering handkerchiefs and breeding. Reading a horticultural magazine would have been the closest I would have been allowed to gardening. My days an empty parade of shallow social events. No, I rather think Lord Talbot made the best choice for both of us." She had read the newspapers. Indeed, in those first months when the wound to her heart was raw, she couldn't help herself. She devoured every detail of the highly anticipated wedding of the man she once loved to a ridiculously wealthy and haughty woman. Then her replacement exceeded all expectations by producing an heir, a spare, and a girl in just five short years.

"You should have friends your own age." It seemed her uncle was not done with the topic.

Fern squirmed on the sofa. "I have many friends in Drake's Bend."

That loving but sharp gaze never wavered from her face.

"You know what I mean. The trio, as bewitching as they are, are not the sort of friends I mean. You are young and should be off having wild adventures with a group of friends."

"Firstly, I rather think *one* wild adventure was quite enough, thank you. Secondly, a group of friends? I'd struggle to find even one. We both know that no well-bred woman could dare to be seen with me, or she would be tainted by the stench of scandal that will always cling to me." When her uncle, the earl, had sponsored her debut in London, Fern had been surrounded by new friends. But it transpired those relationships were as delicate and easily damaged as camellia petals.

Before Ambrose could muster an argument for her venturing beyond the village's boundary in search of companions, Fern jumped to her feet. "I like the friends I have in the village. None of them judge me for either my behaviour or trouser wearing."

Ambrose arched a pale reddish-blond eyebrow but let the matter rest.

After a quiet dinner, George placed a mug of hot chocolate in her hands, and Ambrose shooed her out of the dining room. It was her routine to spend the evenings in her study, engrossed in the latest horticultural news from around the world while the two men played chess or backgammon.

Tonight, their conversation about dragons declining in numbers sparked a memory. She pulled down a bundle of her father's old notebooks. The books detailed his travels around the world and his botanical findings. Sorting through them, she found the last one that had been beside him on the desk at the time of his death.

Fern read and re-read her father's journals, hoping for some clue as to what happened that fatal day. Hope burned inside her that one day, she could clear her father's name. Others believe he took his own life by drinking a poisonous concoction, unable to carry on without his beloved wife. Fern suspected another hand had slipped the toxin into his tea.

If only she could prove it.

Opening the cover, she traced a fingertip over the drawing on the front page—a dragon curled around a rowan tree. Not just any sub-species of rowan tree either, but the rare *Sorbus celmsgeul*. Its scientific name drawn from two old words. Cèl, meaning mystic or hidden, and sgeul, or story. Commonly, it was known as the kelmsgale.

That tree had been the reason her father had settled in the quiet little village. At its heart stood an ancient specimen that had seen kings rise and fall. The tree was the last of five that had formed a natural nemeton.

Tucked into the notebook was a large sheet of folded paper. Fern laid it on the desk to reveal a map of England. Over its surface, her father had drawn the known stands of kelmsgales in a deep-green ink. Trees were painted over in silver as they died or were cut down. Now, the map seemed to identify ghosts as silver spectres lingering near waterways and lakes. Only a few vibrant specimens, further away from populated areas, were left.

Notes were scribbled in the accompanying book. Some were cryptic, as though he feared who might be peering over his shoulder. Fern couldn't shake the belief that there was a connection between her father's death and what he had been studying. The particular type of rowan had always fascinated him, and they had tried, unsuccessfully, to grow seedlings.

"Dragon numbers diminish, as do the kelmsgales. Did Father find a connection?" Fern traced the outline of the remaining tree in Drake's Bend. Once, it and its companions had grown at the edges of the village green. Five trees like the points on a star.

She turned to the back of the notebook, and just before the blank pages, an ugly scar marred the book. Four pages had been torn out. The jagged stubs of paper jutted up like broken twigs.

George thought they were simply pages where her father made a mistake and he tore them out and tossed them on the fire. Ambrose entertained Fern's more fanciful idea—that whoever poisoned her father took the pages with them.

But what secret about the kelmsgales had been worth her father's life?

She turned back to a coded page she couldn't decipher and studied the neat script as she drank her hot chocolate. When letters and symbols marched across the page in tune to her weariness, Fern folded up the map and closed the notebook, putting it back on the shelf.

"I wish you had confided in me, Father," she murmured to whatever ghosts might linger in the room.

She called out goodnight to her uncles on her way past the drawing room, where the two men engaged in an intense game of backgammon. Then she made her way up the staircase to her bedroom.

As she undressed and climbed under the blankets,

Ambrose's words drifted through her mind. *You should have friends your own age.*

Yes, she admitted from under the security of a pile of blankets. She would like one true friend. Someone who understood her, and who didn't judge her against the ridiculous standard that some man had come up with. But any such person would have to be as damaged as her, and she wouldn't wish such a fate on anyone simply to fill the void in her life.

THE NEXT MORNING OVER BREAKFAST, the family discussed their plans for the day.

"I'm going to see Ben. I need a part made for the trolley I'm building," George said. Ben was the local blacksmith, and the trolley was something Fern had requested to make it easier to move larger potted plants in her greenhouse.

George might have been born noble, but he had the soul of an inventor and liked nothing better than to use his hands to create things. A trait much appreciated by their household.

"I have an article to finish writing for the *Midnight Chronicle*," Ambrose said as he sipped tea. He earned a small income by penning articles and stories for the seditious periodical that gave a voice to those who society tried to silence.

Fern munched the last piece of her toast and then licked her fingers. There was much she wanted to get done today. "I'm off to see the Moray sisters. The cuttings I have for them now have enough growth to plant out."

"Let's reconvene at supper time." George gulped the last

of his coffee as he rose from his chair. He claimed a swift kiss from his partner and then strode out the door.

Fern followed behind, slipping out the kitchen and heading for her greenhouse. There, she carefully placed three pots in her basket and used an old shawl to stop them from banging against one another. She had received the cuttings of a rare blue rose by post, and had managed to get them to strike. The stems now had sufficient leaf and root that they could be planted in a sheltered spot.

With the plants secure, she walked back through the garden and out the side gate to the packed dirt yard before the stables. Then she wandered along the drive and past the smaller cottage that housed the Bentley family of six. The Bentleys took care of Nemython House and its residents.

Fern's home occupied the south-west corner of Drake's Bend. Rowan Oakby had purchased the home thirty years ago and brought his bride to the village surrounded by dense forest and lush meadows.

In no hurry, Fern closed her eyes to listen to the lyrical birdsong as she trod the familiar road. She played an old game, taught to her by her father. Drawing a deep breath, she tried to identify the sweet fragrances swirling in the air.

"Phlox, sweet pea, and alyssum," she muttered before opening her eyes and scanning the greenery for the wild-flowers.

A deep-pink sweet pea clamoured over a willow fence and turned its face to the sun. Phlox of the palest pink and white alyssum were scattered among the taller grasses at the side of the road that bordered the river. The waterway mean-dered through the middle of the village, and Fern approached the southern bridge. Her footsteps rang out on the wood as she crossed over to follow the road on the other side.

Not far along the east bank, bordered by the river on one side and the forest on the other, were the picturesque cottages occupied by the three sisters. Two dwellings with white-washed walls nestled close to each other, and were enclosed by a stone fence. The garden was a riot of spring colour and greenery, with flowers and vegetables grown alongside each other. Chickens scratched in the dirt, weeding and fertilising as they searched for insects and seeds.

Fern walked up the path and found the trio sitting on a bench in the sun. The Moray sisters were affectionately referred to as the three witches, given their similarity to the crones in Macbeth. They all possessed the ability to cast magic, and they used their skills to help the locals in different ways.

Despite the warmth in the sun, the women were wrapped in woollen shawls of muted purple, navy blue, and an earthy green. Their hair had turned a pure white, and their faces were lined with years of knowledge and experience. No one knew exactly how old they were, since there was no one to ask as they were by far the oldest residents of the village. They were rumoured to be triplets, and while similar in appearance, they were still different. As though the lives they had lived and decisions they had made had altered identical clay to produce three different pots.

"Good morning!" Fern called out as she approached.

"Did you see the dragon yesterday, Fern? I think it was the largest we've had hereabouts in five years," Nona said. The eldest of the three, or she certainly acted as the oldest,

Nona was also the tallest. Which meant she barely came up to Fern's shoulder.

Before Fern could answer, Decima, the middle sister, shook her head. "It's been longer than that. It's ten years since Drake's Bend last saw one of such a size. Why, three men could have ridden on its back with space between them to lay out a picnic."

The third and youngest crone, Morda, with the milky gaze of blindness, let out a sigh. "I remember as a wee girl when they were a common sight in the skies around Drake's Bend. Back then, some used to land right on the village green to bathe in the river. We children would sit on the bridge and watch."

"That must have been a marvellous sight." Fern sat on the grass at their feet as the women reminisced. How she would love to see a dragon paddling along the river. She wondered what ducks made of such much larger companions. "It's a shame they no longer sun themselves in the village."

"It's not just dragons disappearing. My hands don't hold as much magic as they once did. I can hardly summon enough motes to light a candle these days." Nona stared at her arthritis-gnarled hands.

Motes were the base material of magic. Nona once explained to Fern that just like dust motes, teeny wisps of magic danced in the air. Those with the gift could both see the golden motes and pluck the glowing specks from the air and mould them to do their bidding. If you were powerful enough, and could gather enough of them, spectacular things were possible.

"I'm not sure you were ever the brightest flame, Nona." Morda cackled and slapped her sister on the back.

Ten years ago, Morda, who was gifted with the sight, had taken Fern's hand and plucked a mote from the air to cast a vision of what awaited her in London. The crone had warned Fern to guard both her heart and her tongue. Advice she had disregarded. Never again would she ignore the warnings of the old women.

# CHAPTER 4

As the women spoke of old memories, a faded one rose to the surface of Fern's mind. Her mother's face, laughing as she helped her young daughter dig in the soil. Sadly, no amount of magical motes was powerful enough to bring back lost loved ones. Fern breathed out the lingering sadness left by her memory and smiled at the banter as the sisters bickered back and forth. Under the teasing, they obviously cared for each other deeply.

"Wait until the kelmsgale flowers. Then we will be able to harvest enough motes to last us through winter," Decima said.

The flowers of the kelmsgale were said to release a pollen that contained tiny specks of magic. Except only those with the gift could see the phenomenon. The witches would collect motes in jars and store them on shelves to use when needed. Fern wished she could see both the amazing spectacle of the rare tree exhaling magic with its flowers, and the specks trapped like fireflies in jars.

"I have the blue roses for you, Nona." Fern lifted the scarf from around the pots and cuttings in the basket. "They should put down good growth over summer and will flower in another year or two."

"You are a treasure, Fern. Help me up, and we can find the best spot for them." Nona leaned on her cane.

Fern stood and took the old woman's arm, helping her to her feet. Nona was the healer of the trio. She had asked Fern to try to obtain a blue rose because of the healing properties of the hips left after the rare blooms had dropped their petals. It had taken her many months to barter with the gardener who protected the only blue rose in England, *Rosa caeruleus*. The canny horticulturists had demanded an equally rare specimen from Fern in exchange for five lengths of stem. She had sent him the sole cutting of the lunanavis she had managed to grow. Fortunately, all five cuttings she had received in exchange had struck roots and then tiny leaves had sprouted. Two were now growing in Fern's garden, the other three were for Nona.

"I think against the cottage would be a good spot. They will receive plenty of sun, and the stone will keep their roots cool." Fern gestured to the lush border that ran the length of the larger cottage that Decima and Morda shared. "If I place them either side of the kitchen door, you could give them a little extra water in the morning."

Once they decided on a spot, it didn't take her long to have the cuttings in their new home. Morda and Decima approached as she finished. Morda reached out a hand and Fern took it.

The old woman leaned in close, her head barely reaching

Fern's chest. Her bony fingers tightened in the fabric of Fern's sleeve as she tugged her lower. "You are nearing a fork in the road, child. If you want answers, you must walk a dark and dangerous path."

The seer's words rippled cold through Fern. She had so many questions. Primarily which path would lead her into the dark so she could avoid it? She placed her dirt-stained hand over a gnarled one and managed a smile as she asked, "Is the other path one of ease and comfort? Because I'd rather take that one if it's an option."

Decima and Nona chortled behind them while Morda tightened her grip on Fern's hand. "Nothing worthwhile was ever easily won. You, Fern Oakby, would never be content with luxury and laziness."

Fern kissed a wrinkled cheek. "You are probably right about that, Morda." But she wouldn't object to a little occasional luxury.

Waving goodbye to the sisters, Fern carried on along the road with her now-empty basket, and over the northern bridge into the centre of the village with its row of shops. She purchased a few items Mrs Bentley had requested from the general store, and with a full basket, she wandered to the village green nestled in the curve of the river.

Fern's gaze was drawn to the kelmsgale tree. The ancient specimen stood tall by the river. Its boughs spread out, and its dense leaves offered shelter from sun and rain. The tree flowered for only a few days once a year in late summer, with golden blooms shaped like a cupped hand and similar to a magnolia. The village always celebrated the event each year, but it was some months away yet.

As she walked past the stumps that were all that remained of four other kelmsgales, recent conversations weighed on her mind. The diminishing dragon numbers. The loss of kelmsgales. The witches losing their magic.

For millennia, dragons and magic had been an integral part of life, not just in Drake's Bend, but across England. The thought of losing such wondrous things saddened Fern deeply, even if George and others said it was natural. As science and industry rose and made England great, dragons and magic receded like the tide.

She tried to convince herself that George was right. As science explained more about how their world worked, the veil of mystery was pulled aside and magic retreated from whence it came. Like a spider startled by a curtain being flung open and throwing a dark room into light.

She approached the tree and sat with her back to the rough bark, facing the river. The old sentinel was the heart of their village. Her father had estimated it to be at least five hundred years old. Now, it was the last one left for many miles.

The spring breeze teased tendrils of her hair. Tilting her head back, Fern gazed at the bright-green foliage. She tried to imagine the days gone by when entire families of dragons had bathed in the river before climbing up the bank to sleep in the circle of ancient trees. It was, after all, how the village came by its name. The area was so called because of the dragons who frequented this particular curve in the river.

Or they did. Decades ago.

While those in London marvelled at modern advancements and machines, Fern mourned what was lost in the wake of progress. Why couldn't there be a way to safeguard precious flora and fauna, even as they marched onwards through the nineteenth century? If scholars were so enlightened and intelligent, surely they could determine how to preserve the most magical parts of their world so future generations could also marvel at them?

It struck her as odd that the kelmsgales seemed to wither and die alongside dragons. But that didn't make any sense—fauna did not affect flora in such a manner. How could the old tree have any responsibility for the loss of dragons or vice versa? Not unless the creatures were stripping the trees to nubs, or destroying their roots. Or perhaps the trees were poisoning the dragons. But there was no evidence of any of that. Nor would dragons of old have lounged under the spreading boughs after swimming in the river if the tree were toxic to them.

Nor did any of it explain the waning of magic. While the pollen released some motes into the air, it augmented the natural magic already floating around, unseen by most of the population. It wasn't like the flowers were the *only* source of magical motes. Wasn't it?

Then an idea made her sit bolt upright. What if there was a connection? Could the slow fading of magic be responsible for the death of both the trees and mythical creatures?

An image shimmered in her mind. Her father's notebook with its drawing of a dragon curled around a rowan. But what if they were only two sides of a triangle, and the third was magic?

"Had you made a similar connection, Father?" Fern whispered to the silent tree.

But even if Rowan Oakby had been investigating the loss of the kelmsgales and however they might be impacted by dragons or magic, how could that have resulted in his death?

"Who would murder someone over a tree?" she murmured to her father's spirit, wherever it might linger. There was one mystery science still couldn't explain—what happened once a soul left its mortal remains?

Not finding any answers to her multitude of questions among the rustle of foliage or the burble of water, Fern picked up her basket and wandered home.

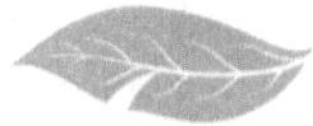

THE NEXT MORNING, a stack of mail awaited Fern when she took her place at the kitchen table. A steady flow of correspondence came to their corner of rural England. Mostly Fern received orders from head gardeners of grand estates who needed a rare plant to grace their master's garden or conservatory. Sometimes, they ordered seeds or cuttings to grow on themselves. Such as when she exchanged the lunanavis cutting for stems of the blue rose.

Other requests were from apothecaries and alchemists who required the rare and sometimes dangerous plants she grew as ingredients for their spells and potions. Occasionally, botanists who had known her father wrote to enquire if she would consider selling his collection, or part with a specimen the scholar simply had to have.

And sometimes...somebody reached out with an intriguing flora-related problem that had flummoxed their staff. Today, one such letter was nestled among the orders. She mulled over the short paragraph written in a neat hand devoid of any flourishes.

"What are you staring at so intently, Fern?" Ambrose asked.

She waved the thick paper through the air. "Lord Warrington asks me to investigate a patch of dead ground cover and hedging on his estate. Apparently his head gardener has replaced both, more than once, but they continue to expire. He wants it fixed urgently before some fancy house party next month. I will head out there today."

"His estate isn't too far away. A two-hour ride at most, is it not?" Ambrose said.

George huffed. "It's going to rain this afternoon. Be prepared to stay overnight. Even Warrington wouldn't throw you out during a storm."

"I'll pack what I need." Her fingers drummed against the worn wooden table as she made a list in her mind of what to take. The other letters could wait until she returned, either later that evening or tomorrow.

After a hearty breakfast, Fern went to her study and grabbed a thick journal of her father's that detailed sicknesses and pests that blighted plants in their district. In her room, she surveyed her wardrobe with a critical eye. She caressed a silk gown, a relic from her season in London. Closing the wardrobe door, she reached for a pair of sturdy trousers, a practical linen shirt in a deep cream, and a tweed waistcoat.

A small, rebellious smile twitched at the corners of her lips as she considered the scandalised expressions her attire provoked outside their secluded community. She had little patience for the superficial constraints of their society, and today was no exception.

"Stodgy old biddies can tut all they like. I won't be bound by their antiquated notions of what I can wear when there is honest work to be done," Fern muttered.

With nimble fingers, she secured her shirt cuffs and buttoned up the waistcoat. She grabbed a swirling, long woollen coat from the hook behind her door. It would offer some protection from wind and rain if George's prediction of a storm transpired.

Next, she packed a change of clothes, in case she got dirtier than usual on the job. Satisfied with everything she had shoved into her voluminous satchel, Fern headed back down the stairs and through the kitchen. She hoped Lord Warrington had deep pockets to pay for her time and expertise.

Before heading to the stables, Fern detoured to the greenhouse to grab her favourite trowel. Then she did up the buckles on the bulging leather satchel as she passed through the garden gate to where her mount waited.

Fern had a particular love for the dark bay mare that George had acquired for her some years earlier. With a swirling white mark that started above her eyes and curved down over her nose, and one white sock, she had a gentle temperament. But she was still a mare and possessed a strong opinion about many things, which endeared her even more to Fern.

William Bentley, the oldest son of Mrs Bentley, had saddled up the horse.

"Thank you, Will," Fern said as he passed her the reins.

Her uncles had come out of the house to see her off. George legged her up and patted the mare as though he would miss the horse more than Fern.

"Do you really think it will rain?" Ambrose asked George as he stared at the clear sky.

"The last of the cheese says it does before nightfall." George stuck out his hand.

"Throw in the last of the walnut loaf and you have a deal." Ambrose shook the offered limb to seal their bet.

Fern swallowed her laughter, waved goodbye, and tapped her heel against the mare's sensitive side. The horse popped into a rhythmic trot as they headed along the road and away from the village, then she urged the mare into a steady canter.

As she rode, Fern pondered what might be causing the problems at Warrington Manor. The unexplained death of the ground cover and hedge was either something plaguing the plants or the soil. Possibly there was a third option—deliberate sabotage, but people rarely committed crimes against shrubs.

At the halfway point in her journey, Fern slowed the mare to a walk and approached a creek that curved close to the road. The water flowed gently, and the bank was low enough for the horse to wade in for a well-deserved drink. Fern dropped to the ground and led the horse over the lush grass before tying the reins in a knot so the mare didn't stand on them.

While the horse bent her head to drink deeply from the pristine water, Fern walked up the bank a few paces to where a tree had been hacked down at shin height and left a comfortable place to sit. She traced a fingertip along the concentric circles. As a child, her father had told her how the story of a tree was contained inside it. The rings revealed the age of the tree, growing conditions, and even recorded events that affected the surrounding environment. But sadly, the story was only visible once a tree was felled.

"Why were you cut down, my friend?" she asked the stump.

There were more rings than she could count, and the tree had to have been over two hundred years old. There didn't appear to be any evidence of disease at the outer edges. Firewood, perhaps. Travellers might have made camp, and cut the tree down to keep them warm at night and cook their supper.

Curiosity nibbled at her to name the tree. It would seem odd to others, but she had to know why the quiet sentinel was reduced to a low piece of rustic furniture. Pushing aside the grass by her boots, Fern searched for clues. The cut had weathered but there was no sign of rot. She guessed it hadn't been more than a year since someone took an axe to the tree. The bark appeared too similar to many other aged trees, with the grooves and gnarls earned over the passage of time. Her gaze settled on a nearby mound of grass. It might hold dead leaves from the tree that could reveal its identity.

Fern needed to see leaves, flowers, or fruit to aid in identifying a plant. George could look at a piece of wood, run a finger along the grain, and do the same. Fern thought his ability unnerving. To her, it was like recognising someone by reading entrails, since he had to study the inside of a tree.

Getting off the stump, she knelt on the ground and pushed aside the tufts of grass. As her hands parted the thick stalks, her fingertips skimmed a thin branch. Closing her grip, she tugged it free, hoping a few leaves clung to it still. A gasp caught in her throat as dappled sunlight rippled along the *branch* in her hand.

Fern had grabbed a bone.

With more care, she peeled aside the grass to reveal a sad mound of bones. A skeleton—curled upon itself as though the creature had snuggled close to the trunk before breathing its last. A very distinctive skeleton. One with a long tail tucked back over its muzzle and delicate wing bones pressed against its side and a unique stripe of dorsal spines.

A dragon.

# CHAPTER 5

"You poor thing. What happened to you?" Fern asked the skeleton. In size, the creature had been similar to a wolfhound. It must have been a juvenile dragon who had met with some accident. Or had disease snatched the dragon's life before it had a chance to reach full size?

With reverence, she placed the bone back among the ribs. Rising to her feet, Fern brushed twigs and seeds from her trousers. The scene before her conjured to mind the drawing at the front of her father's journal. But instead of a snoozing dragon curled under the lush foliage of a tree, she stared at the ghosts of those comrades. A skeleton and a stump.

"Which of you died first?" she wondered. Did those who felled the tree slay the dragon? Or perhaps they had discovered the creature injured or sick and had put it out of its misery.

The sky above darkened, and Fern couldn't dally any longer. On her way home, she could stop and pay her respects. She led the horse to the stump to use it as a mounting block, careful to use the opposite side to the skeleton.

Back on the road, the mare picked up a canter. The forest pulled back from the road, and a sharp wind pursued them. Less than an hour later, Fern finally rode between the ornate gates of Warrington Manor. The mare dropped to a trot as they headed along the driveway.

Fern stared at the manor as her horse halted. The estate loomed before her like an expensive mausoleum. Its grandeur and size were both awe-inspiring and intimidating. She felt a twinge of unease at the stark contrast between the sprawling manor and the cosy village of Drake's Bend, as though ghosts of her past rose up and danced along her spine.

She reminded herself that his lordship was paying for her expertise, and she would earn enough to keep George in cheese and walnut loaf for some weeks. Dismounting, she glanced up at the many windows of the manor and thought a pale face looked down upon her, but then it was gone.

A brisk breeze rustled through the trees, tugging at the edges of her trousers. Fern stared at the dark clouds scudding across the sky. "George will win that bet with Ambrose. It looks like a storm is brewing. Let's see how much I can get done before it rains."

Rubbing her arms to dispel a shiver, she led the mare around the side of the house in search of the kitchen entrance.

Once, she might have been greeted at the front door if she were paying a social call. But those who dirty their hands, either men or women, went to the tradesmen's entrance. As she made her way around the house, Fern marvelled at the meticulously tended gardens, no doubt the work of at least half a dozen groundsmen. The stretch of lawn alone would have kept a man busy full time, on his knees snipping at it with shears. By the time he reached one side, the grass behind him would have grown, and he'd have to start all over again!

They crossed the expanse of cobbled yard that stretched from the rear of the house to the outbuildings. The warm scent of freshly baked bread drew Fern closer to the kitchen door, propped open with a boot scraper to let the breeze into the stuffy room. Within was a bustling hive of activity. Cooks and scullery maids hurried about in a well-orchestrated dance. The warm breath of the mare feathered over Fern's neck as the curious horse also peered in through the door.

A footman spied her and rushed out to either greet her or to evict the horse before it entered the kitchen.

"Can I help you?" he called out.

"I am Miss Oakby. Lord Warrington engaged me for a garden-related problem," she said.

"Of course. I'll have the lad take your horse." He gestured to a young boy sweeping the cobbles, who put the broom aside to do as instructed. "His lordship said you might have to stay overnight, and a room has been made available for you, if you will follow me."

Fern handed over the reins to the boy and fell into step behind the footman, who lacked the age or gravitas to be the house's butler, even though he acted as if he were in charge.

She was shown through the kitchens and up a narrow flight of stairs. All the while, she wondered where she would find herself staying. The blood of a noble family ran through her veins, making her too good for the servants' quarters. But her ruined status meant she wouldn't be placed anywhere near the family or in the rooms reserved for guests.

After ascending another set of stairs, her guide showed her down a darkened hallway. Then he stopped and pushed open the door. "In here, miss. I'll find the head gardener, Mr Corby, and have him meet you down in the kitchen shortly." He paused, his hand on the doorjamb. "He is a...gruff man, Miss Oakby. But he takes special care of the grounds here."

"Gruff? Well, I deal with someone like that every day, but thank you for the warning. I'll be quick, so I don't keep him waiting." Fern entered a smallish room with plain decoration and simple furniture. It looked the sort of place a lady's companion or governess might be given.

She dropped her satchel to the single bed pushed up against the wall. Unbuckling the straps, she rummaged inside for what she needed. First, she tugged out a short apron and tied it about her waist. Next she tucked the book and trowel into the apron's pockets. She left the long coat on, in case the sky released a downpour while she was outside.

Fortunately, the route back to the kitchen hadn't been too difficult to memorise. As she traversed the manor's corridors, several staff members crossed her path, their reactions to her presence ranging from wide-eyed astonishment to barely concealed smirks. She wondered if they knew about her reputation, or if it was merely her brazen demeanour that earned her such varied responses.

Soon Fern emerged from the dim servants' stairs into the kitchen. A dour-looking older man stood by the back door, his arms crossed over his chest and a cloth cap pulled low on his wide brow. Of average height, he had a broad chest and thick arms. He glared at Fern as she approached.

She took a deep breath, mentally steeling herself for the encounter as animosity rolled off the man already. He could glare all he wanted. It made no difference to her. She had faced far worse in her life, and would not be deterred by the disdain of one man.

Plastering a smile on her face, she said, "Mr Corby, I presume? I am Miss Oakby. Lord Warrington asked me to look at your dead plants."

The scowl on his face deepened, and his top lip pulled upward in a sneer. "You're supposed to be an expert on gardens?"

"My father was Mr Rowan Oakby, the renowned botanist. I had the privilege of learning at his side and maintain his garden of rare and exotic species." Fern held the man's gaze and refused to look away. *Her* pedigree and experience were impeccable. What was this boorish oaf's claim to botanical knowledge? That he could chew grass?

Mr Corby snorted. "Your father knew an azalea from a camellia. You're just a trousers-wearing oddity."

She didn't move or bat an eyelid. "And yet...I'm the one Lord Warrington sent for to fix the problem. Which rather implies that you failed, doesn't it?"

The gardener took a step towards her, and his hands clenched into meaty fists, but when she didn't flinch or back down, he stopped. Instead, he snarled. "His lordship will hear about this!" He turned on his heel and strode out the door.

"And a pleasure to meet you too," Fern said to the empty

space where he had stood moments before. Drawing a deep breath to settle her raised temper, she followed him outside.

The wind had picked up in the short time she had been inside, and dust eddies swirled through the courtyard and snatched up loose dirt and leaves. Mr Corby walked off without a backwards glance. Fern hurried to catch up with him while, at the same time, trying not to look as though she chased him to the curious servants who watched. It was a hard thing to pull off, but she congratulated herself on not having to run thanks to long legs and trousers.

Having made it across the yard, she slowed her pace to take in her surroundings. Let the man complain to Lord Warrington. She would report how instead of assisting, he stormed off and refused to show her the area of concern in the sprawling grounds. If she got lost, it could take her weeks to find the right spot on her own, and she doubted his lordship wanted to pay the sort of bill that would result from wasting her time.

The drop in temperature outside must have chilled Corby's foul mood, as he stopped by a low hedge and pretended he was trimming a bit of unruly growth. "Don't know what possessed his lordship to send a girl to do a man's job. Bet the chit has never even held a spade before," he grumbled to the plant but loud enough for Fern to hear.

She bit her tongue, and with effort, resisted the urge to respond to his obvious baiting. Instead, Fern surveyed the estate with a critical eye. Focusing on the hedges lining the path, she noted the expertly trimmed shapes with a begrudging admiration. A rose garden burst with immaculate blooms, and a Boston ivy on one wall was kept in check and resembled a swath of verdant curtain. In another space, annuals and perennial flowers in muted tones enhanced the tranquillity of a pond. The man was clearly skilled. But his churlish demeanour left much to be desired.

At length her reluctant guide paused by an arch cut in a tall yew hedge.

"You maintain impressive grounds. I understand that it is seen as a slight for Lord Warrington to bring in someone else to tend a problem. Particularly someone younger," Fern said, hoping to soften the man's hard edges.

He grunted and narrowed his eyes suspiciously. "I've worked here since I was a wee lad and know this estate like the back of my hand. I don't need your help. I've told his lordship it's most likely the hounds peeing."

Fern had to admit that would do it. If all the dogs on the estate relieved themselves in the same place, the urine would poison both grass and hedges. "Have you tried fencing them off so they find somewhere else to go?"

He huffed and walked through the yew to the other side. "I'm not daft. We did that, but the cunning things are drawn by the scent and push through."

Fern followed his broad back and emerged in a sheltered space. In the middle was an ornate fountain, now disused, and its pond holding a few inches of green muck. Paths of a soft creeping thyme separated the fountain from beds with sickly perennials. A bench sat to one side under a bower being claimed by an enthusiastic pink rose, the only bright spot in the subdued garden. On the opposite side, an oak tree spread its boughs.

As Fern walked along the fragrant path, the problem

became evident. A patch of thyme was sickly yellow and spread over the ground like a dropped bowl of custard. The tendrils of disease curled around box hedging, and those plants also yellowed and wilted. It certainly appeared that dogs relieving themselves were the problem.

"We've dug it up and resown the thyme, but it still dies. So does the hedge. I've replaced that three times now, twice since I insisted all the dogs be kept out of the garden." He crossed his arms, and a smug smile flitted over his face as though he was confident of her failure, even as he *dared* her to find the source of the problem.

The plants were wilted and sickly, their once-vibrant hues now dull and lifeless. Fern knelt on the creeping thyme and ran a hand across the dead and brittle leaves. There were visible signs of an imbalance in the earth, and the silent cry of plants in distress.

Mr Corby continued to share what he had tried to remedy the problem, though his tone remained dismissive and tinged with annoyance.

If she discounted incontinent dogs, what else might be responsible?

"Certain plants can have adverse effects on one another when planted too closely together. It's called allelopathy." Fern tried to keep her tone conversational despite the head gardener's continued antagonism.

"Allelo-what?" he scoffed. "Sounds like some made-up nonsense to excuse poor gardening."

"Have you moved any plants into or out of this area in the last three months? It is possible the natural balance here has been upset." Standing, she walked a slow circle around the fountain, examining the beds and hunting for any plant that appeared to be out of place. Like a cuckoo in the nest.

"Nothing has changed here for years. Her ladyship likes it just as it is. It's her favourite spot to sit when she's in residence." At long last, his tone softened as he mentioned Lady Warrington.

"Have you considered the possibility of a curse?" Fern's thoughts raced with theories and ideas. "The upcoming house party is important, is it not? Could there be anyone seeking to damage Lord Warrington's reputation for the beauty of his gardens?" Although, why anyone would curse a path of ground cover, a stretch of buxus, and a few perennials was beyond her. The Moray sisters would mutter about magic being imprecise, and perhaps the culprit missed their intended target, like the spectacular rose garden they had passed through.

"A curse? Is that the extent of your blasted expertise, suggesting a silly curse?" he scoffed, clearly unamused by the notion.

Fern took a calming breath and refused to let Corby's dismissive attitude derail her investigation. After all, the plants were suffering and required her assistance.

"Regardless of your personal opinions, I have been engaged to consider the cause of distress in this area. As part of that, I will keep an open mind if you could try to do the same," she said evenly.

"Listen to you putting on all those fancy airs. Don't expect me to kiss your boots because you're going to fail," he said, clearly irritated by her refusal to engage in his petty jabs.

"Your confidence in my abilities is truly touching," Fern retorted, rolling her eyes as she turned her focus back to the ailing plants beside the fountain. All the surly man did was increase her determination to prove him wrong.

She knelt by the dying hedge and parted two brownish-yellow plants to get a better look at their stems and roots. The soil had an odd discolouration and appeared a deep red when the light struck it.

"Curious," she murmured.

The head gardener, still fuming, leaned in to see what had caught her attention.

She dug her fingers into the soil and lifted a small clump. Opening her hand, she spread the dirt over her palm. It left a dark stain on her skin, the colour of rusty water. Or blood.

"When you replaced the hedge and ground cover, did you notice anything strange about the soil?" She held her hand up for his inspection.

He took a pinch between his thumb and forefinger and rolled it on the tips, watching the stain that emerged when he squeezed. "Well, it wasn't that colour. It was waterlogged. That fountain was damaged years ago. Her ladyship likes it broken. She calls it her secret ruin. I figured the last of the water was draining out of the basin. Me and the lads added a channel angled back to the yew to redirect the water before we replaced everything."

Fern straightened, an answer already forming in her mind. Part of her was disappointed it proved so easy. "That looks like rusty water. I suspect some internal part of the fountain has rusted and possibly recent rain washed it out. The iron and manganese will be affecting the plants."

Curling her fingers around the soil, Fern brought her hand closer to her face and sniffed. There was something else about the dirt that bothered her.

"Oh!" A sharp odour hit her nose and stabbed up behind her eyes, causing her to jerk her hand away. There was definitely something stagnant and rank under the fountain.

# CHAPTER 6

Mr Corby sniggered. "The soil has a whiff about it. We thought we had disturbed some old rotten eggs when we dug it up."

"Thanks for the warning." The horrible man could have said something before she bent over the fistful and inhaled. With her fingers curled over the soil, she noticed another thing about it. It was warm. A combination of things had combined to kill the roots of the creeping thyme and hedge.

"If you're as clever as his lordship says, I'm sure you can find your own way back to the house when you're done. I have more important things to do than play nursemaid to you." He strode off through the hole in the yew.

A rumble sounded overhead, and the clouds darkened to the blue-black of a bruise. "That storm is not far off," Fern muttered. There was no chance she would make it home before the weather broke, so she may as well learn all she could before rain drove her back to the manor.

She dropped the handful of dirt to the ground and

brushed her hands against each other before leaning on the stone basin of the fountain. The once-ornate structure had become a sad sight to behold, with chipped edges and cracks running along its surface like spiderwebs. No wonder Lady Warrington called it her *ruin*.

In the wide and shallow basin, stagnant water cast a sickly green hue. Fern's nose wrinkled at the unpleasant stench that wafted from the still water. The fountain would be gravity-fed through underground pipes. Somewhere on higher ground would be the reservoir that supplied the water features on the estate.

A sigh heaved through her. She would have to get dirtier than usual to investigate. She took off her coat, not wanting to get it covered in muck, and rolled up the sleeves of her shirt. A shiver rippled over her exposed arms, and the wind became colder.

Reaching in, Fern felt around in the green, velvet-like algae. Somewhere would be the inlet pipe that sucked up the water to recirculate. Most likely there would be a valve or pipe that had deteriorated over the years. If a puddle formed around the metal, it would rust. If there was a push of water from the reservoir and it couldn't surge up the central urn due to a blockage, it would have to find another means of escape...like out among the hedging plants that surrounded the fountain.

Her fingers found the hole, approximately two inches in diameter. "In for a penny, in for a pound," she said before shoving a digit in as far as possible. Crooking her index finger, she tugged, and a blob of solidified muck fell from the pipe. A swirl cut through the water as it trickled downwards.

With that blockage cleared, she grabbed hold of the three-foot-tall urn for balance and stood on the edge of the basin to peer inside. The pipe that should have burbled fresh water appeared clear, although the urn was filled with fallen leaves from the oak. Possibly leaf matter had broken down and wedged itself into the pipe, but she didn't want to try cleaning it out while precariously balanced. If she toppled, she would end up covered in pond scum. She might wear trousers, but she didn't want to be filthy and smelly if she could avoid it.

Stepping down to the ground, Fern returned to the other thing she noticed about the soil. It was warmer than expected. She wondered if there might be a thermal spring in the area. One venting in a new direction might have created the problem and accelerated the rusting of the fountain's mechanism or pipes.

"Time to talk to Lord Warrington," Fern said to the threatening sky. Fat droplets of rain began to fall, splattering against the sides of the fountain and the lime path. The rich scent of wet earth filled her nostrils as she took one last glance at the broken fountain, its murky water now swirling with the fresh liquid falling from the clouds.

Fern hurried through the garden as it grew darker and the rain turned from occasional droplets into persistent drizzle. She only took a wrong turn once on her way back. Fortunately, she had been intent on taking in the layout of the garden as she followed the gardener, and was able to navigate by reciting what she passed.

"Left at the rose garden, straight on through the night blooming room..." she said under her breath.

By the time Fern trotted across the cobbled yard, the sky had darkened with a premature twilight. The kitchen was alive with activity as they prepared for the evening meal. The smell of roasting meats filled the air.

Fern strode in and soaked up the warmth and delicious aromas. Someone here would be able to show her through to his lordship. What she needed was a high-up footman or...her gaze alighted on a man who was calm and composed among the chaos...the butler. He surveyed his domain like a conductor standing before an orchestra, poised to correct any sour notes in the performance.

"Excuse me," Fern called out, her voice barely audible above the clattering pots and shouted instructions.

When he turned to regard her, his aged face betrayed no surprise at her damp appearance or muddy boots. "Miss Oakby, how may I be of service?" he inquired, his tone formal and measured.

"I need to speak with Lord Warrington," Fern replied.

"Of course. I assume you wish to change first?" He arched one impeccably groomed eyebrow.

Fern glanced down at her trousers. They were clean and serviceable, and she had avoided any splashes of rancid water, although there were damp spots over the knees where she had knelt on the ground. Why would she change out of them? Admittedly her boots weren't that clean after hurrying through the gardens, but any mud would have stomped off by the time she reached wherever Lord Warrington was tucked up.

"No, I do not wish to change. Thank you. Now, where will I find his lordship?" she replied.

The eyebrow arched a little higher as the butler waited for her to realise her attire was unsuitable and to rush to her room to put on a gown. After several seconds of their stare-off, he caught on that neither her mind nor clothing would be altered.

"Please, follow me." The butler led Fern back through the servants' hall and out into the wide and opulent corridors of the main building. The walls were adorned with tapestries and old paintings. Vases held cut flowers, and provided splashes of colour against the dark walls.

He stopped outside a door not far from the main entrance hall and rapped on the polished wood. "Lord Warrington, Miss Oakby requests an audience with you."

"Enter," came the muffled response from within.

The butler opened the door, revealing a sumptuous study. One entire wall was shelving lined with leather-bound volumes and illuminated by flickering candlelight. A rug in swirls of rich blue and pale cream covered the floorboards and stretched from side to side of the room.

"Miss Oakby. I trust Corby showed you the problem area that I need fixed before next month." Lord Warrington looked up from the papers in his hand, and his eyes widened as he took in her dishevelled condition. "Good grief, Miss Oakby! You have some nerve to present yourself in such a state before me." He gestured up and down at her with a flourish of his hand.

"The storm is not far off, milord, and I hurried through the grounds. I apologise for any mud still clinging to my boots." She chose to ignore what actually bothered him about her appearance. Trousers.

He narrowed his eyes and huffed. An action which made him resemble his rude head gardener. "Despite your muddied reputation, you are the niece of Lord Ashwood. What would the earl say if he saw you clothed in such a ridiculous fashion?" He tossed the papers to the desk and laid his hands on them, as though to shield the letters from her scandalous attire.

"If my uncle wants any say in my wardrobe, then he should provide the funds for it. Until then, I will wear what is appropriate for my work. Do you wish to hear my findings, or would you prefer to discuss the latest fashion and what well-bred young women are wearing this season?" She clasped her hands behind her back and dug her nails into her palms. The sharp bite helped keep her face serene as she stood her ground before Lord Warrington's obvious distaste.

This was why she rarely ventured beyond Drake's Bend or into polite company with its strictures and expectations. It always struck her as odd how peers made demands of those beneath them with absolutely no regard as to whether such demands were feasible or practical. Even more ridiculous, society expelled her from their ranks, and they *still* expected her to follow some ludicrous and antiquated rules that governed every aspect of their lives.

"Very well, but this is most irregular and unseemly, Miss Oakby." He pushed his chair back and partially turned to watch the storm rolling towards his estate.

"You hired me, Lord Warrington. Surely you expected an *irregular* woman?" While she didn't want to antagonise him to the point he didn't pay for her work, Fern had to needle him just a little bit. He couldn't employ her and then condemn her for working.

"Of course I knew that due to your circumstances, you continue the work your father started. But I expected to find you..." He narrowed his gaze as though squinting might transform her trousers and muddy boots into a muslin gown and indoor slippers.

Since he couldn't find the right word, Fern suggested a few to complete his sentence. "Penitent? Submissive? Wearing sack cloth?"

He made a noise in the back of his throat like a dog challenged over a bone. "None of this is solving the ugly blight in my garden. What have you discovered that has defeated my gardener?"

"There is an odd red tinge to the soil around the fountain, and given the overall state of the thing, I believe you have a rusting and leaky pipe. The minerals in the rust will be adversely affecting the surrounding flora as they leach into the earth. There was also an unusual warmth, but I cannot explain that without examining underneath the fountain." It might have simply been that the drop in temperature had made the soil feel comparatively warm in her hand.

Lord Warrington leaned forwards in his chair, a look of genuine concern etching itself across his features. "Corby never mentioned that it might be rusty water. He thought it was the hounds...doing their business. Are you certain?"

"As certain as I can be without dismantling the fountain. I suspect recent rain might have pushed the foul water through blocked pipes. Mr Corby said the damaged area is enlarging, which would be consistent with something seeping through the soil. You could keep replacing the plants, but if it is the fountain at fault, nothing will flourish until the leak is dealt with." Not unless they planted something that loved iron and manganese like azaleas and rhododendrons.

His lordship rapped short nails on the desktop and muttered under his breath before reaching a decision. "Since you are here, you may as well make certain. You can pull the fountain apart. Get Corby to make it work again while you are at it," Lord Warrington said.

Fern bit the inside of her cheek, certain that Mr Corby would love to hear he was taking orders from her now. "Will her ladyship mind? Mr Corby said she liked it in a derelict state?"

"I will deal with her ladyship. We have proper ruins for our guests to explore. We don't need smelly water in that fountain spoiling the garden." He pushed off the desk and rose to his feet.

Fern wondered what could have gone wrong with the network of pipes hidden beneath the earth that channelled water from the reservoir to the fountain. The old oak that stood in the corner rustled its leaves in her mind. Its roots might have disrupted the ground, or sought out the pipes in dry weather to suck moisture from them. "As you wish, Lord Warrington. Once Mr Corby and I have correctly identified the source of the contamination, the soil can be replaced so the new plantings will flourish. All in time for your house party next month."

As they discussed the work to be done, the storm grew closer and gathered strength. Eerie shadows flitted across the room as the candles swayed in response to the gusts outside.

"You had better stay the night. I'll not send you out in that. You and Corby can start early in the morning, and you should be done by tomorrow afternoon. But I think, Miss Oakby, that you should have a tray in your room," he said.

Fern occupied a desolate wasteland in society. As the niece of an earl, she could have sat at Lord Warrington's table. Except she was considered *ruined* and had been cast from their ranks. Yet, since she was of noble birth, she couldn't sit at the servants' table either. Isolation in her room was the compromise.

"Of course, Lord Warrington. I shall begin at dawn, once the storm has passed, so I do not impose overly long on your hospitality." She would have preferred to be tucked up in the solid walls of Nemython House back in Drake's Bend. Away from home, she worried what damage the storm might do to her garden. She would have to trust that the walls and forest would protect the exotic plants and greenhouse.

"You may select a book from my library to read, if you wish. There are some botanical volumes my father collected." He waved his hand in what Fern hoped was the vague direction of the library.

"Thank you, Lord Warrington." Dismissed, Fern retreated from the study. As she stepped into the corridor, the wind howled around the manor, rattling the windows and raising the hairs along her arms. The storm was here, and with it, an ominous sense of foreboding that rippled through her bones.

Fern hurriedly navigated the dimly lit corridors back to her temporary accommodation. She closed the door and crossed to the window. Rain now lashed the panes, and rivulets of water flowed down the glass. To fill in the time before her dinner arrived, she put away her apron and tools. Then she toed off her boots and collected the thick notebook before settling at the little table under the window.

Flicking through the pages, Fern scanned dense lines of text in her father's neat hand that accompanied the drawings. The book had a section about the health of soil and ailments that affected plant growth. Re-reading the chapter and comparing it to what she had seen would help confirm her diagnosis or lead her in another direction.

There was another reason to read her father's notes. The familiar tidy handwriting and words were faint echoes of him, and for a little while, she had his company once more to alleviate the hollow ache inside her.

CHAPTER 7

FERN'S STUDY was interrupted by a scratching at the door
that sounded like a trapped mouse. It turned out to be the
timid knock of a young maid delivering a dinner tray. The
young woman didn't utter a squeak, but stared with wide-
eyed curiosity as though she expected to find the odd guest
had horns and a tail. Fern smiled, thanked her politely for the
meal, and closed the door while the girl still peered into the
room. No doubt she was terribly disappointed not to find
cavorting demons dangling from the corners or whatever
nonsense they spread about her below stairs.

Fern took the tray to the table. Someone had set the fire
while she had been outside, and she had lit it for the companionship of the crackling flames. The flicker of the candles
across the walls made the room seem intimate, rather than
small. The aroma of roasted vegetables wafted from the plate.
Solitude gave her plenty of time to sort through events in her
mind. Taking a bite, she let her thoughts roam as she stared
without seeing out the rain-lashed window.

Despite her disdain for the trappings and strictures of society, part of Fern still longed to bask in the glow once more. She traced the rim of her plate with her fork, lost in memories that danced before her eyes of one glorious season in London. Grand ballrooms, exquisite gowns, a handsome noble taking her hand...on the surface, it had a fairytale appeal. Until you peeked beneath the veneer and saw the rot underneath.

"I suppose it is better to be an outcast than trapped in a stifling gilded cage," she muttered. To think she had once dreamed of being a part of London society. Her life would have been a monotonous routine of shallow entertainments, tedious conversations, and the ever-watchful eyes of society's elite. Pretty fripperies like a new parasol would have been the highlight of her year.

Instead, her passion for botany offered a balm against the harsh judgements of others. In the quiet embrace of nature, Fern found solace and purpose. The natural world provided a constant sense of wonder to replace the disillusionment and boredom that settled like a heavy fog over most young ladies once the glamour had worn off.

Fern's reverie was interrupted by the increased tempo of the rain. It pounded against the windows as if a thousand tiny fists were demanding entry. The storm lingered over the estate. The wind howled through the trees below, their branches swaying and creaking in a frenzied dance.

"I've not seen a squall like this since last winter." Fern placed one hand on the cool glass and worried about her garden.

As the storm intensified and lightning streaked across the

sky, there came a particularly loud clap of thunder that made her jump in her seat. The raging weather amplified her need to escape the confines of the room, and she paced back and forth.

"I shall venture out and find the library," she decided. Discovering what books the previous Lord Warrington had collected on the subject of flora would be a welcome distraction from the thunder and lightning.

Fern picked up the candle in its holder and ventured out of the bedroom and down the darkened hallway. It took a few wrong turns before she found the library. Her instincts told her it would be somewhere on the ground floor, not too far from Lord Warrington's study, as she recalled the vague direction of his hand gesture when he said she could borrow a book.

When she pushed open the ajar door, what she found was nothing short of grandiose. Towering bookshelves lined the walls, their wood polished to a gleaming shine that seemed to drink in the flickering candlelight. The scent of old parchment hung heavy in the air, mingling with the faint tang of leather-bound tomes. Fern had found a sanctuary of knowledge and insulation against the squall buffeting the house. Her restlessness was settled by the presence of the books, and she let out a long-held breath.

Approaching one shelf, she trailed her fingers along spines, letting history and wisdom seep through her skin. Books were a connection to the past, and those who had come before her. Botanists, philosophers, poets, historians, mathematicians, and even novelists, all invited her to spend time with them.

"There might even be some of my father's work here," she whispered.

Fern's curiosity blossomed as she perused the shelves. Each volume she discovered held a secret or a tale waiting to be uncovered. How would she pick just one to take back to her room? Excitement surged through her as she uncovered a dusty volume on rare botanical specimens, its pages filled with delicate illustrations of plants she had never even heard of before.

"Oh, you are exquisite," she told the book as she closed it again and clutched it to her chest.

A loud clap of thunder startled her, and she nearly smacked herself in the face with the heavy tome. What she needed was a comfortable spot to marvel over her find, and the library was more welcoming than her little room. Someone had lit the wood in a fireplace that stood as tall as Fern, and the flames threw a warm glow across the room.

As Fern took the book to the armchairs before the fire, more thunder rumbled outside and shook the manor's very foundations. A gentle, stifled sobbing followed in the silence after the crack of lightning, barely audible over the howling wind and pound of rain.

Odd. Storms didn't usually whimper, and besides, the noise came from inside the library.

Fern placed the botanical book on a chair and set off to investigate the sound. Rounding one stack, her attention fell on a shadowy alcove between two towering bookshelves. There, pressed into the spines of books was a figure clutching their legs to their chest and a face buried in their knees.

Ghost or real person? Fern wondered.

She took a cautious step closer, to discover a woman with a tangle of dark hair falling around her bowed head. Her shoulders heaving in great sobs. Another bang of thunder made the woman flinch, and her cry turned into a warble. She wore no dressing gown over her nightdress, suggesting she had left her room in a hurry. Books lay scattered around her, as if she had been seeking refuge among their pages.

Fern approached slowly, not wanting to further frighten her. "Hello? Is everything all right?"

The woman looked up, startled. Brown eyes widened and were filled with terror in a pleasing, heart-shaped face.

"I...I'm sorry," she stammered, trying to wipe her tears away as though embarrassed at being discovered in such a state. "I just...the storm. I can't..."

A crack of lightning made her cry out, and trembles raced over her body. She pressed her face to her knees and fisted handfuls of nightgown as she shook.

Fern softened, her curiosity giving way to empathy. She had never been one for social niceties, but at that moment, she decided that the other woman needed a friend—someone who would stand by her as the storm raged outside. Something Fern wished she had possessed ten years ago.

She sat on the floor across from the terrified woman, and not so close as to cause her more anxiety. Fern drew her knees up and leaned against the books. It took a moment to find a comfortable spot as hard edges dug into her spine.

"I don't like storms. That's why I came here. I imagine all these books are like solid stone bricks, creating an impenetrable wall between me and what is happening outside." She glanced along the row as a flash of lightning illuminated the library for an instant.

The woman nodded and whispered, "Me too."

"I'm Fern Oakby. Lord Warrington hired me to investigate sickly plants by a fountain." She didn't expect a reply, but hoped the woman would listen to her voice and not the frightening crash of thunder.

"Mill...Millicent Carlisle," the other woman said between cracks of lightning.

"Pleased to meet you, Miss Carlisle." Fern wondered who the woman was, that she dashed through the house in only her nightgown like a spectre. Assuming she was flesh and blood, her soft voice seemed too polished to be a servant. Nor could she imagine any maid fleeing to the library when they had a robust pantry to take shelter in. A friend of the family, perhaps? She tried to recollect if his lordship had any children who might require a governess.

"Mrs." Millicent drew a shuddering breath. "I am Mrs Carlisle."

"My apologies. Are you here with your husband visiting Lord Warrington?" Fern asked. She thought if she kept asking gentle questions of Millicent, it would give her something else to concentrate on.

She turned her face on her knees to stare at Fern. "No. I am widowed. Bertie is my brother. I live here now." She spoke in bursts, as though she mustered her courage for each short sentence and then uttered the words between claps of thunder.

"I am sorry." Fern struggled for a change of topic. Asking about a dead husband wouldn't help with the tears or panic.

She noticed how Millicent's gaze darted to the windows every time lightning flashed, followed by a flinch at the subsequent thunder.

"You have a lot of books here. Were you looking for anything in particular? Perhaps I could help, if you like?" She picked up one and read the title. It appeared to be a gothic novel. The next was a romance. The third was *Northanger Abbey* by Jane Austen.

"It appears you were seeking an escape among the pages. Perhaps I could find a travel memoir with lots of drawings? I love reading those, and we could escape together to a warmer country without such storms." Fern had lost herself in novels and let them sweep her away to other places and times when she sought to run away from her troubles.

Millicent raised her head and brushed her hair away from her face with one hand. She sniffled and took a shaky breath, attempting to compose herself. "I love stories. Especially ones with smart heroines and dragons. Do you like dragons?"

Fern picked up a book that had landed upside down, and she could practically hear its stretched spine screaming for help. "Yes. I live in Drake's Bend, and our village got its name centuries ago from the dragons who used to sleep by the curve of the river. I like stories of enormous dragons who people could ride for days and days as they soared over strange new lands." Although, if she were honest, rare botany fired her imagination as much as any winged lizards.

One by one, she made a pile of the discarded books, asking the frightened woman quiet questions about each. As Fern made a stack, Millicent helped her, using one hand while her other remained curled in against her stomach. Fern peered from the corner of her eye, wondering if Millicent had some injury to her arm. Then she spied something papery. She couldn't quite make it out, but the other woman appeared to be sheltering something with ears and a tail.

"What do you have there?" Fern asked.

"Oh. This. I made a dragon from paper." Swallowing a sob, Millicent sat a little taller. She shifted her hand, which had stopped trembling as Fern drew more of her attention, and she paid less heed to the storm.

"Oh. That is exquisite," Fern said.

The little dragon was about six inches tall and even had papery wings that were tucked by its body and a long tail. Fern had as much patience for paper crafts as she did for embroidery.

"I never got the hang of paper quilling or folding, even though I know noble ladies are supposed to do such things." Fern bit the inside of her cheek before she made a rude comment about the skills noble women were forced to acquire. Millicent was obviously a much better student than Fern had ever been.

"Long ago, I found a book about origami. It's Japanese paper folding. Watch this." Millicent tugged on the paper dragon's tail, and its wings flapped up and down. A faint smile touched her full lips, and her breathing seemed more regular now.

"That is clever. I much prefer something that can move to pages glued stiff and mounted like paper-quilled pictures." Origami might be a worthy distraction for her during the long winter months, when snow and cold kept her inside with only brief visits to the greenhouse. There might be a book that showed her how to make replicas of flowers.

"I don't like storms. Or loud noises. Or lots of people." Millicent kept her gaze fixed on the paper dragon as she spoke. "Bertie says I'm just being silly and hysterical, but I can't help it. Truly." Her voice became small on the last few words, as though she often had to defend the reactions of her body and mind.

"You must detest balls almost as much as I do." That wasn't entirely true. Fern loved dancing and music. It was the cruel gossip that she disliked.

"They were torture. All those people crammed inside, and all shouting to be heard over the music. Peter, he was my husband, allowed me to leave when I couldn't take it any longer and I was overwhelmed. I miss him terribly." Millicent leaned her head back against the books, and a single tear rolled down her cheek.

"Did you lose him recently?" Fern had tried to avoid the topic, but if Millicent raised the spectre, surely she could ask just a few questions about the deceased spouse to ease the curiosity itching at the back of her mind.

"Three years. You don't know who I am, do you?" The shudders had stilled and when she opened her eyes to regard Fern, the tiniest hint of interest simmered in their depths.

"No. Sorry. Should I?" She hadn't kept up with society gossip, but Ambrose did. How he loved his periodicals, detailing all the latest scandals from London.

Millicent looked away. "Well, no point in dredging it up now. Better it stay buried in the past."

Except when someone dangled a carrot like that. How

could she not nibble? She would ask Ambrose what he knew about the widow Mrs Carlisle as soon as she got home.

"Thank you, Miss Oakby, for talking to me. I haven't felt this calm during a storm in a very long time." Millicent placed the dragon in her lap to pick up another fallen book.

Fern rather liked the intimacy of talking to someone while huddled among the books as a storm lashed the house. They were like two adventurers on a boat in a rough ocean. "You are welcome. Sometimes, all we need is a gentle reminder that we are not alone in our struggles. I also came to the library to find sanctuary against the storm. But you must call me Fern. I'm not one to adhere to the rules of society."

The tiniest smile tugged at the other woman's lips. "And you must call me Millie. I always thought that Millicent sounds like something medicinal you take for a horrid cough."

Fern swallowed a laugh, in case she startled the woman and sent her spiralling back into panic. "At least you're not named after a dull plant that hides in the shade."

"I think ferns are quite lovely. Understated, and with a quiet dignity. Not showy like some flowers." Millie drew a few more deep breaths and anchored herself in the conversation.

"I don't think anyone would ever describe me as understated or possessing quiet dignity. But I don't really mind my name. I like all sorts of plants. My father was a botanist, and he was named after a tree by his mother." Now that she thought about it, her uncle didn't have a botanical name. Or he might have, but never used it that she could remember. Fern's paternal grandfather probably named his heir and let his wife pick the name for the second son.

Only now did she realise it had quietened down outside, and the thunder was a distant rumble. "I think the storm has blown over. Will you be all right now? It's just I have to be up very early and could do with a few hours' sleep."

Millie nodded. "Yes. Thank you. I will return to my room too."

Together, the women placed the books back on the shelves and said their goodnights. Millie took the candle and led the way, looking like an ethereal figure haunting the manor, like a character from a gothic novel.

# CHAPTER 8

After an eventful evening, Fern slept soundly. She awoke as the first light of dawn peeked through the curtains of the small room. It took her a moment to orientate herself in the unfamiliar surroundings before remembering where she was. She stretched her limbs and sighed, shaking off the lingering heaviness left in the wake of the storm. Determined to confirm the fountain had contaminated the garden so she could return home that day, she flung back the blankets and rose.

From the satchel, Fern pulled out a clean shirt, then she tugged on her trousers. Last, she laced on her boots, eager to be outdoors and survey any damage caused by the fierce weather. The servants would already be up, busy cleaning and cooking and doing dozens of other tasks that their noble master probably never even noticed.

Next, Fern packed the few things she had brought with her into the satchel and flung it over her shoulder. Since she didn't intend to stay at the manor another night, the bag could be left in the kitchen or by her mare's stall in the stables. Picking up the tray from her dinner the night before, she walked through the house and down the dim servants' hall.

Below stairs, a maid gave her a startled look as she placed the tray on a bench. Already, staff darted across the floor as they hurried to prepare a feast for the two people residing in the house. Avoiding a footman carrying a wooden tray with the silverware, Fern stepped outside.

The damp, earthy scent of rain-soaked soil greeted her. A low mist clung to Warrington Manor and obscured the tops of trees. Fern struck off in the general direction of the old fountain, surveying damage caused by the tempestuous weather on her way.

The air was fresh, washed clean by the night's rain, but the scent of upturned earth and broken foliage hung heavily around her. She pulled her coat tighter against the chill as she walked. Moving through the gardens, she appraised the damage. Branches and leaves littered the pathways, and several new plantings had been tugged loose of the soil, roots exposed to the morning air. She felt a pang of sadness for the lost plants, each one a living thing that had not withstood nature's fury.

The flowerbeds, once meticulously maintained, were now a jumble of petals and stems. The vibrant colours of the blooms were dulled by splashed mud, making the once-cheerful garden appear forlorn. Fern crouched down, gently lifting a sodden dahlia flower, its petals bruised and heavy with rainwater.

Continuing her survey, she noticed the larger trees had

fared better. Deep roots anchored them against the wind's onslaught. However, a delicate climber that scrambled over an arbour had become another victim of the storm. Its stems were torn in many places, tendrils hanging loose and bereft of their blooms.

She moved through to the next garden room—the walled space that sheltered the glorious roses. As Fern walked the lime chip paths and inspected the roses, she noted that apart from torn petals, there was little damage. For all their delicate appearance, roses were surprisingly robust. Probably due to the hard pruning undertaken by the groundsmen, that removed any leggy growth prone to snapping.

A rustling caught her attention, and Fern stared at the length of wall at one side. Her feet halted, and she frowned. She had hurried through the area the previous day, trying to keep apace with Mr Corby, but she couldn't recollect seeing the unusual and vigorous vine that completely obscured the stonework. Her memory suggested a Boston ivy had been in that spot.

She must have been mistaken. The climber did in some ways resemble an unusually aggressive Boston ivy. Its tendrils creeping and twisting like serpents in search of prey. But they were thicker than normal. What should have been stems no wider than her finger, were instead sinewy ropes like fore-arms. Even its leaves seemed almost malicious in their expanse, like an invading army that had claimed the entirety of the wall for itself. Larger than her hand, the leaves were a deep green mottled with crimson, as though a painter had splashed red at them. It created an eerily beautiful sight that both fascinated and unnerved her.

"Odd. I don't remember seeing you yesterday." How on earth had she not noticed that it was no common ivy? Given the arresting nature of the climber, it should have stopped her in her tracks. As it just had. But it had to have been there the day before. Such plants didn't just spring from the earth overnight like a magical beanstalk.

She must have been intent on catching the grumpy gardener and trotted right past the unusual creeper.

"Curiouser and curiouser. I've never read of such a variety of Boston ivy. Father would have been fascinated to study you," she murmured to the plant.

As Fern reached out to touch one of the leaves, she hesitated, her fingers hovering above the splashed surface. Her impulsive nature tended to lead her into precarious situations, and for some reason, a soft voice of caution made her pause.

Some plants had leaves coated in toxins, like the fine hairs of a stinging nettle. Or the resin emitted by poisonous ivy. She didn't need her hand swelling up or turning red because she touched something she shouldn't have. The red splotches might be a warning sign from nature.

"I think I will consult Mr Corby about you first. Just in case you are some species of poisonous ivy." Fern curled her fingers into her palm and kept them well away from the glossy leaf.

As she turned to continue on to the fountain, something jarred against the mass of foliage and caught her attention. Peering closer, and without touching the ivy, she noticed a leather glove such as gardeners commonly wore, jutting out from the undergrowth like the wilted petals of a forgotten flower.

Grasping hold of an empty finger, she eased it free of the ivy's suckers. The worn leather seemed strangely heavy in her grasp, having soaked up the overnight rain. "One of the groundsmen might have misplaced you, perhaps in a hurry to get indoors yesterday. I'll ask Mr Corby to return it to the owner." She tucked the glove into the pocket of her coat before carrying on her way.

"Miss Oakby!" called an unfamiliar voice.

Turning, she found a young, and what she'd describe as *weedy*, groundsman, his face flushed with exertion as he ran along the path. "Beggin' your pardon, miss, but we can't seem to find Mr. Corby and wondered if he was with you. One of the beech is tore up bad, you see, and we need to know if we try and save it or cut it down."

"No. He's not with me," Fern replied, but the lad wasn't listening to her.

His gaze had drifted sideways, and his mouth formed an O of surprise. He raised one hand and pointed. "Blimey! Where did that come from?"

Then he stared at her, as though he expected either an answer or a confession that she had just tossed the climber over the wall.

"Are you new? This ivy has surely stood in this spot for several years given the thickness of its growth." A new employee might take many months to learn all the wonders held within the grounds of an estate as large as Warrington Manor.

The lad shook his head. "I've been a groundsman here for

two years, miss, and I ain't never seen that before. This stonework used to be covered in a regular ivy that was only about eight foot across. Mr Corby ordered us to keep it under control with hard pruning, and its trunk was no thicker than your wrist."

A chill rippled down Fern's spine as she stared at the creeper with renewed interest. Bending, she peered under the leaves to spy a trunk broader than a man's thigh. "Are you sure? You might be thinking about another wall in a different place."

"Oh, no, miss. I swear that weren't this big yesterday." The lad kicked at the leaves. A ripple ran over the foliage, followed by a thud.

Fern and the lad stared at the grass by the tree trunk-like base. Now, a boot sat beneath the ivy.

"That's Mr Corby's! You can see the splash of blue on the toe from when he painted the pergola." The young groundsman's voice trembled with recognition.

Fern leaned in closer. The rolled edge of the leather had a sky-blue line across it.

"Huh. It sounded like it dropped through the ivy. Perhaps Mr Corby lost it during the storm and a gust of wind blew it over the wall." A storm that could tear branches off hundred-year-old oaks could certainly throw a boot through the air. "Is this also Mr Corby's?" Fern reached into her pocket and retrieved the leather glove she found earlier.

"Could be, I suppose. But all gloves look alike, don't they?" He shrugged.

Fern turned it over but there were no paint splashes like on the boot. Next, she turned the open edge over and peered inside. "Someone has written a large C in here." Most likely a grumpy gardener who marked his possessions so no one else took them.

Fern swallowed a lump that formed in her throat. Could the storm have snatched up a boot and a glove? Her initial curiosity about the plant morphed into a cold suspicion. Still reluctant to touch the ivy, she found a broken branch caught up in a nearby shrub. She used the woody length to poke at the climber, feeling somewhat silly for prodding at it like a slumbering bear. Did she expect it to drop the other boot?

Back and forth she dragged the branch until the end snagged on something and broke off. Fern stared at the snapped piece of wood, wondering what to do next when the vine quivered all over. As the leaves shook, it exposed a monstrous flower pod, shaped like a fig but much larger. If this were a fig, it would feed a family of six as it was twice the size of Fern's fist.

The pod twitched and pulsed like a cat about to vomit on the best rug. Then its glossy maroon skin split open with a sickening, wet cloth-tearing sound. Fleshy petals peeled back to reveal a dark interior, and it expelled a small, glistening white object. Whatever it was, it landed with the soft plop of a raindrop in a patch of mud.

Without thinking, Fern stepped closer and crouched down for a better look. The open flower pod emitted an odour of decay that reminded her of the *Stapelia lepida*, or the starfish flower, a carnivorous plant that lured flies close by mimicking the stench of rotting flesh. Now that she thought about it, she could see the similarity between its fleshy five-starred flower and the one before her. All it lacked was the distinctive blood-red spots on a pale, skin-toned background.

"Could you possibly be a climbing variant of *Stapelia lepida*?" she wondered aloud.

"What's that?" The lad stumbled backwards.

Fern paused, wondering if he was asking about the starfish flower or whatever had fallen from the ivy. She decided curiosity demanded she investigate the thing lodged in the mud first. Reaching out with her stick, Fern flicked the white object clear of the dirt.

Once lying on the grass, it had a vaguely familiar shape with rounded ends. "It looks like a bone."

One that had been stripped clean and gleamed wetly in the early light. She couldn't place what animal it had come from.

"You mean that plant ate sommit?" The young groundsman took another step backwards, as though he feared the vine would lash out and ensnare him.

Fern rolled her eyes and reminded herself that not every groundsman had the same advantage as her, with a renowned botanist father to impart the knowledge of a lifetime. Many started in the job without knowing anything about flora or gardening.

"There are many carnivorous plants. The *Stapelia lepida*, or starfish flower, has a flower very similar to this one. Another better-known one is *Dionaea muscipula*, or the Venus flytrap. Both commonly consume flies, but their blooms are nowhere near as large as this fellow." Fern pointed to the flower with her stick, the petals closing back up to form the fig-shaped pod. "It's highly unlikely that this was deliberate. I suspect a hawk flying overhead might have had a meal in its talons and dropped the bone into the flower due to the storm. The plant has now spat it out, perhaps because the bone is foreign to it." Fern said the words to reassure the startled boy, but a voice whispered this was no accident. If a hawk dropped its dinner, what stripped the bone of all flesh and sinew?

A small bone and a boot were insufficient evidence to draw any conclusions about a possibly carnivorous nature of the unusual climber. Both items could have been picked up by the storm and simply ended up caught in the dense foliage.

Fern wracked her brain for what she knew of carnivorous plants. The largest known specimen was the giant montane pitcher plant. While that species had been known to consume frogs or rats, what undulated before her was no pitcher plant. As she reviewed what else the greenery could be, another groundsman came racing through the storm-damaged garden.

Tall and wiry, his face was deeply tanned from years of labouring outside. He skidded to a halt beside her and the young lad, his eyes wide at the sight scrambling over the wall. Shaking his head as though he sought to clear his vision, he turned to the younger groundsman. "Have you found Mr Corby yet? His lordship is up early and asking for a report about the grounds."

Before the lad could reply, the vine shuddered violently once more. With a sickening squelch, it dropped something heavy onto the wet ground. A second boot landed with a dull thump, and it was all too clear this wasn't a storm-tossed item. A leg bone protruded grotesquely from the top of the boot.

All three of them took a jump back, and the younger lad pressed a hand to his mouth as his stomach rebelled at the sight.

"While it is possible that Mr Corby might lose one boot accidentally, he probably wouldn't misplace his tibia." Even as she stared at the bone and boot, Fern's brain refused to believe the vine was responsible. She glanced up at the surrounding trees. "Did Mr Corby take a saw with him when he set off to inspect the gardens this morning? It might be possible he was up a tree, sawing off broken branches when he suffered a horrible accident."

"That looks snapped, not sawn." The older groundsman pointed to the jagged tip. "And if he did saw off his own leg, where's the rest of him?"

"A very good question. We're also assuming it belongs to Mr Corby. What if someone stole his boots during the night and had a misadventure? We need to inform Lord Warrington and continue the search for Mr Corby," Fern said with a quiet authority that brooked no argument. "No one is to touch either the plant or boots until his lordship is told."

"I'll go!" The young lad didn't need to be told twice, and he sped off and away from the terrible vine before Fern could reply.

"I'll gather tools to hack this thing back, in case it's hiding anything else," the second man said.

While Fern waited, she studied the vine. It was unlike anything she had ever encountered in her botanical studies. If the plant was in any way responsible for Mr Corby's disappearance (not that she could believe it, but it was an interesting hypothetical question), what could have caused such an aberration in nature?

*The storm.* The lad said the vine had not been there the day before, but only a normal ivy. That fit Fern's recollection of when she had passed through the garden. The climber before her hadn't been there until the terrible storm lashed the estate.

Her scientific curiosity warred with a growing sense of horror as she imagined what might have happened to the grumpy head gardener. The implications were disturbing. This wasn't just about sickly plants around a fountain anymore—it was something far darker...and deadlier.

# CHAPTER 9

Fern didn't have to wait long before Lord Warrington, garbed for riding in breeches, polished boots, and a fitted coat, strode through the gap in the hedges and along the paths of the rose garden. The two groundsmen trailed behind him, the older one pushing a wheelbarrow clattering with tools and shears, ready to mount an assault on the interloping ivy.

"What's all this fuss about? I was about to ride out when the lad waved his arms and rambled on about some plant eating Corby." Lord Warrington stopped and placed his hands on his hips to glare at the monstrosity that pulled the eye away from the beauty of the roses. "Who planted this ugly thing in my rose garden?" He fixed an accusing stare on Fern, as though he suspected her of sneaking the ivy onto the grounds in her satchel.

"From what your men have told me, it seems that the Boston ivy that was originally here has transformed somehow during the storm. As for Mr Corby, we have found his boots... and what appears to be a tibia." Fern pointed to the boot sitting upright at the base of the climber, which undulated to an invisible breeze. The leaves rippled, and more of the fig-like flower pods emerged from the foliage.

As his lordship's gaze fell upon the creamy arrow pointing upwards from the boot, his face paled to the colour of milk left too long in the sun. His hand flew to his mouth, and he turned away sharply, fighting the urge to retch.

"God in heaven." He gasped, scuttling backwards a few steps to steady himself against a nearby plinth holding a marble bust.

The swaying plant stilled. A lone flower pod rotated like a head towards where his lordship stood.

"I wondered if Mr Corby might have had a horrible accident while sawing back broken trees this morning?" Fern raised the most likely explanation.

It was a little too early in the morning to suggest a head gardener eating monstrosity now reigned over the rose beds.

Lord Warrington straightened, drawing on whatever reserves of fortitude he possessed. "Moyles, assemble the grounds staff. Finch, gather the stable lads. We must search the estate. Every inch. If Corby is missing a leg, we need to find the poor man," he commanded, sweeping his arm over the expanse of his holding as if rallying troops for battle.

"Yes, milord." Moyles nodded to his master and then trotted off with the younger lad in his wake, leaving behind the wheelbarrow of tools.

Lord Warrington turned to Fern, his lips thin and tight, lines drawn around his eyes. "Miss Oakby, you must examine this...this monstrosity. We must know if it conceals...anything else. I shall address the staff."

Lord Warrington strode away, probably before the ivy spat out any more body parts. His mutterings drifted on the still air until he disappeared through the yew, and Fern was left in an eerie silence.

"Right. Time to trade the stick for something more robust." Fern tossed the remains of the twig over the wall and approached the selection of tools gathered by Moyles.

She picked a pair of gloves. They were thick leather things that should protect her hands from any potentially toxic substance the ivy might secrete, unless the plant sucked them off. Next, she picked up a long-handled rake and a pair of shears. As foolish as she looked using gardening tools like a sword and shield, she wasn't going to stick her hand among the leaves until she learned more about her opponent.

Using the rake, Fern drew it across the layers of foliage so she could peer beneath. The leaves were thick and almost rubbery. Their surface was slick with moisture from the storm. She worked methodically, starting at one end and combing the ivy with the rake. Prising apart one spot revealed another clue. A fragment of cloth was caught within the sinewy grasp of a tendril. The fabric was torn, but unmistakably similar to the dark-brown coat Mr Corby had been wearing the day before.

Using the end of the shears, Fern lifted the scrap and tugged it free. The piece dropped to the ground next to the boot. With painstaking care, she continued her work. The vine seemed almost sentient in its stillness now that it was being closely examined. Each time she freed another piece of fabric—mercifully there were no more bones—it felt like unwrapping secrets that were never meant to be revealed.

Fern remained focused on her task while she pondered how such an extraordinary plant came into existence during the storm. Was it possible that Mr Corby had met his end caught in its tendrils, or was there another explanation entirely? The questions circled in her mind like carrion birds as she peeled back another leaf.

The tines of the rake snagged against a particularly dense clump of leaves and flower pods. Fern adjusted her grip on the handle, her muscles tensing as she prepared to pull back the covering foliage. The head of the rake was stuck, and the ivy held fast. Fern refused to lose a game of tug of war to a plant and gave a determined yank, peeling away the stubborn veil of green.

As the leaves parted, a grotesque tableau emerged from the shadows beneath the vine. Mr Corby—or what was left of him—lay enmeshed in a cocoon of fibrous tendrils that had wound around his form like pythons constricting their prey. His remains appeared skeletal within the confines of his heavy wool coat. His shirt and trousers underneath were shredded as though he had been set upon by knife-wielding pixies. His flesh had been stripped away by either the carnivorous plant's insidious embrace or the suckling mouths of the flower pods.

Fern's mind immediately wondered how to prove that the flower pods devoured flesh like the star-shaped mouths of the starfish flower. Could she stomach sacrificing a mouse to advance her botanical knowledge of the rare specimen before her?

No, she decided. Not a mouse. Possibly a rat, though, because few people liked them. As long as someone else caught it and then dangled it before the vine like offering a morsel to a hungry snake.

Fern tightened her grip on the wooden handle and steeled herself to carry on. She prodded at the vine with the tool, rapping on the woody arms and demanding it relinquish its hold on the unfortunate gardener. Like a nocturnal creature exposed to sunlight, the tendrils recoiled from the metal teeth of the rake and unwound from around its prize before retreating back into the thicket.

Released from the web that had been holding him upright, the clothed skeleton fell to the ground with a muffled thunk, like a gentle reminder of mortality that echoed through the quiet of the garden. Thankfully, the long coat did a fine job of keeping him *intact*. Mr Corby now lay on his back. Hollow eye sockets stared up at Fern with an accusatory emptiness. Did his mortal remains plead with her for justice, or was it a mocking grin, convinced she was out of her depth and she'd never solve the puzzle of his death?

Her gaze hardened, and she leaned on the handle of the rake. There was no escaping it now—this wasn't a fatal gardening accident while limbing up a tree, nor any murder committed under cover of dark and concealed in the lush greenery.

This was something far more sinister.

As she waited to attract the attention of the staff sent to search the grounds for the no-longer-missing man, Fern resolved that the monstrous creation would yield its secrets to her. Once she had learned all she could, she would write to the botanical society about her incredible discovery. Perhaps they would finally admit her as a member and give her a standing ovation for her work.

"What are you?" Fern said to the vine. Curiosity and morbid fascination warred with a slither of horror inside her.

She stared at the foliage, tendrils, and flowers as she tried to determine how the plant had reduced the head gardener to a pile of bones in only a few hours. Suckers on the tendrils had possibly resulted in the tearing of his shirt and trousers. Did the flower pods contain some sort of dissolving liquid that had reduced Mr Corby to a palatable feed for the plant?

"That might explain your incredible overnight growth if Corby acted as a fertiliser once consumed." Ensuring she stayed out of reach of grasping vines, Fern knelt down to examine the exposed bones. There didn't appear to be any teeth marks, although that didn't reassure her much.

At length, she heard men combing the grounds and calling out for Mr Corby. Not that the poor man would ever reply. Fern waved her arms.

"Over here! I have found Mr Corby!" she shouted. Then her mind stuttered. What if it was someone else? No, that wasn't possible. The younger man, Finch, had confirmed the boots were those of the head gardener. She pushed the very idea of there being *another* body concealed in the vine from her mind.

Four men hurried over with a mix of concern and curiosity written on their lined faces. One man she recognised, the older groundsman Moyles. The others appeared to be men pulled from their work in the stables.

"Where is he?" Moyles looked around, then he noticed the shape behind Fern. He froze, his hand outstretched and his attention fixated on the sight laid out at the base of the climber. He let out a long sigh. "That's him all right. That coat is an old one of his lordship's that Mr Corby always wore when out in the rain or cold. What happened to him?"

The others huddled in a loose group and gawked at the pile of bones and shredded clothing dressed in a finely tailored great coat that had once been Mr Corby. The men's faces paled under their weathered skin. Finch, who appeared to be barely out of boyhood, clutched his stomach as he fought back his breakfast. Again.

"Mr Corby was held tight under the growth. When I rapped on the tendrils with the rake, they released him." Fern pointed to where she had found the man cocooned by twisted wooden arms.

"We need to burn it to the ground!" one man said to murmurs of agreement from the others.

"No one is to touch it until Lord Warrington has been advised." Fern raised the rake, ready to defend bones and vine if necessary. Both discoveries needed to be carefully examined. While she didn't want anyone else to meet the same fate as Mr Corby, no one was going to deprive her of a chance to present a paper on the ivy to the botanical society.

Then another thought wriggled and itched in the back of her mind. If one such horror had sprouted overnight, might there be others? "During your search, did any of you find any other similar vines or unusual plants in the gardens?"

The men scratched chins, muttered among themselves, and shook their heads.

"Storms usually pull stuff down. An old oak split and fell

on a fountain," said one of the older men, a sturdy fellow with a face like weathered bark.

"The one with the dead creeping thyme and buxus?" She recalled the large specimen that had shaded the secluded room much loved by Lady Warrington.

"That's the one." He pointed to the eastern side of the rose garden.

"Bother. I'm going to have a look at the damage. But nobody is to go near this vine. Give it a wide berth. Do you all understand?" Fern pointed to each man with the rake.

"What about poor Mr Corby? It ain't right that he's lying there like that." Finch pulled his cap from his head and twisted it in his hands as he darted glances at the skeleton.

"Fetch something to place over him until Lord Warrington returns," Fern said.

Moyles stayed to act as guard. Finch rushed to fetch a canvas to drape over the remains. The others returned to their jobs, now that the search for the missing gardener was over.

Satisfied that no one would be foolish enough to tackle the vine, and if they did, Fern hoped it was satiated for the moment, she struck off through the rose beds to investigate the next room. Her boots crunched over the debris strewn across the path—scattered reminders of the storm's ferocity. The bright scent of torn branches and sap mingled with the acrid tang of charred wood from a lightning strike.

The tall yew hedges that framed the secret nook stood watch over the room beyond, their dark foliage ruffled like dishevelled hair by the strong winds. As Fern entered the secluded nook, she discovered the damage was worse than she anticipated. A lightning strike had split a heavy limb from the oak in the corner. The branch lay across the fountain like a giant's discarded club. The blow had shattered the fountain's basin and split the stone. What had once been broken was now ruined.

Fern knelt to survey the damage to the destroyed water feature. "There will be no fixing you now."

The unexpected silver lining of this particular storm cloud was it afforded her a peek at the mechanism and pipes beneath the fountain. With care, she levered a chunk of stone out of the way. As she peered into the hole, a faint, raspy cry pierced the stillness, at odds with the noises one expected from a wrecked fountain.

Fern paused, head cocked to one side as she tried to place the sound. Her heart skipped a beat as it came again, from… *beneath* the fractured remains.

"Hello?" she called into the hole she had created. "Did you fall in?"

The cry rasped again, barely audible, as though whatever made the sound was exhausted. An animal might have sought shelter from the storm, wormed its way under the fountain somehow and then become trapped when the branch came down on top of it.

She tried to place the cry. A cat or fox, maybe?

"Don't worry, little one, I shall fetch help, and we will get you out of there." She ran back to where Moyles stood by the vine. "I need your help! There is some small animal trapped under the fountain." She gestured back over her shoulder.

The groundsman eyed the vine, and the now canvas-draped object.

"I don't think either are going anywhere," she said when he hesitated.

Nobody could help Mr Corby now, but some poor creature hovering on the brink might still be rescued and revived.

With another backwards glance at the vine, Moyles followed her. She hurried along the path, not quite running but setting a quick pace.

In the sheltered corner, Fern pointed to the downed branch and the crushed stonework underneath. "I pulled out a broken bit to make a hole, trying to see the pipes below, when I heard a cry. A fox might have crawled in last night seeking shelter and got trapped."

"Let's see what we can do," Moyles said.

Together, they set to work. The branch was too heavy to be dragged away, and would need to be sawn into pieces. So instead, they chipped away at the chunks of stone beneath it. They hauled lumps out of the once-elegant water feature and made a pile on the path.

Finally, they had cleared enough debris to reveal a small opening that one determined botanist could fit in—if she crawled on her stomach and kept her arms extended before her.

"Are you sure about this, miss?" Moyles asked, his face crinkled in worry. "You don't know what's in there. What if it's like the other thing?"

"You think the vine that ate Mr Corby might have underground runners that ensnare creatures and drag them within reach of the main plant?" Now she said it out loud, she wished she hadn't.

# CHAPTER 10

Fern wondered how Mr Corby had ended up in the deadly python-like embrace. Had a tendril snatched him as he walked past in the dark, or had the head gardener lunged at the interloper for invading the roses? She could well imagine the grumpy individual wrestling with the carnivorous plant.

"It could have runners." Moyles paled under his sun-weathered skin. His Adam's apple bobbing up and down against the neckerchief tied below it. "We don't yet know how it got him."

"I assure you, I have no intention of being dessert for some overgrown ivy. How about you can hang onto my ankles and haul me back out if I shout for help?" It wasn't the best plan, admittedly, but anything else would mean more delays while they summoned extra men and equipment. One quick peek in the hole to satisfy her curiosity couldn't be too dangerous, surely?

Moyles brushed his hands against the sides of his coat, his

fingers dipping into a pocket. "This might help." He held out the stub of a candle, no more than two inches square. Finding his tinder box in another pocket, he lit the tiny bit of wick.

"Thank you." Fern placed the stub inside the hole before a draft snatched the tiny light. The flickering glow elicited a faint, reedy cry from below.

"I'm coming in," she said to whatever made the noise. "And I expect you to behave. I don't want to be scratched, bitten, or eaten. Otherwise, I shall leave you there."

Fern knelt down and lay on her stomach before the dark hole. She peered into the opening. The cool stone pressed against her cheek as she angled her head to catch a glimpse of whatever lay trapped within.

"Stay close," she instructed Moyles, whose hands hovered near her ankles, ready to yank her backwards should anything untoward happen.

Cautiously, Fern crawled further into the hole, using her elbows and knees to propel her along. Every few inches, she pushed the candle forwards. The light fought bravely against the encroaching darkness as she advanced downwards inch by inch. Her eyes adjusted, and shapes formed in the shadows.

Another weak cry reached her ears, a pitiful sound that spurred her onwards. Another half a foot and a foul stench crammed itself into the space and jabbed sharp fingers up her nostrils. Fern screwed up her nose, but the odour persisted. She wriggled deeper, her fingers brushing against something soft but chilled. She had expected to find fur. Not a fox or cat then.

Recoiling slightly, she steadied herself before sliding the

stub of candle along the dirt. The flame flickered with her inhaled breath, and then the small circle of light caressed something leathery-looking and greyish, like a discarded sofa cushion.

No, not leather. Scales.

She reached out a tentative hand and touched the creature again. Bones moved under skin, and the shape emitted a barely audible gasp. Breathing in shallow snatches against the stench, Fern cobbled together a horrible story out of what she had discovered.

The trapped animal had been down here far longer than just the previous night. It was starved and lying in its own filth. Only now did she recognise the shape when a wing gave a shiver-like flutter against its side.

*Dragon.*

The world contracted to the cramped darkness and the feeble life that trembled under Fern's touch. A dragon. The very creatures who quietly vanished from their world. Now one huddled before her. Deathly sick and pitiable.

"How did you end up in here?" she asked, not expecting any answer. "Moyles, it's a dragon," she called over her shoulder.

A gasp echoed her astonishment from outside the hole. "A dragon, miss? Are you certain?"

She bit back a retort of *No, actually, as I frequently confuse foxes and dragons. Which ones have wings, again?* "Yes. And it's alive. Although barely."

Fern assessed the situation the best she could. She couldn't leave the creature here, or it would perish. The dragon was small, likely only a hatchling not long out of the shell. Like the one she had found perished by the tree stump at the river. From what she could make out, this one's scales were dulled by starvation and possibly injury.

She manoeuvred to get a better look at it, inching forwards until her face hovered near its snout. Two silvery eyes, barely open slits due to its weakened condition, met her gaze.

"Hold on, little one, for just a bit longer. I will get you out. I promise," she whispered.

The dragon rolled its head to one side, and its dry and cold muzzle nudged against her hand—but whether in understanding or by accident, Fern couldn't tell.

Having made a promise to the deathly sick dragon, Fern had to make good on her word. She wriggled backwards until daylight flared across her vision.

Moyles was crouched by the gap and helped her to her feet. "Did that plant eat a dragon too?"

Considering the robust Mr Corby had been skeletonised by the plant, she couldn't see the small dragon being left intact. Unless the ivy couldn't bite through scales. There was a thought for another day. "Doubtful. I'd say it's been stuck for some time and was trapped before the carnivorous vine appeared. While I would guess it is only a youngster, it's still far too wide to fit through that hole. We need to make it bigger."

Fern planted her hands on her hips and considered the problem. They needed the fallen branch out of the way before she could extract the dragon. Raised voices came from elsewhere in the garden. One cultured voice was instantly recognisable—Lord Warrington.

"His lordship is back," Moyles said. For a moment, the groundsman was torn about what to do.

"Let's advise him of the latest development," Fern said. Then, down the hole, she called to the hatchling, "I'll be back with help, I promise."

She took off after Moyles, his figure receding into the distance, hastening towards the commotion where Lord Warrington's voice carried over the morning air. Back through the hedge tunnel, she wound her way to the rose garden and the monster that had taken over the stone wall.

Lord Warrington and a group of men stood by the covered remains. One of the bolder groundsmen lifted a corner of the canvas, revealing the coat-wearing skeleton.

"This can't be him, surely? The man only went missing last night," Lord Warrington said.

"There's no one else missing from the estate, milord," the canvas-lifter said. Short and robust, he had arms that spoke of long hours of hard labour. Possibly relating to heavy horse harnesses if he had been pulled from the stables.

Lord Warrington made a chuffing noise in the back of his throat and crossed his arms. While his feet stayed in place, he leaned away from the dead man.

Fern laid out the evidence for the deceased's identity. Pointing from the woollen coat to the boots sitting by the body. One boot had a tibia jutting up, the other with the splash of blue paint. "Finch said those boots were most defi-nitely those of Mr Corby, and I found a leather glove among the leaves with a C written inside it. And Mr Moyles recog-nised the coat, which he said is an old one of yours, Lord Warrington, that you gave to Mr Corby."

"Dogs might have done this," another man piped up, rubbing the back of his neck.

"There aren't any teeth marks that dogs would have left. Besides, I found him trapped inside the vine. Under all that foliage, he was wrapped in tendrils like arms, holding him upright. When I tugged on them, they let go, and what was left of Mr Corby fell to the ground," Fern explained, her voice steady despite the incredulity that met her every word.

Lord Warrington's brows arched high in scepticism, and he exchanged a glance with his groundsmen. "Plants do not consume men," he said flatly.

"Plants *do* consume flesh, and there are many types of carnivorous plants. The smaller ones dine on flies and small insects. But there are varieties known to eat frogs and rats." It pained Fern to have to explain everything. If a crusty old man from the botanic society told them there were man-eating plants, they would have believed him without hesitation.

"A frog is one thing, a robust man quite another," Lord Warrington said, his look of disbelief still in place.

"It's only a question of scale," Fern replied. "This could be the botanic discovery of the century. The name of this estate will be known worldwide for this unique specimen." She couldn't keep the excitement from her voice. While the death of Mr Corby was a gruesome and horrible thing, his name would be remembered as the first known victim of the terrible vine.

His lordship huffed. Possibly, a reputation for man-eating plants wasn't one he wanted to be attached to his grand estate. Although it would be a highlight of his upcoming house party, so long as no guests stumbled into the plant.

"Oh! There is also the matter of the trapped dragon. I need men to help free it." Fern's exhilaration at the discovery of the vine almost overrode the urgency to free the sick dragon.

"Dragon? What dragon?" Lord Warrington spluttered and glared at Fern, as though she were solely responsible for the destruction of his immaculate gardens and unexpected things that kept popping up in it.

"Lightning brought down a branch of the oak by the fountain in the little room favoured by Lady Warrington. When I peered into the hole, I found what I believe is a trapped dragon. I suspect that is what has been killing the plants. The poor thing is knee-deep in muck that has seeped through the surrounding soil." Now that she thought about the creature's dire situation, it made sense to her. Which meant it had been down there for weeks. Probably surviving on insects and water dripping from a leaky pipe.

"How did a blasted dragon get under my fountain?" He rounded on her, demanding answers.

Fern shrugged. Her speciality was flora, not fauna. "I can only assume it crawled into a tunnel somewhere and got stuck. Can I have help to get it out?"

Lord Warrington waved a dismissive hand as his attention was drawn back to the leaves that undulated like a ripple over wheat. The same fig-shaped flower pod as before seemed to track his movements. "Yes, yes. Get it out before it dies and creates an awful stench. Take Finch and Moyles."

Before she left, she had one more question. "What will become of the vine?"

"The men will hack it to the ground, of course. It quite

draws the eye away from my roses, and I cannot risk it harming Lady Warrington or eating one of my guests." He turned away from her to make his way back to the house.

"You can't!" Fern shouted. "This is a new and unknown species. It must be studied."

He swivelled, and a cold gaze fixed on her. "You can study it to your heart's content *after* it is cut down. You were hired to find why the plants around the fountain were dying, Miss Oakby, not to interfere with the running of my estate."

Fern chewed the inside of her cheek. To destroy such a terrible beauty was a crime in itself. But the decision was Lord Warrington's to make. Not hers. She would take away as many samples as she could carry of its leaves, roots, and flowers to examine later. She might even be able to get a cutting to strike if she didn't let the ends dry out. Before she said anything she might regret later, she nodded.

"Yes, Lord Warrington. I will free the hatchling so the soil around the fountain can recover in time for your party." She bowed her head and clenched her hands together to stop herself from tugging her forelock.

"Come along, Moyles, Finch," she said once Lord Warrington had stalked away.

First, Finch and Moyles fetched a three-foot-long saw with handles at each end. Then they set to work in the secluded garden. The men took an end of the saw each and cut through the fallen branch section by section, to make it more manageable to remove.

Fern took off her coat and rolled up her sleeves. As each lump of wood fell to the ground, she dragged it to one side. It took time, and sweat beaded between Fern's shoulder blades before they had the tree trunk cleared away.

Next, they turned their attention to what was left of the fountain's basin. The two groundsmen hauled away chunks of stone, enlarging the hole to reveal the workings beneath the water feature.

Fern dropped to her knees, brushing aside dirt and stone fragments with hurried hands. Now she had sufficient room to crouch down and waddle into the space, rather than crawling on her stomach. Curling into a ball, she crept into the tunnel, relying on the light coming over her shoulders rather than the stub of candle. Soon, she reached the spot where she had last seen the shivering creature. Her fingers found scaly hide that seemed much cooler than it should have been.

"I'm going to have to hold onto you, to drag you out. But I need you to keep still or you might scratch me," she whispered to the youngster.

Gently, she slid her arms around the creature's middle, being careful of its delicate wings. The dragon didn't—or couldn't—resist as she tugged it free from its earthen prison. Inch by inch, Fern scooted backwards, part-carrying and part-dragging the limp creature. She thought it would be heavier given its size, but remembered reading in a book that dragons had hollow bones like birds, which aided them in flying. But still, it was much larger than a dog, even as scrawny as it was with sunken ribs. Nor did she want to break a wing as they flopped around at its sides.

Waddling backwards and trying not to further injure the hatchling took longer than she thought. Eventually, Fern emerged into the light and Moyles rushed to help. The dragon lay limp, splayed wings and eyes glazed over in pain.

"I have you now, little one. Please don't die on me," Fern said. She had failed her father in his final hours; she'd not fail this dragon. "Let's get it into the wheelbarrow."

Now that Fern could see it properly in the daylight, she wondered if the poor thing would survive for long. Its sides heaved in irregular, shallow breaths and it was dangerously close to starving.

"What happened to you?" she murmured as she slid her hands under its head and shoulders, while Moyles handled the hind with its drooping tail.

Between the two of them, they laid the creature in the wheelbarrow with its head curled next to its body and its tail placed carefully within so it didn't get trodden on.

"I think I know what happened," Moyles said as he picked up the handles of the wheelbarrow, and Fern walked alongside as they began their journey towards the stables. "His lordship had a hunt about a month ago. The dogs had the scent of something and chased it to ground close to here. The huntsman had an awful job getting the dogs out of the garden while Lord Warrington yelled about his roses. I wonder if this little dragon was their quarry. It might have been looking for somewhere to hide and found where the pipes for the fountain are exposed."

Fern considered the idea. A terrified creature being pursued by a pack of dogs might have squeezed into the small space. How long did it wait for the dogs to pass, only to realise once they had, that it couldn't turn around and get back out? "That does seem likely. The poor thing will have a long road to recovery." That raised more questions in Fern's mind. Was the dragon male or female? Who would give it the care needed to put flesh back on its frame? Would the dogs come looking for it again?

As they passed through the rose garden, men prepared to hack back the monstrous man-eating vine. The groundsmen wore thick leather gloves, their faces set into grim expressions as they held axes and saws. The tale of what happened to Mr Corby would have spread, and no one would want to find out how, *exactly*, the vine stripped the flesh from his bones.

## CHAPTER 11



Fern surveyed the rose garden, which now lacked the skeleton as a gruesome ornament. Mr Corby had been taken away and, hopefully, would be placed somewhere well away from hungry dogs until he could be buried.

"Could you please leave the flower pods intact? I'd like to study one," Fern called out, pointing to the cupped globes of maroon.

"We'll try, Miss Oakby." A man touched the brim of his cap in acknowledgement before swinging his axe over his shoulder. Another man held a curved pruning saw to remove the thick limbs.

"Thank you," Fern said. There would still be much to learn about the vine, even once it lay scattered across the ground in hundreds of bits. She could collect cuttings and leaves once the sickly dragonet was settled in a stall and had something to eat and drink.

As they continued across the grounds, Fern decided that she knew the exact place for the dragon to get better. At

Nemython House. Ambrose would be delighted to have a mythical creature to lavish attention on, and George would have practical ideas on how to aid its recovery. Luckily, there were a few dragon-related books among all the botany ones in their library. Not to mention the Bentley children would all be keen to pitch in and watch the dragon night and day until it was on the path to good health.

In the yard, Fern straightened her spine as Lord Warrington emerged from the stables, where he must have overseen a temporary resting place for Mr Corby. His lordship's gaze fell to the pitiable form in the wheelbarrow. The juvenile dragon was all scales and feeble limbs as it lay in a coil of its own misery. A knot tightened in Fern's chest at the poor thing's plight.

"Lord Warrington," she began, taking charge of the conversation before he could. "This creature will need around-the-clock care if it is to be nursed back to life. That is care I am willing and able to provide."

Lord Warrington stared at the creature that lay deathly still. "Ghastly things. What was it doing under my fountain?"

Fern blinked as the conversation detoured, and she glanced at Moyles. How the dragon ended up stuck had been his idea. He could share it with his employer.

The groundsman cleared his throat. "I think your hounds had the scent of it last month, milord. I reckon they must have chased it onto the grounds, and it found a hole where the pipes run."

"When your huntsman called the dogs back, the dragon must have realised it couldn't turn around in the small space and was stuck. I suspect the poor thing has been subsisting on water from a leaky pipe and whatever insects it found." Fern rested a hand lightly on a dull, grey side.

"So this has been killing my plants?" Lord Warrington arched one eyebrow.

"Indirectly, I believe so, yes. Possibly, it heated the water and ground, trying to flame its way out. Then, as the days and weeks passed, there was...um...bodily waste that seeped into the soil and poisoned the growth. With the creature removed, the ground will heal, and the sick plants can be replaced." Fern held her tongue between her teeth to stop herself from saying more. If his hounds hadn't terrified the poor hatchling in the first place, it wouldn't have got trapped!

Lord Warrington hummed as he thought. Then a greedy gleam entered his gaze. "I can't think of another garden with a pet dragon. We could chain it up in one of the follies."

Fern let out a gasp and curled her hands into fists. No one would be chaining the poor thing up while she drew breath. But a different approach might elicit the response she needed. "Of course, if that is what your lordship wishes to do. I imagine it won't take any more than two or three men around the clock to care for the little thing. I'm sure there are areas of your grounds that can be left unrepaired after the storm while they tend the dragon. When is your house party?"

It took all of her self-control to plaster an interested expression on her face.

"Three men you say?" His lordship squinted at the hatchling.

"The dragon is too weak to eat or drink and will need water dribbled into its mouth. Someone might have to chew its food, also, like mother birds do." She wasn't sure about that bit, but it sounded good and time intensive.

"Let us assume I allow you to care for this creature at your home. What's in it for me? I will no longer have a curiosity to delight the ladies during my party." The cunning light remained in his eyes.

Fern had little to offer except for a man-eating oddity. "When I write up my study of the vine you shall, of course, receive all credit as having discovered the rare specimen. I am sure the botanical society in London will wish to host a gala to honour your discovery." It made her blood boil that the old men who ran the society would fawn over Lord Warrington, but overlook the woman who did all the work.

His lordship stroked his chin, clearly enticed by the notion of attaching his name to such a discovery. A slow smile tugged the corners of his mouth, and he waved his hand at her. "Very well, Miss Oakby. I entrust this dragon to your care. You can bring it back when it is recovered, and I have a place for it to inhabit."

*Like hell,* she thought. Aloud she said, "Thank you, Lord Warrington. I will need the use of a cart to convey the creature back to Drake's Bend. Along with samples of the vine that I will need for my study and to write my paper all about it."

As she calculated how long it would take the slower cart to return to Drake's Bend, a journey she hoped the little creature would survive, her thoughts were interrupted as Lord Warrington continued to speak.

"My sister had quite the reaction when I told her about the vine and Corby." He shook his head, a troubled look passing over his features. "She went as white as a sheet and became quite agitated. But then Millicent was always highly strung. I have ordered her to stay in her room until that monstrosity has been dealt with. We can't have her fainting at the sight of it."

Fern considered what little she knew of the lord's sister. Would a propensity to panic at loud noises and crowds make her scared of a vine?

"I'm sure many gently-bred women would be shocked to learn a staff member met such an end, and that the thing responsible has sprouted in your rose garden." Fern wasn't such a woman. She was fascinated by the ivy, and she had enough sense not to stick her fingers anywhere near it.

Lord Warrington huffed. "I shall go see what progress they have made on removing it. Blasted shame to lose the Boston ivy. What do you think became of it?"

"It might yet be underneath, or it could regrow from the roots. They are hardy things." Fern cast a worried glance at the dragon. They needed to get it to drink a little fresh water.

Dismissed, Fern turned to follow Moyles when a figure burst from a side door of the manor and ran across the yard. She recognised Millicent Carlisle, the woman she discovered in the library the previous night. Ribbons of dark hair streamed behind her like pennants in the wind. Her gown, though of fine make, hung off one shoulder in dishevelled abandon. She hurtled towards Lord Warrington with a fervour shining in her eyes.

"Bertie! Bertie!" Millie yelled with a high-pitched note of panic. "You must stop them! Stop them at once!"

Lord Warrington's mouth tightened at the spectacle of

his sister yelling and running. The thin line turned into a grimace when she seized his arm with both hands. "What is all this screaming about, Millicent? The staff are watching, for goodness' sake, and you look an absolute fright. Have you been taking your tonic? The doctor told me it would control these histrionics."

"No, you don't understand!" Millie's eyes were wide, and a tear trickled down one cheek as she shook her brother's arm. "That mysterious vine. The one you said your men would cut down. They must stop! You must stop them NOW!"

Warrington's face was a mask of aristocratic annoyance as he addressed Fern. "Miss Oakby, please excuse my sister's theatrics. She is not well, you understand, and she needs to return to the house."

Before Fern could reply, Millie shouted, "I'm not mad. You must believe me. Just make them stop! They cannot cut it down!" Her voice rose in pitch, and she tried to pull her brother in the direction of the rose garden.

Lord Warrington prised her hands off his arm and held her wrist in a tight grip as he spoke between gritted teeth. "Enough of your nonsense, Millicent. This is not some scene from one of your absurd novels. Go back to your room, or I will have two of the men escort you there."

Millie wrenched free with a burst of vigour and darted towards the rose garden. Her skirts kicked up behind her as she ran with determination—like a debutante in pursuit of an eligible bachelor.

Lord Warrington pinched the bridge of his nose, muttered under his breath about being saddled with kin, and then he set off after his sister in a quick-paced walk—as he refused to run in front of the staff.

Fern was torn. Part of her needed to know why the other woman had a sudden interest in the vine being saved (a course of action she agreed with) but the dragon needed urgent care. "Make the dragon comfortable in a stall, Moyles, and then fetch fresh water. You will need to dribble a little into its mouth. I'll be along shortly."

Having issued hasty instructions, Fern took off after the others at a run. She wasn't going to miss out on what was happening by dawdling at a dignified walk. In the rose garden, Fern wove through clusters of staff who were tasked with cutting down the vine. Now, they stood back to watch the unfolding drama, creating a semi-circle grassed stage for the players.

"Stop at once!" Millie grabbed the arm of the man wielding a pair of shears who stood the closest to the strange growth and tugged him, unresisting, backwards.

Worry lines, deep enough to plant potatoes, furrowed the forehead of the man Millie pulled away from the vine. The poor man was probably concerned he would lose his job because the noblewoman yelled at him. The other groundsmen had confusion etched on their faces as they stared at their master's sister and then at his lordship.

"Don't touch it!" Millie let go of the man and placed herself between the plant and the groundsmen. Her arms were outstretched as though she was trying to form a protective barrier.

Lord Warrington sliced through the throng of staff to bear down upon his sister. "This is quite enough, Millicent!

You are causing a scene." His voice cut through the murmurs of the assembled staff like a scythe.

He turned and scanned the crowd, which contained a few curious staff from the house. He pointed to a woman dressed in black with a chatelain pinned to the waistband of her skirt that identified her as the housekeeper. "Jones, take Mrs Carlisle back to her room at once and ensure she drinks her tonic." Then he gestured to a tall footman who stood by the edge of the path. "Assist Jones."

But Millie would not be so easily moved. Her voice broke as she tried to control her sobs. "Bertie, you must understand —the storm last night, it transformed something else. Something most marvellous came alive and is connected to that vine. Each time they cut into the plant, he suffers as well."

"You mean there's another one INSIDE the house?" Lord Warrington roared as he lunged at his sister, grabbing her by her upper arms to shake her.

Alarmed gasps raced around the crowd.

"No! Not a vine. This is a small creature, who fits within my hands like a kitten. He deserves a chance to live. Please. Just give me a chance to explain, Bertie." Tears streaked down her cheeks, catching in the hollows of her throat as she looked up at her brother with pleading eyes.

Fern found herself stepping closer, drawn by Millie's desperate plea. There was a sincerity in the other woman's tearful eyes that could not be feigned, and empathy for her plight pulsed inside Fern. Despite their different positions and dispositions, they both knew what it was to be disregarded.

Lord Warrington exhaled sharply through his nose and

glanced around at his staff, who watched the spectacle with rapt attention. With a resigned sigh, he nodded curtly. "Very well. But this conversation will not be held here for all and sundry to gawp at," he conceded with ill grace.

While Fern wanted to rush back to the deathly ill dragon, curiosity held her in place. What other creature had been brought to life by the storm, and how was it possible when magic waned across the country? She would have to trust that Moyles would do as she instructed, as she needed to know how something inside the house was linked to the terrible ivy outside. She would need to include such an effect in her study of the carnivorous plant.

Lord Warrington's features pinched into a scowl as he ushered his sister away from the prying eyes of the staff.

Millie turned and locked gazes with Fern. "Miss Oakby, you must come too. My friend is connected to the vine that... consumed poor Mr Corby."

Fern glanced to the distant stables and silently asked the little dragon to hang on for a while longer. "I cannot be too long."

The staff parted as Lord Warrington propelled his sister back to the house and through the front door. A novelty for Fern, who followed close behind. Across the tiled floor, he led them to his study. The door slammed shut behind them with an ominous thud. Only in the sanctuary of his domain did Lord Warrington let go of his sister. He crossed his arms over his chest, his foul mood making him an imposing figure against the backdrop of leather-bound books and dark wood.

"Now," he said, his voice a low growl as he fixed his gaze on Millie. "Explain this nonsense."

Millie perched on the edge of an armchair, her back ramrod straight as she took a deep breath. Her chest rose and fell in rapid succession as she tried to compose herself, and her hands combed through her long hair, which had become tangled in her flight through the garden.

"Last night, in the library, I made a paper dragon. Do you remember Miss Oakby?" Her voice trembled.

"Yes. I remember." It was a clever thing, with wings that moved when she pulled its tail. "Origami, I think you said it was called?"

Millie nodded, and she sighed, as though relieved that someone believed any part of her story. "Well...this morning, I discovered that he is...alive."

"Alive? Are you saying we have another dragon here? In the house?" Lord Warrington's voice grew in pitch and volume. He loomed over his sister, a wild look in his eyes. "This will NOT do, Millicent. I have had enough of your silliness destroying MY reputation!"

# CHAPTER 12

MILLIE SHRANK into herself and hugged her arms around her chest. A faint tremor shook her body.

Fern stepped forwards, placing herself between the towering lord and his quivering sister. She stared at a vein throbbing in his lordship's temple and thought he needed a calming tonic far more than his sister.

*Men,* she huffed, *were often the ones to get hysterical and lose control of their emotions.*

"I don't think yelling is going to achieve much, do you?" She glared at him and refused to budge.

Lord Warrington puffed out his cheeks but held his silence. With a warning look that she hoped made him stay silent for a little longer, Fern knelt down beside Millie. She laid one hand on the other woman's arm and said in a gentle tone, "Tell us what happened, Mrs Carlisle, when you woke up this morning? Why do you believe the paper dragon is tied to the vine in some fashion?"

"After...after we talked in the library, I returned to my

room. I put the origami dragon on my bedside table. To watch over me while I slept. This morning, an odd huffing noise woke me. When I rolled over, there he was. Staring at me," she spoke quickly and in snatches while darting glances at her brother, who stood with an annoyed look on his features.

Lord Warrington snorted. "Of course it was looking at you, Millicent. You just said you placed it by your bed."

Millie took Fern's hands and, ignoring her brother, spoke directly to her. "That was the noise I heard. He was huffing warm air over my face. He looks rather different to how I made him too. Bigger. Stronger. But it is most definitely my little paper dragon at his core."

"Bigger and stronger, but the same at his core?" Fern rolled those words around in her mouth. "Just like the Boston ivy that used to cling to the wall in the rose garden. It has been encased in something bigger and stronger."

"By Jove." Only now did his lordship's shoulders relax, and he turned to place one hand on the mantel. "Could that have been a magical storm? Although why would it take a paper toy and my ivy and transform them into monstrosities?" He stared into the fire, expecting it to have the answers to his questions.

Millie sat a little taller in the chair and let go of her knees. "Squib is no monstrosity!"

"Squib?" Fern's brain was having difficulty keeping everything straight.

"Yes, Squib. That is what I have called him." Millie's eyes brightened, and the fear retreated. "It is a clever pun, you see. A squib is a short, satirical piece of writing. Admittedly, I made him from a much longer work but..."

"Good grief, Millicent. Stick to the point." Lord Warrington pinched the bridge of his nose.

Fern suspected the noble's sister had brought on many headaches. Perhaps it was just as well Fern was an only child. Imagine if she had an older brother—he might likewise be afflicted. Her uncle certainly considered her a thorn in his side and had made it clear she was to have no contact with him or her cousins.

"Could we see him, please?" Fern asked.

"Oh." Millie sat back in the chair and narrowed her gaze at her brother. "Only if Bertie promises that Squib will not be harmed. Nor will he try to take him off me."

Lord Warrington likewise glared at his sister. The standoff appeared well practiced, as though the siblings had done them many times over the years.

Fern didn't have time to sit and see who gave in first. She wanted to ask Moyles how much water the sick dragon was able to drink. The kitchen might have a little bone broth that would be more nourishing. She needed to move things along.

"I'm sure Lord Warrington won't hurt Squib if, as you say, he is small and made of paper." Fern shot the lord a look that simply dared him to contradict her.

He grunted. "So long as the thing isn't going to devour the staff, I promise not to toss it into the fire. Fetch this creature of yours."

Millie yelped at the idea of a pyre for Squib. Then she pushed off the chair and rose. "Very well, I shall fetch him."

The other woman hastened away. An awkward silence ensued as Lord Warrington pushed papers around on his desk as they waited. Fern stared out the window at the manicured lawns and wondered what type of grass seed Mr Corby had preferred for such even and lush growth.

After five minutes, the door burst open, and Millie returned, cradling something to her chest. It appeared as though she carried a small chicken. A head stuck up past her fingers, but the face was more rounded with a muzzle, rather than a beak.

Millie opened her hands and held them a short distance from her body, but not so far that she couldn't snatch the creature back if her brother lunged for it. A dragon perched on her palms. When he stood tall and unfurled his neck, he reached some eight inches in height and was similar in size to a kitten. Or a chicken.

Lord Warrington's eyes widened, and he took an involuntary step forwards. His posture, once stiff with disdain, was now relaxed with fascination. "I'll be damned," he muttered under his breath, the veneer of his snootiness cracked under the weight of genuine amazement.

The dragon's wings quivered, and he turned to Millie and emitted a questioning trill, as though seeking her reassurance that he wouldn't be tossed on the fire.

"No one will hurt you. I promise." Millie stroked a parchment-like side with her thumb.

The creature retained remnants of his original construction. His skin was the mottled beige of thick paper. Written words of a deep purplish-black were etched into his hide. The looped script gave the appearance of scales across his body. Where his tail curled, sentences spiralled down to a pointed tip. Squib's eyes gleamed with an ink-dark intensity as he surveyed the room.

"He's beautiful." Fern leaned closer, entranced by the tiny dragon.

The previous night he had been a lovely piece of folded paper, made with undeniable skill. But the storm had transformed him while holding onto his origins, just like the vine. Squib had grown in size, and while still appearing delicate, at the same time he had a bulk and solidness that made Fern wonder if he had a paperweight inside him. And yet, he moved with an organic fluidity like a natural creature that defied his paper construction.

At her inspection, Squib reared back on his haunches, wings fluttering in a display of miniature grandeur as he emitted a soft huff of heated air that warmed Fern's face. She hoped it was some sort of greeting and not an attempt to roast her before being eaten. Admiring him brought to mind another tiny dragon she had seen years ago, and Fern wondered if the creature before her was a new type of pixie dragon.

"Isn't he marvellous?" Millie cooed at Squib as though he were a child who had performed some magnificent feat.

Fern nodded, barely trusting herself to speak. Magic was dwindling in their world, and dragons were dying out. Yet here stood Squib—a dragon made of paper and ink, who lived and breathed. Her trip to Warrington Manor had spiralled far beyond her expertise. The Moray sisters might know how a storm turned the paper-folded creature into something real.

Putting aside the matter of Squib, there was a larger and hungrier problem that needed to be dealt with.

"As marvellous as Squib is, I don't see how he is related to the vine, apart from the fact they were both altered last night by the storm," Fern said.

"Ah. Well, about that..." Millie squirmed on the spot and then, needing to do more with her hands, she gently set Squib down on the desk. She pressed one hand to her temple, the other sat on her hip. "I wrote a story, you see. It was a grand, gothic adventure, set in the grounds of this wild and overgrown..."

"Millicent." Lord Warrington cautioned his sister with a single word.

"Oh, right. The point. I wrote a story about a monstrous vine that ensnares the beautiful heroine. But it is supposed to protect her until she is rescued. No one gets eaten!" She flung herself to the nearby chaise, and Squib jumped into the air and glided over to her, landing on her chest.

"Your story came to life." Fern put the pieces together, but she was still a long way from understanding. "And how does Squib fit into this narrative?" Although she had an idea. The previous night, Millie had been surrounded by hand-written pages torn from a journal.

"My writing is terrible. Just like Bertie always said. And no publisher would ever be interested in my novels." Millie made a whispered admission filled with pain. "So I tore the pages out of my journal and made Squib with them instead."

Fern drew in a deep breath and counted to ten inside her head, before she let Lord Warrington know exactly what she thought of his abominable treatment of his widowed sister. "I'm sure that's not true at all about your stories," she said instead.

"I never put it quite like that, Millicent. I said you should put away your silly scribblings and turn your mind to what a well-bred lady is supposed to do." The scowl remained on Lord Warrington's face.

Fern thought calling someone's creative outpourings *silly scribblings* sounded just as horrid as telling a writer no publisher would ever be interested in their work.

"Let's leave aside any discussion about the literary merits of Mrs Carlisle's stories for the moment. It seems that the tale came to life in two very different ways. Her creative imagining now sprawls over the rose garden wall. While the physical work, the actual pages she wrote it upon, became Squib the pixie dragon." Now Fern understood how the two were connected. This brought them back to the reason for being in his lordship's study. "You said the men had to stop cutting the vine because it affected Squib."

"Oh, yes. My poor little friend has been gravely injured." Millie rose from the chaise, and Squib hopped up her arm. She extended her hand and pointed to one hind leg. "You can see the cuts in his leg. They appeared when the men began to hack at the vine. Poor little Squib cried most horribly, just as if he had always been flesh and blood. He even bled!"

Now that Fern looked closer, there were a series of deep cuts along the dragon's flank and a dribble from them like spilt ink.

"Yes, well, this has all been terribly entertaining, Millicent, but the vine has to go. It's quite ruining the rose garden, and I can't afford to lose any more staff. Miss Oakby, tell the men to get back to work." Lord Warrington sat at his desk and picked up a letter.

"No!" Millie cried out. She curled her arms inward and

hugged Squib to her chest. "Don't be monstrous, Bertie. If they hack the vine down, it will turn Squib into nothing but tiny scraps of crumpled paper."

Lord Warrington sighed and looked up from his correspondence. "You really are self-indulgent, Millicent. You are concerned for a silly paper toy when I have lost my head gardener. The thing must be destroyed before anyone else is lost."

"Squib is not a toy! He is real and...my friend." Millie laced her fingers to form a protective wall around the creature.

Squib trembled against her palms, the slices in his hind opening and closing like fish gills, and a fresh drop of ink-like blood formed along the cut.

*Her friend.* A pang shot through Fern, and she understood why the other woman so fiercely defended the paper creation. Then an old memory rose to the surface of her mind. Of a small pixie dragon who died because of something she had done.

"He's a pixie dragon. Not a toy." In her mind, she saw a lizard-like creature with tiny wings who curled around an unremarkable little violet that had once lived in Kew Gardens.

"A what?" Lord Warrington tossed a letter to his desk.

"A pixie dragon. They are a very rare and tiny species of dragon. There are not many of them seen by humans. Being so small they are usually somewhat timid and preyed upon by larger creatures." Fern imagined that whatever magic shot from the storm combined the origami form and a pixie dragon to create Squib. Just as a Boston ivy and a carnivorous plant, possibly a *Stapelia lepida*, made the new vine.

"See! He is as real as you or I." Millicent stood a little taller at the news.

The fate of the sickly creature pulled at Fern, but now she had two very different dragons to try and save. "Lord Warrington, we must consider the scientific implications of what has happened here," Fern interjected before the noble could bury himself in his correspondence or another standoff erupted. "A creature and a plant have been born from your sister's creativity and a unique storm that was laced with magic. We're witnessing an anomaly that has never been seen before, and you wish to destroy it without studying it first? The newspapers will vie to interview you and place the story on their front pages. Society will be abuzz with talk of it."

Lord Warrington leaned back in his chair and drummed his fingertips on the rolled arm. "Miss Oakby, while I appreciate that the scientific community would be interested in my discovery, surely you aren't suggesting we let this infestation continue unchecked? I will not sacrifice more staff just to save a few sheets of used paper."

"I would assume your staff are too intelligent to throw themselves at the vine since we now know it is carnivorous," Fern retorted. "Rope off the area so that no one ventures too close while we approach this methodically. There may be a way to sever the vine's connection to Squib so that one can be destroyed without harming the other. That would also give you time to alert the botanical society and the newspapers."

Any delay she could wring from the noble would give her time to study the vine and prolong little Squib's life.

Millie nodded vigorously, and Squib swayed in her hands. "Yes, that sounds most sensible! Please, Bertie. Just give Miss Oakby a few days to find a satisfactory solution for everyone."

A few days? Fern thought it would take months, or even years, to truly understand what had happened at Warrington Manor and to figure out how to undo it. On the verge of blurting that out loud, she met Millie's gaze and the other woman mouthed a silent, *please?*

She blew out a sigh. She could try. For the sake of Millie, the tiny creature, and her fascination for the man-eating monstrosity. And for the pixie dragon she had once failed. "Allow me a few days, Lord Warrington. I shall take the sick dragon back to Drake's Bend and place it under the care of my uncles. Then I can search my botanical library for any mention of such an anomaly, or seek the assistance of a magic user or alchemist for a way to break the bond between the two. This discovery is of such importance I suspect the Prince Regent himself will wish to hear about it."

"The Prince Regent, you say?" Lord Warrington tented his fingers. He studied the two women before him for several long moments. "I shall grant you a week. My men will have plenty of other areas in the garden to fix before the party. It won't take them more than a few hours to hack down the criminal vine and plant something pretty along the base of the wall when your time is up."

"Oh! Thank you, Bertie!" Millie rushed around the side of the desk and kissed her brother's cheek.

He grabbed her wrist in his larger hand. "But this is the last of your nonsense, Millie. I have engaged a nurse to attend to you and expect her here tomorrow or the day after. You will take your tonic every day, as the doctor instructed, or there will be consequences."

Millie sucked in a gasp, but whether from the order or the tight hold, Fern couldn't tell. In that moment, she decided that not only would she save the sickly dragon and the paper one, but she would find a way to free Millicent Carlisle from the reign of Lord Warrington.

# CHAPTER 13

"Thank you, Lord Warrington. I shall leave as soon as I can." Fern bowed her head and left the study.

Millie hurried after her and touched her arm. "Thank you for trying to save Squib. After my husband died...well, I don't have much that is mine, nor do I have a friend here. It truly was magic that brought Squib to life, and how can we allow such a gift to be destroyed?"

Fern scratched the pixie dragon under the chin, marvelling at how while he appeared to be crafted from paper, his hide was soft and warm like silk. "It doesn't matter that he is small. Squib is alive, that means he deserves a chance to live."

The other woman smiled and squeezed her arm. "We are fellow adventurers on this path of discovery, are we not? Now, what's this about a sick dragon? Is it a real one?" Her eyes were wide with curiosity and a glimmer of excitement.

"Real, but terribly ill. It had been trapped under the fountain and is close to starving, but I am hopeful of nursing it back to full health," Fern said as they walked along the hall.

"It will need bone broth. And a name. It is terribly rude and impersonal to refer to the creature as it. This is turning out to be most marvellous. Yesterday I was alone and bored. Today I have not one, but *two* friends, and I'm about to meet a real dragon." Millie linked her arm with Fern's and steered her towards the kitchen. Squib had hopped up to her shoulder and sheltered against her neck and under the fall of her hair.

*A friend?* The words dripped warm honey through Fern's insides, and she rather liked it.

On the way through the kitchen, Millie asked the cook for a mug of bone broth and a teaspoon. The old woman smiled fondly at the younger one.

"You'll need more than a mug to put meat on your bones, Miss Millie." She addressed the widowed woman as though she were still a child sneaking into the kitchen for a warm biscuit. Grabbing an earthenware mug, she ladled from a pot on the back of the range.

Millie took the mug and cupped it in her hands. "It's not for me, Mrs Brown, but a sickly animal."

Before the cook could ask more questions, Millie pushed Fern towards the back door. Fern retrieved her satchel as she passed and slung the strap over her head.

Across the courtyard, they hurried to the dimly lit stables where shafts of sunlight pierced through windows set high in the stone walls. Solid wooden half-walls divided the stalls. The top halves were made of iron bars to stop horses biting one another. In a small end stall, nestled in fresh hay, lay the juvenile dragon. Its scales were a dull grey, and it was curled upon itself.

Moyles stood by the stall door, wiping his hands with a rag. "She's taken a bit of water, and her breathing is easier now," he reported.

"She?" Fern queried.

"Aye, it's a lass," Moyles confirmed.

Fern crept into the stall and knelt beside the creature. She was made of leathery skin stretched over bones. An air of hopelessness washed from her too-still form. How long had she cried for rescue, and no one heard her? The poor thing must have resigned herself to starving to death, trapped in the narrow tunnel and unable to escape. Entombed alive. And alone.

Fern would need to find a way to reassure the dragon that she was safe and that they would help her recover.

The dragon's nostrils twitched, scenting the bone broth carried by Millie.

"Good. She can smell the broth," Fern said.

"Oh, she is beautiful, even in such a state," Millie whispered with reverence in her tone. She took Squib from her shoulder and placed the pixie dragon on the dividing wall. He hopped along to peer down at the much larger version of himself.

Millie knelt on the other side of the dragon. "Do you think she will drink?"

"She might be too weak. But we can dribble a little into her mouth and see if she will swallow. I'll hold her head, Millie, if you will try to feed her." Fern cradled the delicate head on her lap. The creature's eyes fluttered open for a moment, revealing liquid pools of mercury flecked with bright blue, like a sapphire set in silver.

"Come on, girl. Have a little taste for Millie," the other woman crooned, placing a spoon of broth at the edge of the dragon's mouth and letting the warm liquid trickle over a blue tongue.

Nothing happened at first, and worry knotted inside Fern. What if they were too late? She thought of the skeleton she found on the ride out to Warrington Manor. The world lost too many dragons, and yet, so many people seemed oblivious to their plight. How much poorer their world would become without such creatures in it.

Millie refilled the spoon and let more trickle over the dragon's parted lips. The creature's throat brushed against Fern's hands.

"She's swallowing. That's good." She glanced up and shared a relieved smile with Millie. "She needs a name. Something befitting such a creature."

The dragon opened her mouth wider, and her eyelids fluttered briefly before closing once more. She was trying, Fern thought. That was encouraging.

"How about Eurydice?" Millie suggested as she spooned more broth into the dragon's open mouth. "A beautiful and mythic figure doomed to shadow. But now freed."

"Eurydice," Fern repeated softly, stroking the creature's neck as she swallowed the nourishing soup. The name felt right—a beautiful literary name for a creature plucked from the pages of a gothic novel. Later, when the dragonet had recovered and they were better acquainted, her name could be shortened to Riddy.

Millie dipped the spoon into the broth again, murmuring encouragements as if she were coaxing a story's protagonist back to health. Squib, from his vantage point on the wall, craned his papery neck and watched every droplet of broth vanish into Eurydice's mouth.

Silence reigned in the stables, with only the occasional shuffle of hooves or soft nicker from a horse.

"I think she's had enough," Fern said when the frail dragon turned her head away from the offered spoon.

"She's barely drunk half of it." Millie held out the mug to show Fern.

"After so long with very little, perhaps it is best not to force too much into her. Her breathing seems more regular even for the little she swallowed." Fern stroked the sinuous neck, marvelling at how the scales warmed and no longer had the chill of a vegetable plucked from the cold store.

Fern rose to her feet and turned to Moyles. "Lord Warrington has said I can have use of a horse and cart to take Eurydice back to Drake's End. Could you find a groom to hitch one up, please? I shall leave my mare here overnight and return for her tomorrow."

"Aye, miss. A small cart will be best. You don't want her sliding around. There's a little gig her ladyship uses that will give the dragon a smoother ride." Moyles touched the brim of his cap and went in search of a groom to relay the instructions.

"I'll find some old blankets to make a soft pallet. Eurydice must be as comfortable as possible," Millie said.

Fern watched Millie hurry away, her skirts swishing against the straw-covered floor. The woman might have a dramatic nature, but she had a heart that bled ink and compassion in equal measure.

While she waited for the gig and horse to be ready, Fern found the stall with her mare and explained to the horse that she would return for her. Then she leaned on the wall to watch the dragon sleep. Her shallow breaths grew steadier, a sign that she clung to life yet.

Fern's thoughts tangled together. A deadly vine that was connected to a dragon. A drawing in her father's notebook of a dragon curled around a type of rowan. The old words to a nursery rhyme that her mother used to sing.

"Rowan leaves and dragon's breath are the key to life and death." A shiver erupted along her arms as she murmured the words. Were flora and fauna entwined like Mr Corby in the monstrous ivy?

The ring of shod hooves on cobbles pulled her from overgrown memories. Moyles appeared at the stable entrance, a wiry groom at his side leading a sturdy bay mare harnessed to a small gig.

"All ready for you, Miss Oakby," Moyles called out.

Millie returned moments later, arms laden with blankets she'd pilfered from linen closets and trunks. "These should cushion Eurydice and keep her warm."

The gig had a small area behind the seat, large enough for a load of shopping from the market or a juvenile dragon. They lined the tray with a thick quilt and rolled blankets on either side to act as bolsters.

Together, Moyles and the groom gently lifted Eurydice and carried her to the gig, laying her on the makeshift bed. Millie fussed, tucking in the blanket to ensure the dragon didn't slide around and damage her delicate wings or thin body.

Fern dropped her satchel on the driver's seat and then climbed up into the gig.

"Here's the leftover broth. She might drink a little more if you stop along the way." Millie passed up a flask of nourishing soup. "I want Eurydice to get better, but I don't want to lose Squib." Millie wrung her hands together, and her brow was wrinkled.

"We are going to save both, big and small, remember? I'll be back in a day or two. I need to make sure Eurydice is settled and eating, and I have to consult my books. I will find a way, I promise." But the words rang hollow inside her. What did she know of how to sever a magical link between a deadly plant and a paper creation?

Fern guided the bay mare out of the stables, along the driveway, and away from the estate. Soon, they were on the familiar road to Drake's Bend, with the rhythmic clop of hooves providing a steadying cadence to her thoughts. She checked on Eurydice periodically, ensuring the dragon remained safely cushioned within the blankets.

At the halfway point, Fern tried to offer the dragon a little broth from the flask, but she turned her head, and her eyelids remained closed.

"Stay with me, Eurydice, please." Fern urged the mare onwards as fast as she dared. While she didn't want to jostle the sick creature, she also didn't want to walk the whole way and take hours to get home.

Upon arrival at the edge of the village, Fern guided the mare along the road towards Nemython House. She took the driveway that ran between her home and the neighbouring cottage of the Bentleys to the stables at the rear. George was chopping wood in the yard, and he swung the axe into the block as she drew the horse to a halt.

"What happened to your mare?" He brushed off his hands as he approached.

"Nothing. She is enjoying a short stay at the Warrington stables until I return," Fern said as she hopped to the ground. "I needed the gig for a very sick passenger."

Ambrose was drawn from the house by her arrival. The two men followed Fern to the back of the gig where Eurydice lay.

Fern peeled back a covering blanket, and Ambrose gasped. He extended his hand towards the still creature nestled in the fabric. "I say, it's a—"

"Dragon," Fern said before Ambrose could finish. "She's sick and needs our help. She has been trapped beneath a fountain for some weeks with nothing to sustain her."

George's eyebrows were knitted together in thought. "She'll need to be fed slowly, or she'll become worse. But let's make her comfortable first."

Taking an end each, they lifted the quilt from the gig with the dragon secure within it. With care, they walked to the stables and arranged a bed in an empty stall. The dragon's eyes fluttered open briefly, a glimmer of recognition flashing in their depths when her gaze alighted on Fern. Then her lids closed once again.

After they settled Eurydice in her new quarters, they went to the warm kitchen. Mrs Bentley made tea while Fern recounted events at Warrington Manor. She spoke of the dead plants surrounding a malfunctioning fountain and the warm, coppery sludge in the soil. Her tale continued with the ferocious storm and the sad discovery the next morning of Mr Corby entwined within an unnatural vine. She finished with how the storm damage had uncovered Eurydice's plight.

Her uncles listened intently, their faces grim at times, as she detailed her encounters with Lord Warrington and Millie's exaggerated, but not entirely unfounded, fears about cutting down the climber and how it would destroy Squib.

"Magic swirls around you, Fern. A simple botany job has unearthed not one but two dragons and a cursed plant." Ambrose sipped his tea, and his eyes gleamed. Fern could see him penning his story for the *Midnight Chronicle* behind that keen gaze.

"Magic." George snorted into his mug.

"How else do you explain the horrid plant that sprung from the ground overnight and devoured that poor gardener?" Ambrose asked his partner with a wave of his teacup.

George was silent for a long moment before answering, "Man-made fertiliser."

Ambrose stared at George. "You are horrid. Why on earth have I put up with you for over thirty years?"

Fern poured herself more tea from the pot and inhaled the fragrant blend before guiding the conversation back on track. "I have two dragons to save. Somehow. How do I destroy the vine without also destroying the little papery pixie dragon?"

She floundered beyond her depth and could practically hear Mr Corby chortling to himself as she struggled. Fern hoped that Eurydice would respond the same way as any starved creature, with small but frequent nourishing broths, until she gained enough strength to eat on her own. But how to save a delicate, tiny dragon connected to a deadly plant?

Not to mention that in a few days' time, Lord Warrington would order the destruction of the climber with the unnatural and horrific appetite. Part of her already mourned the loss of a rare and unusual specimen. She had a mission to save the dragons, but was there some way to save the ivy and have it available for botanists the world over to study? It could be enclosed behind iron bars to make sure no one ventured too close. A keeper could throw it the occasional piece of meat, like how lions and tigers were fed.

But until she examined a seed pod and knew how it propagated itself, the plant might scatter spores across England on the wind. They could find themselves battling the botanical nightmare in every corner of the land. That would be a terrifying tale for Millie to write.

Fern blew across the surface of her tea. Her mind was too tired from recent events to tackle everything at once. In such times, there was one course of action to take. She had to make a list.

"I need paper," she announced to her uncles and left them discussing whether magic or science was responsible for the uproar at Warrington Manor.

In her study, she fetched a sheet of paper and a pencil. Then she made a short list:

> 1. Nurse Eurydice back to health
> 2. Sever bond between Squib and the vine
> 3. Save Squib for Millie

*4. Rescue Millie from her horrid brother.*

Did she dare add *Save the vine* to the list? The plant also needed a name. Something that reflected its origins as a Boston ivy, or *Parthenocissus tricuspidata*, and its similarity to *Stapelia lepida*. Lord Warrington would probably demand it be named after him.

Staring at her list, Fern wrote more comments under each item. Now she was home, her family would muster around the sick dragon, and if love and care alone could bring about a recovery, little Eurydice would be on her feet in no time.

Whatever connected Squib to the plant was more problematic. She would talk to the Moray sisters. The magic casters, with their decades of experience, might know what happened and how to fix it. Once free of the vine's grasp, Squib would be saved.

Fern drew a line under *Rescue Millie from her horrid brother*. That needed a different approach. Assuming the widow even wanted to be rescued. Or that rescue was possible. Most widows had little option except to rely on the charity of family. Fern had been fortunate in that after she ruined herself in the eyes of society, she had a loving home and the knowledge to earn an income.

She tapped the end of the pencil against the paper as she thought. Stealing Lord Warrington's sister away would have to be left until last and, ideally, until after she had been paid for her work. Since Eurydice was sleeping in the stables, and she still had plenty of time to call on the Moray sisters before dark, Fern turned her mind back to the vine. Or a tiny part of it.

# CHAPTER 14

WHEN LORD WARRINGTON had ordered his men to cut back the vine, they had managed only a few slashes through the tough and fibrous vine before Millie had dashed from the house, yelling for them to stop. From what little they had severed, Moyles had scooped up a small cutting from the end of a tendril and had dropped it into a jar for Fern.

Opening her satchel, she drew the container out that held a six-inch length of vine, with a single leaf attached. As she held it up to the light, the tendril writhed against the glass, as though it sought a way to escape.

"Let's take a closer look at you." Collecting a sketch pad and her box of pencils from her study, Fern carried everything out to her workroom at one end of the greenhouse. She dropped everything on the bench that ran under the long, rectangular window and perched on the stool.

The first thing she did was draw the bit of climber. At times, the cutting tapped on the glass with its leaf, like a prisoner banging a tin cup against the bars that held them. Fern frowned in concentration as she examined the wriggly specimen. On closer inspection, the dark-green leaf had veins of burgundy that appeared almost black. The lighter-red splashes were randomly placed, like when a leaf turned for autumn. She made a few sketches, trying to capture the exact shape and colouring.

Then she made a sketch from memory of how the plant covered the wall and the horrid mystery it hid beneath its hand-sized leaves. Another quick sketch was of the five-petalled flower pod that opened to reveal a gaping mouth-like centre that lacked a visible stamen.

"I wonder how you fertilise your flowers?" Fern asked the tendril as she waved the pencil before the jar. The leaf tracked the movement and swayed like a tiny dancer.

When she was satisfied with her drawings, Fern moved on to a more scientific examination of the cutting. From the shelves that lined the wall beside her, she selected a pair of elongated (and substantial) tweezers. Peering under the bench, she found a stout pair of leather gloves, their surface weathered from frequent use, and tugged them on.

Prepared, Fern unscrewed the lid of the jar, releasing a faint, earthy aroma from the imprisoned sample. Using the tweezers, she extracted the cutting, handling it as though it were a dangerous weapon that might try to poke out her eyes.

She placed the cutting on a wooden tray, where it immediately began to twist and writhe, like a rat's tail, whipping its leaf around. For a moment, Fern worried that with its frenzied motions, it might escape and scuttle across the greenhouse floor. What would she do if it burrowed in the rich, loamy soil in the raised beds? To ensure it remained a prisoner, Fern leaned on the tweezers to hold it in place.

"What is your secret?" She posed the question, half-hoping the plant would wave the leaf and signal its answer.

Her gloved hand remained steady, pinning the restless cutting to the tray. With her free hand, she picked up a magnifying glass and examined the piece of vine. While the colouration was unusual, she didn't find any clues as to what continued to animate the length of tendril.

"I hope you are not so alive as to feel pain," she said to it.

Putting down the magnifying glass, she reached for a scalpel. She paused, wondering if the cut she was about to make would likewise be inflicted upon Millie's companion.

Muttering an apology to Squib in case he felt what she was about to do, Fern sliced along the long side of the tendril. A thick, viscous sap oozed from the incision. Grabbing a vial, she scooped up a few drops for later analysis. When she held it to the light, the liquid had a deep purple-to-black hue that reminded her of the inky blood that had seeped from Squib's cut flank.

When Fern could learn no more from the sample, she dropped it back into the jar and screwed the lid on tight. The cutting continued to wriggle, but its movements were sluggish. Almost as though the oozing sap had drained its life force.

"Now, what to do with you?" she said to the cutting as she surveyed her workroom.

She would need to secure it somewhere safe, in case the wriggly sample managed to escape the jar and crawled out like a monstrous caterpillar. But before she stowed it away, she first wanted to show it to the Moray sisters. Fern collected her drawings, the vial of sap, and the jar, and headed back to the house.

After putting her drawings and the vial of sap on the desk in her study, Fern took the jar with its unusual captive to the kitchen. George was now missing, and Ambrose and Mrs Bentley were watching a pot on the stove.

"That won't boil with both of you staring at it," Fern called out.

"Good. We don't want it to. This is broth for Eurydice," Ambrose said.

"If you don't mind doing without me for an hour or so, I'm going to visit the Moray sisters and seek their opinion of events at Warrington Manor." Fern approached the stove and peered into the pot. A thin, brown liquid simmered to a gentle heat and wafted the faint aroma of beef.

"George is sitting with Eurydice. You go consult Macbeth's witches." Ambrose waved her away.

"I'll try not to be too long." Fern took her coat from the hook by the back door and pushed her arms into the sleeves as she headed outside again.

Before she left, she poked her head into Eurydice's stall to reassure herself that nothing terrible had happened to the dragon. Seeing that George read to the sleeping hatchling from a book (no doubt using science to explain why dragons weren't magical), she set off for the quaint cottages of the sisters, wanting to be back home before dark fell.

Fern walked as fast as she could without breaking into a run, along the road and over the bridge. There was no sign of the sisters outside, and she rapped on the door of the larger of the two cottages.

Nona opened the door and grinned at seeing her. "Fern! Do come in. Have you come to check on the roses?"

"No, I have encountered a problem at the Warrington estate that is most definitely magical, and I need your help," Fern said as she stepped inside the warmth and shrugged off her coat.

The snug cottage had a low ceiling and heavy oak beams that made it feel as though you walked into a comforting embrace. Blankets and pillows in lush purple and deep green added a splash of colour. Candles burned in wall sconces, and Decima and Morda were seated in worn armchairs by the fire. An old blackened pot hung over the open fire on a hook, and a mouth-watering fragrance wafted from whatever was within.

Fern reached out and touched blind Morda's hand in greeting as she dropped to an overstuffed pillow on the floor between the chairs. "What's in the pot? It smells fabulous."

"Vegetable soup, with Decima's secret ingredient," Morda said.

*Bacon*, Decima mouthed to Fern, and she winked.

Nona fetched a tin mug and ladled soup from the pot before handing it to Fern. She took a sip and savoured the hearty taste, then started recounting her tale. Once more, she told of the fierce storm that transformed the Boston ivy into a terrible thing. And the origami construction turned into a papery pixie dragon.

When she finished, she fetched the jar from where she had wedged it in her coat pocket and handed it to Decima.

The middle of the sisters held the jar to the flames and peered at the prisoner that wiped its leaf against the glass.

Nona, whose eyes were as green as a deep forest, cleared her throat. "That was no ordinary storm. It was a nexus of magical energies. Rare and powerful. We were awake all night, brewing spells made all the more powerful by its touch."

"We have not felt such a storm in over two decades," Morda said, stretching her hand out.

Decima picked a cup from the low table and placed it in her sister's hands. "Weather is a fickle mistress, and we cannot predict when she might bless us with such a tempest."

Fern drank a little more of her soup and mulled over their words. "Does that mean it was the storm alone that created the carnivorous plant and brought Squib to life? That it wasn't Millie's story about it?"

"The ways of magic can be unpredictable, especially with such natural events. The energy in the storm might have been drawn to Mrs Carlisle's desires and fears. Her story, indeed her very wishes, became the conduit for the magic," Nona explained.

"If the storm created them both, pulling from Millie's imagination, how do I break whatever connects them? Lord Warrington will destroy the vine in a few days, and the little dragon will likewise be...killed." While it might seem silly to some to bother about a pixie dragon who was once folded paper, the means by how Squib came into being didn't matter.

Squib was far more than just paper and words. He existed. He had feelings and intelligence. And he was loved by Millie. Fern would fight just as hard to save Squib as she did for Eurydice. Why should size or species dictate the value of a life? Their society had enough people squashing others as worthless or undeserving. It was time someone started tearing down their preconceptions.

The three sisters passed the jar between them. Each taking their time to stare at the cutting, or in the case of Morda, she clasped it between her hands and hummed.

While Morda communed with the plant, Nona shared her thoughts. "This is more than a piece of a vine and also more than magic. There is something else at play here, but I cannot fathom what."

"I sense a metallic touch in its creation," Decima said.

"Metallic? There could be a high iron content in the soil." Fern tried to make sense of their findings.

Nona took the jar back from her younger sister and held it to the light. The cut Fern had made with her scalpel had stopped oozing purplish-black sap, but the leaf had smeared it up one side. "There may have been something more than the primal energy of the storm involved in its creation. Does Mrs Carlisle craft magic?"

"I don't think so. She didn't say anything about being able to see motes." The ability was a rare trait. If the other woman had such a gift, most likely, Lord Warrington would have had her using it to his advantage. Or Millie might have mentioned it when she asked Fern to save Squib.

Morda moved in her chair, her milky gaze finding Fern's. "Remember, every spell, every bit of magic, comes at a price. The bond forged between the vine and the paper dragon is a reflection of an intertwined fate. Before you break what connects them, you must first understand the true essence of the story Mrs Carlisle created."

"I don't understand. What do you mean by the true essence of the story?" Fern's quick trip to Warrington Manor to look at a dead patch of creeping thyme had veered into animal husbandry and now headed down a literary road.

"Mrs Carlisle's secret desire. The one that remains unwritten and yet hides among the words inscribed on a page and flowed over the paper creature. You must seek the truth that is not seen," Morda said.

Fern blew out a snort. Why were seers always so...cryptic? Long years of experience had taught her there was no point pressing the old woman for a simple answer. She wasn't capable of giving one.

Her older sisters cackled in laughter, and it took no imagination at all to see them tossing frog's legs into a boiling cauldron under a full moon while they waited for Macbeth to ride past.

Fern finished her soup. "I will see if Millie will let me bring Squib to you. You might be able to learn something from the little dragon." Not that she had learned much from their examination of the bit of vine. Other than she had to understand a hidden story before freeing Squib of whatever hold the plant had over him. Somehow. Pocketing the jar, she thanked the sisters for their help.

On the walk back to Nemython House, Fern mentally scanned the bookshelves in her study. Her father had collected numerous rare volumes over his lifetime. As unlikely as it might be, it was possible that another such plant had burst into life during a previous magic-laden storm.

When Fern slipped through the back door, Ambrose and Mrs Bentley were conferring over a range of ingredients laid out on the bench. After hanging her coat on the hook and removing the jar, Fern approached.

"Did Eurydice take any broth?" she asked.

"No. Poor thing has been asleep. I think George's science book bored her into unconsciousness. Daniel is out there with her, and I told him to let me know the instant she wakes. We are keeping a small pot warm on the stove for her," Ambrose said.

Fern spied a fish on a board, its sides scraped of scales and a hole in its belly where it had been prepared for cooking. "I take it George went fishing today?"

"Yes. He's trying to get back into my good books. He caught a trout, and Mrs B is going to do something marvellous with it." Ambrose rubbed his hands together, and his eyes sparkled.

"I would if you lot would give me room to work." Mrs Bentley waved her ever-present knife.

Ambrose took Fern's arm and drew her away from their busy cook. "How went the visit to the three witches?"

"They said it was more than botany and a magic storm but couldn't really tell me what other than something metallic." When she returned to Warrington Manor, Fern would take a soil sample from around the vine. "I will secure this cutting so it doesn't escape, and then go see Eurydice." Fern held up the jar, and the leaf continued to decorate the glass with its sap.

Ambrose shuddered. "Yuck. And you say that ate a man?"

"You know how ivy takes over entire buildings and eats the stonework? Now imagine what a magically transformed one did to a gardener." Objectively, it was terribly fascinating. So long as one was observing how the plant consumed its meal and wasn't the main course. Or dessert.

"Go put that thing away, and I'll spoon some broth into a bowl for our special patient." Ambrose gave her a push in the direction of the door.

In her study, Fern placed the jar in a safe built into the back of a shelf and turned the key. Then she returned to the kitchen and grabbed a shawl to drape around her shoulders to stave off the descending chill of evening. With the bowl warming her palms, she headed out the back door and set off towards the stables.

Inside the barn, a lantern had been lit to softly illuminate their newest house guest.

"How is she, Daniel?" Fern asked the youngest member of the Bentley family. At only twelve years old, he worked as hard as his older siblings.

"She hasn't woken, Miss Oakby." The lad was huddled in a blanket in the corner, his attention fixed on the dragon.

Eurydice was nestled in the opposite corner to Daniel. Curled into herself, shivers wracked her body despite the thick blanket covering her dull grey scales. Her eyes fluttered open as Fern approached, and with great effort, she lifted her head a mere inch before dropping back to rest on her front legs.

# CHAPTER 15

Fern knelt in the hay next to the sickly dragon. "It seems our patient is awake." Although barely, given her sluggish movements. While she wanted to think the dragon woke because she sensed the person who had freed her, Fern suspected it was the rich aroma wafting off the broth that had tickled under her nose and roused the creature.

"Why don't you go home, Daniel, and get some rest? I'll stay with her," Fern said to the lad as she made herself comfortable and crossed her legs.

The boy looked torn—fatigue and fascination warring inside him.

"Eurydice will still be here tomorrow, and I will need you to watch over her when I have to return to Warrington Manor." Fern caressed the dragon's snout as she balanced the bowl on her knee.

"Yes, Miss Oakby. I'll take good care of her while you are gone. I'm going to ask my friends to help too." His eyes were wide as he stared at Eurydice.

Fern suppressed a smile. News had probably already spread of their unusual guest. Dragons were so rarely spotted these days that the villagers would be curious to see one up close.

"You can tell your friends, but only one can visit at a time. Do you understand? Eurydice is sick, and we don't want to further stress her by turning her into a spectacle." Fern kept a stern edge in her voice to ensure the lad knew he wouldn't be charging his friends to stare at the recovering creature.

"I promise, miss." He nodded solemnly, then ran from the barn in search of his supper.

Once they were alone, Fern scooped up some broth with the spoon and held it out to Eurydice. The dragonet sniffed at it warily before lapping at it with a long, blue tongue.

"Good girl," Fern murmured. "Keep drinking, and you'll soon be able to explore the forest around here and grow big like you are meant to."

Over the next hour, spoonful by spoonful, Fern managed to coax Eurydice into drinking more of the broth. Although it was clear that every movement was an effort for the dragon. More than half of the nourishing meal remained in the bowl when Eurydice closed her eyes and drifted back to sleep.

Fern repositioned the blanket around the dragon, ensuring she was tucked in and warm. The shivers over Eurydice's too-thin skin had stopped after drinking the hearty broth. Then she put the bowl down to pick up a pronged fork, scooped the soiled straw into a barrow, and replaced it with fresh.

William arrived as Fern finished tidying up in the stall.

He carried a pillow, a blanket, and a bucket that held something for him to eat, drink, and a book.

"Evening, Miss Oakby. I'll watch over the little one until morning. It'll be no different than staying up with a colicking horse," he said as he set his things down in the corner previously occupied by his younger brother.

"Thank you, William. She has just eaten and gone back to sleep. If she wakes during the night, she might be thirsty, and you will need to hold the water bucket for her. No beer though." Since he mentioned treating her like an equine with colic, Fern thought it prudent to mention that the common remedy for horses, beer to relieve the twist in their gut, might not work on a dragon.

"Da thinks he might have an old journal that mentions tending to dragons, written by his great-granddad back when nobles sometimes kept one with their horses." William fluffed up the straw to make a comfortable spot for himself.

"Oh, that would be brilliant if he can find it." It was odd to think that once, grand houses had a few dragons lounging on the lawn. Fern's fingers worried at the spoon as she lingered. Part of her didn't want to leave, but she also needed to solve the issue of the murderous plant at Warrington Manor, or the viscount wouldn't pay her.

"I'll be back first thing in the morning. Or probably during the night if I can't sleep," Fern called out. Worry about the little creature would most likely drive her from her bed to ensure Eurydice still breathed.

Passing through the kitchen and staying out of Mrs Bentley's way, she dropped the bowl on the bench and retreated to her room to change before dinner. After removing her trousers and shirt, Fern scrubbed her hands and face. Then she tugged on a clean gown in a light-brown wool.

"Dinner!" George hollered up the stairwell. There was no need for a supper bell when one had George's large lungs.

After a delicious meal of roasted trout and vegetables seared in butter, Fern took her hot chocolate and retreated to her study. Standing with her hands on her hips, she stared at the books jammed into the shelves.

"If I were a rare and highly unusual plant with a taste for grumpy men, where would I be?" she asked the books. Her gaze alighted on a large and heavy volume with a deep-green cover. Prising it free, she dropped it to the desk. In quick succession, Fern pulled five more books that she thought were the best place to start her search.

With a stack of books to one side and her drink to the other, Fern began. She opened the biggest book, an illustrated treasury of rare and exotic plants that was over two hundred years old. She pored over the ancient pages, searching for any similarities among the drawings to the carnivorous vine that plagued the Warrington estate.

She flicked through every page in the old book without success. Then she placed it on the floor to re-shelf before turning to the next volume. Three books sat in the stack of discards when she reached for a little book, only slightly larger than her palm. This one was a journal her father had collected while on a trip to Eastern Europe.

The language was beyond her ability to decipher since she didn't know Romanian. The journal had always fascinated her because of where it came from, and she had imagined it once residing on a shelf in a spooky castle perched high on a mountain.

The diminutive book had drawings that dominated each page. The text was then crammed into any leftover space and was even scrawled in all sorts of directions around the illustrations. Slowly, Fern studied each picture. With a few quick strokes of their pen, the unknown author had captured flowers, leaves, and shrubs they discovered on their journey three centuries ago.

As she reached approximately halfway through the book, her hand paused, and Fern drew in a sharp breath. Flowing up one side of the page was a vine with a familiar hand-shaped leaf with random splotches. What arrested her attention was the outline of the flower pod, with its petals wide open like a star. Then closed to form a tightly pursed mouth.

The words meant nothing to her except the neat script written sideways at the edge of the page. "*Helix mortifera*," Fern whispered.

Helix was the Latin name for ivy, and mortifera...well, she knew enough Latin to recognise the word for death. Had the unknown explorer found *death ivy?*

Fern leaned back in her chair and stared out the window while she tried to think what else it might refer to. It could be a fatal sort of poisonous ivy. Her gaze slid to the open-mouthed flower. The splotches on the leaves were so unusual; what other plant had such a leaf colouration and distinctive flower?

No. This was no poisonous ivy. This was a plant that had many hungry mouths to feed.

"I need to find someone who speaks Romanian and can

translate the text for me." Fern closed the book and tucked it in her pocket. Her eyes were gritty from strain, and she needed a break. Standing, she arched her back and relieved tired muscles.

She scooped up the discarded books and placed them back on the shelf before going in search of George and Ambrose. She needed to talk through her discovery and decide what to do next. The older couple always listened with an open mind and could offer advice and suggestions.

Fern had slipped off her boots and padded along the hall in her stockings towards the drawing room. The soft hum of voices filtered through the partially closed door, George's deep baritone mixed with Ambrose's lighter tones. They were likely discussing the recent dramatic events.

Pushing open the door, Fern stepped into the cheerful room. The fire crackled at one end, and the candles threw a gentle light over the occupants. George and Ambrose sat in their customary armchairs by the fireplace, each with a glass of port in hand and a chess game in progress on the round table between them.

"Did you find anything?" Ambrose asked as she curled up in the corner of the sofa closest to them and leaned on the rolled arm.

"I think so." Fern pulled the book from her pocket and opened it at the page with the familiar drawing, then passed it to her uncle. "This looks very similar to what is covering the wall at Warrington Manor. The author calls it *Helix mortifera*."

"Death ivy?" George said, and his grey eyebrows shot up.

"That sounds deliciously macabre and not something I'd

want snapping at my fingers." Ambrose passed the journal to his partner.

George studied the sketches and accompanying text. "This is Romanian. I have an old colleague who has spent much time in Romania. He might be able to translate the page, but it will take several days, if not weeks, to get a response from him."

Blast. Fern didn't have days to spare, let alone weeks. However, a translation would assist the paper she intended to write about the plant, and she could credit the person who made the original discovery in the fifteenth century. "Yes, please, George. I can copy the page out if you could send it along and ask for an urgent reply. There might be something in here that will help. Although I am disappointed that I'm not the first to discover the plant, if it is indeed the same."

George rose and poured from a decanter on a sideboard, then he placed a glass in front of her before returning to his armchair.

Fern took a sip of the ruby liquid, relishing the rich, sweet flavour of the port as it warmed her from the inside. "Putting aside what information this journal might bring, I still need to figure out how the vine is tied to Squib. The Moray sisters thought it was more than magic and nature combined. Decima sensed something metallic."

Ambrose leaned forwards in his chair, resting his elbows on his knees as he studied Fern. He ran a hand through his hair, which had faded from the bright red of his youth to a coppery blond. "The problem, my dear, is that you're trying to find a natural explanation for something wholly unnatural."

George grunted from his chair. "It's not some magic trick to entertain children. This is a living thing. It grows; it consumes...gardeners. Fern will find the answer in botany and science."

Ambrose tutted under his breath. "I will make you another bet, my darling pudding. Whatever that little book says, it will confirm the vine is a thing born of the storm, magic, and chaos."

"That just about summarises what the trio said. Mrs Carlisle wrote the story about the vine and then used the pages to make Squib. Then both came to life. If this vine is a thing created from magic and science, how do I turn it back into a normal, non-carnivorous Boston ivy?" She was a botanist, not a magic crafter or a scientist.

Both men fell silent for a moment before they said a name simultaneously. "Seth Drakeman."

Fern blinked at them, taken aback by their unity. Lord Seth Drakeman was something of an enigma in their village. His family had resided in the area for centuries, and a distant ancestor had once been the king's dragon keeper. The role had attached itself to his family in their surname. They were dragon—or drake—men. That role had seen King Henry VIII grant the family large tracts of land and a title in recognition of their service.

Lord Drakeman was a reclusive alchemist who lived alone, apart from his staff, on the sprawling estate that touched the edge of the village. He had little to do with the outside world. No doubt much to the despair of mothers in London. Not only was he an earl who refused to take a noble bride, but it was rumoured he had discovered how to turn base metals into gold and was supposed to be one of the wealthiest men in all of England.

Fern could only recall seeing him once or twice, even though she had lived her whole life in Drake's Bend. Even as a youngster, he hadn't often played with the village children. His father had shipped him off to a boarding school. She did have the occasional interaction with him via letter. He sometimes asked Fern to source rare ingredients for his potions and formulas.

"You want me to go see him? In person?" Fern asked incredulously.

Ambrose nodded at her, an earnest look on his face. "Yes, dear. He's the only one who might have the answers you seek. He's been studying alchemy and magic for years."

Fern was silent, contemplating the suggestion. She had never met him, and the village rarely gossiped about him. Regardless of what he did behind the closed gates of his estate, he was one of them, and they protected their own. All she knew was that he rarely saw people, having suffered a terrible alchemy accident many years ago, and preferred to communicate via letters.

"Given his ancestors were dragon keepers, he might be able to assist you in saving two very different dragons," George said.

"I didn't think to consult him about Eurydice, as there hasn't been a dragon at his family estate for over a century, so he has no experience with them. But he might have journals from when his relatives were responsible for the king's dragons. There might be detailed accounts of how to nurse a sickly dragon or the best way to help Eurydice regain her strength." Fern stared into her glass, wondering if he would help her. There was also another potential obstacle she would have to navigate. "What if I am turned away at the door?"

"Then at least you would have tried. George's Romanian friend and the three witches might yet provide a solution." Ambrose reached out and patted her hand.

"He'll see you," George said with an adamant tone. "No alchemist worth his salt could resist the puzzle you have for him."

Fern leaned back on the sofa. She had nothing to lose from banging on his front door, assuming the gate at the roadside wasn't locked. And there was much to gain if he could save Squib and Eurydice. The previous year, Lord Drakeman had written to enquire if the lunanavis had flowered as he required the stamens. Delivering the precious items should gain her admittance and a little of his time to explain her situation.

Her decision was made. "Very well. I shall go see him tomorrow."

As Fern climbed into bed that night and pulled the blankets up around her shoulders, her mind was filled with thoughts of the mysterious alchemist. Curiosity nibbled at her to see him in person. Rather like dragons, he was rarely spotted and the subject of much speculation. There was also the chance he would snap her head off.

Twice during the night, Fern rose from her bed and crept through the house. Once to harvest the last three blooms from the lunanavis, and another time to check on Eurydice. The young dragon roused in her presence and took a few sips of water but nothing more. It took effort to push down her worries and remind herself that it had only been a day since they had discovered Eurydice trapped under the fountain. The creature's recovery could take weeks.

When morning broke, Fern lay in her bed and stared at her ceiling. There was much to do, but fatigue nibbled at her limbs due to her only snatching a few hours of broken sleep. She had left the damaged lunanavis flowers that bloomed during the storm to set seed, so there were no more to harvest until next month.

"Coffee," she muttered as she flung back the blankets.

Nothing would be achieved that day until she revived her tired mind. If there was one universal truth in their household, it was that a tired person would never be in want of coffee. George always had a brew on the stove.

Fern dressed in trousers and tugged on a warm tweed waistcoat over her shirt. She even laced up soft boots to warm her toes rather than creeping barefoot to the kitchen.

George and Ambrose sat at the table while Mrs Bentley and Alice prepared the meals for the day. George took one look at Fern and poured from the coffee pot at his elbow and offered her a cup.

"You look like someone who spent all night fending off a carnivorous plant in their dreams," Ambrose said, a frown marring his pale forehead.

Fern clutched the mug in both hands and inhaled the dark brew. "And to think that only the other day, you thought I lacked excitement in my life." There were days that Fern could see the appeal of having nothing more taxing to do than a spot of embroidery.

# CHAPTER 16

George met Fern's gaze over the rim of what appeared to be a tankard of coffee. "I checked on our patient at dawn and took out a little broth. William was getting her to drink it."

Fern took a sip of coffee and nodded her thanks to Alice as the young woman (who bore such a startling resemblance to her mother it was as though her father had no input in her creation at all) set a plate in front of her. With coffee in one hand, Fern picked up a rasher of crispy bacon in her other hand and chewed the salty length.

"After breakfast, I'll head out to Wyndham Hall and visit Lord Drakeman," she announced after swallowing her mouthful.

Ambrose, who had been engrossed in his copy of *The Gentleman's Magazine*, lowered the page, his eyebrows arching like well-pruned hedges. "You cannot call at Wyndham Hall dressed like that." He peered over the top of his reading glasses at Fern's attire.

She gave him a sharp look as if he'd suggested she would

have to change into an ornate court presentation gown. "And why not? I am calling upon him as a botanist in need of his expertise, not a debutante expecting a marriage proposal."

George huffed. "Dressed like that, they'll send you round back."

Fern drew a breath to argue and then decided to finish her strip of bacon instead.

"No butler will admit a scruffy worker to his master's presence. You need to at least look..." Ambrose drew circles in the air with a piece of toast.

"Presentable." George finished his partner's sentence.

Fern glanced down at her trousers. Admittedly, they were a bit old, and a stubborn stain from her work in the garden lingered and refused to budge despite how many times they were laundered. Nor had her boots been polished for some time, as she didn't see the point when she would trudge through mud and dirt.

Then another thought occurred to her. This one more distressing than having to wear a gown. "If I'm in a dress, I will have to ride sidesaddle!" She had planned to save time by riding out to the estate. If she couldn't face the sidesaddle, she would have to walk, and there was a high chance she would drag her skirts through the dirt and end up looking just as frightful as if she had stuck with trousers.

The huffing from George took on a distinctly amused tone. When Fern narrowed her gaze at him, he pretended great interest in his coffee.

Fern's mother had been the epitome of grace and style when she rode out sidesaddle. As a child, she remembered watching from a window and thinking her mother some sort of fairy princess. For herself, young Fern had much preferred leaping on her pony bareback, while wearing breeches borrowed from the stable lad, and galloping across the meadows.

Quite apart from inherently rebelling against looking graceful and elegant, Fern simply didn't want to fuss with skirts as she climbed on and off a sidesaddle. She crossed her arms and sucked on her bottom lip, considering whether a tantrum would serve any purpose.

"Lord Drakeman's butler is a formidable guard dog. If you cannot get past him, you won't be able to ask for help with this murderous plant. Or if he has any journals that will help us with Eurydice," Ambrose said gently, mollifying Fern a little.

She heaved a long-suffering sigh and returned to her breakfast. At which point George came to her rescue about one particular point.

"I'm taking Mrs Bentley out to Longshank Farm this morning. We'll drop you off on our way past and collect you on the return journey." He gestured from the cook to Fern with his coffee cup.

Longshank Farm provided both meat and produce for the village and those farther afield. Mrs Bentley and George undertook the trip once a week to stock up their larder.

"Very well. Your offer is acceptable." Not that Fern had many other options. Ambrose was right. If she couldn't gain an interview with Lord Drakeman, she had few other courses of action. Lord Warrington was adamant he would not let the monstrous plant remain in his garden for long just to spare what he referred to as a *paper toy*.

After breakfast, Fern went upstairs to change while George checked on Eurydice and hitched the horse to their cart. She emerged from her room dressed in a gown of soft green wool with a short spencer in a deeper forest green over the top. She made a quick stop in her study to grab a glass vial, gently easing two of the dried lunanavis stamens in, and pushed a cork into the neck.

Outside in the packed dirt yard, Ambrose waited by the stables. A wistful smile played around his lips on seeing her. "I swear that, at times, your mother looks through your eyes."

Fern silently took his hand, squeezed, and reached up to kiss his clean-shaven cheek. Was her mother truly gone when so much of her dwelt in their hearts?

George helped Fern up into the cart to sit beside Mrs Bentley. Space would be a bit tight with three of them on the seat, so Fern perched rather precariously on the outside edge. She hitched up her skirts and tucked them tightly around her legs so they wouldn't catch on anything as they rattled down the road.

The cart lurched to one side as George climbed in and gathered up the reins. With a click of his tongue and a gentle tap of the reins, he asked the horse to walk on. Along the drive and down the road the horse clip-clopped, his hooves echoing as they went over the bridge. They followed the gently winding road that mimicked the path of the river as it meandered through the middle of the village. Fern gazed at the quaint thatched cottages and storefronts that lined the main street.

On the other side of the river, they passed the village green with its old kelmsgale, its branches an umbrella of dense, dark-green leaves. The expanse of grass where they held the market and other village events was edged with wildflowers and clumps of tall grasses.

George guided the horse through the village and out the northern side. Fifteen minutes after they passed the last cottage and the cemetery, he brought the cart to a halt outside a pair of imposing iron gates set into a high stone wall.

"Don't bother helping me, George." Fern grabbed hold of the side of the cart, bunched her skirts up in one hand, and jumped to the ground.

George shook his head at her un-ladylike behaviour. "We'll be an hour or two." Then he clucked his tongue, and the placid horse carried on along the road.

Fern stared at the gates adorned with serpentine dragons guarding the entrance to Wyndham Hall. While they weren't locked, the gates weren't exactly flung wide open either. One side was cracked a few inches, as though it couldn't decide whether to admit anyone or not. Leaning on the black metal, Fern pushed it open far enough to allow her slender form to squeeze through.

Straightening her spine and reminding herself that noble blood flowed through her veins, she set out along the winding drive leading to the main house.

When the house came into view several minutes later, Fern let out a gasp and halted. As a child, she had snuck onto the estate to stare at the brooding house and had forgotten one unique feature it possessed. One end was dominated by a two-storey conservatory with a curved glass roof.

"Oh, my." If she had liked conservatories, which she certainly did not, what a piece of paradise the Wyndham

Hall one must be. She imagined it with exotic soaring palms, delicate trees, and glorious rare orchids from sub-tropical climes.

Then she noted the grime on the panes, and as she approached, she couldn't see any greenery within. Unable to stop herself, she walked up to the conservatory, laid her hands upon the window, and pressed her nose close as she tried to penetrate the gloom. It seemed Lord Drakeman's interests were alchemy, not botany.

"What an utter waste." She admonished the reclusive owner. The conservatory was as ruined as her. Which struck Fern as ironic—since her ruin was facilitated by such a place.

Muttering to herself about wealthy gentlemen who didn't appreciate what they had right under their noses, Fern walked along the gravel path to the double-width front door.

The house loomed over her like a storm cloud, constructed with a dark stone that gave it a broody countenance. No sound came from within as she approached. Nor could she detect any movement behind the lifeless and uninviting windows. Undeterred, Fern grabbed hold of the ornate brass knocker hanging from a metal dragon's mouth and rapped three times.

After several very long and silent minutes, the door creaked open to reveal a butler whose stiff posture rivalled the stone gargoyles adorning the manor's roof. His piercing grey gaze examined Fern from her toes to the top of her head. He didn't say a word, only arched one greying, shaggy eyebrow. His head was entirely bald and possessed a gentle shine, as though she had interrupted him while buffing it.

"I am Miss Fern Oakby, and I am here to see Lord Drakeman," she said.

The butler barely blinked before replying, "Lord Drakeman is not available." His tone left no room for negotiation.

"This is important and concerns both a botanical and dragon-related matter. If he's not home, could I have a look at the library, please? I might be able to find a book that will assist me without any need to bother him." Fern's grip tightened on her battered leather satchel. She refused to carry a decorative, and in her opinion useless, reticule. The embroidered bags were never large enough for even half the items she liked to shove in one.

The butler blocked the door, one hand still on the oak. "Lord Drakeman is not within, and I cannot admit you without his permission, miss."

Blast! From all she heard, he rarely left the estate. Why did he decide to go on a jaunt the one time she needed to talk to him? "When will he return to Wyndham Hall?"

"I did not say he was out. Simply that he is not within." The door closed a fraction.

Fern shoved her boot in the gap before he slammed the door in her face. "This is a matter of life and death."

One side of his mouth quirked for a second before the stone mask fell back into place. "I shall tell Lord Drakeman you called, Miss Oakby." Then he nudged her boot out of the way with his polished shoe and closed the door.

"I have to see him!" Fern shouted at the brass dragon with the ring in its mouth. Indignation surged through her. Now what would she do?

She paced backwards a few steps and stared at the imposing facade. The butler's words swirled through her mind. Not within, but not out. It was a riddle given by the sphinx to those wishing to enter Thebes.

Then the answer occurred to her. "He's here. Somewhere. But not inside." Refusing to be stymied by a grumpy butler, Fern set out to find Lord Drakeman.

She walked around the side of the imposing hall, following the gravel driveway. Pausing at the edge of the house, she surveyed the unruly grounds. These were not meticulously manicured gardens like Warrington Manor, but ones that suffered from years of neglect and disregard. Like what should have been a showpiece conservatory.

An alchemist would not conduct his arcane experiments inside the grand home. Especially not one who had suffered a horrid accident in the past. No, he would need a separate laboratory, somewhere more isolated in case things went awry...or blew up.

She searched the tree line, looking for any small outbuildings placed further away from the house than the barn used to store carriages and the impressive wyvernry—the stone building once home to dragons.

There! On a gentle rise behind a stand of old oaks, she spotted it. A small stone building nearly hidden by the hillside and trees. Fern picked up her hem and hurried through the long grass. Her skirt snagged on a tuft, and she had to pull it free while muttering that Lord Drakeman should graze some sheep around the house to at least get the lawn under control.

As she drew closer, she saw the building was tucked into

the slope of the hill, and turf spilt over its roof as though it had emerged from the ground like a dazed mole. The thick stone walls had only a single narrow window, more like a sideways arrow slit, placed high and to one side of the door. The only way in was made of weathered oak and reinforced with steel strapping and hinges. This was either Lord Drake's laboratory or a storeroom for armaments and kegs of gunpowder.

Fern strode up to the wooden door and, raising her fist, knocked firmly.

The occupant of the odd little building responded quicker than the butler in the main house.

"Go away!" came a hoarse voice from within.

"It's Miss Fern Oakby, Lord Drakeman. I need to talk to you about a most urgent matter!" she yelled back.

For all that Ambrose insisted she dress like a lady, she was now reduced to yelling through a shut door like a fish wife berating her drunk husband.

"Leave my supplies with Quint. I'll send payment when I have time," came the shouted reply.

Fern crossed her arms. She hadn't expected a polite invitation, but the curt dismissal gave her pause. Still, she was not one to give up so easily.

She tried the handle, rattling it this way and that, but it remained firm, and the door wouldn't budge. Next, she walked along the three exposed sides of the building, the fourth being buried under the sloping ground. There were no other windows or doors in the stonework. She even climbed a way up the hill to look down, hoping for a hatch in the roof or a chimney she could shimmy down. While a skylight occupied a large part of the roof and seemed promising, it had a tightly laced metal cage over it with bolts sunk into the stone. Almost as though the occupant sought to keep out anyone intent on breaking in.

Returning to the front of the laboratory, she stared at the narrow window. It was propped open and secured with a latch to allow fresh air inside. In width, it looked barely wide enough for one determined botanist to squeeze through if she positioned herself horizontally.

What she needed now was something to stand on. Like the empty wooden crates stacked on the other side of the building. They had probably once contained supplies that had been taken into the laboratory and were awaiting removal.

One at a time, Fern picked up a box and moved it under the window until she had constructed a somewhat shaky, pyramid-shaped stairway. Climbing up to the top crate, she undid the latch and held the window up with one hand. With her other hand, she swept up her skirts and then squeezed herself long ways through the window.

Within, light flooded a large square table placed directly under the skylight. Benches lined two walls. One side was covered in floor-to-ceiling shelves, crammed with a variety of containers, bottles, bowls, and equipment in no discernible order. The rear was cloaked in dim shadows where the storehouse tunnelled into the earth.

Every available flat space was covered in vials in wooden stands, or metal ones over flames. Glass beakers containing brightly coloured liquids bubbled quietly in the grasp of metal arms, the contents emitting a soft glow or releasing puffs of pale-blue smoke. Strange contraptions whirred and hissed in the corners, and books with worn spines were piled high everywhere. The air was thick with the scent of herbs and chemicals, creating an intoxicating atmosphere.

Fern slid one leg over the window frame and glanced down to see where she would land. Right below her was a row of three small metal cauldrons, all sitting over flames. She would need to place her feet just right so she didn't upset any experiments.

She gave a little push with the foot still balanced on the crate and swung her leg up. As she moved her weight forwards to get one leg through the window, Fern encountered a problem. Her skirts had tangled around the latch. Her weight was now tipped over the window, but if she let go of the ledge to untangle herself, she would tumble on whatever simmered below.

"What the devil do you think you are doing?" came an angry shout. At the square table stood a tall figure clad in a thick, leather apron. A helmet covered all his head, and protective goggles obscured his features. Leather gloves came up to his elbows as he used long tongs to remove something from a box. "You have made a grave mistake, Miss Oakby."

"Of course I have!" she yelled back. "I would never have got stuck if I was wearing trousers!"

# CHAPTER 17

Fern tried to lift her leg, but her knee caught against the fabric of her skirt. When she moved one hand to tug on the material, the shift in her weight nearly unbalanced her and caused her to lurch towards the experiments below.

"Trousers?" the formidable-looking figure said. "You think your mistake was your attire?" He raised the visor of his helmet, and an odd gaze alighted on her.

Fern swallowed a gasp. Lord Drakeman possessed one brown eye and one that was silver. A shaft of bright sunlight stroked the scar on the right side of his face, but it was like no scar Fern had ever seen. Instead of burned flesh, the experiment that had blown up in his face turned a stripe from forehead to chin into...scales.

Scales that appeared remarkably like those on Eurydice.

"Are you going to help me, Lord Drakeman, or shall I fall on whatever concoction you have set on the table beneath me?" Fern called out.

"You got yourself up there. You can damned well get

yourself down on the other side of the window and leave me alone." He crossed his arms and glared at her. His simmering anger was made all the more eerie by the eye that seemed to be made of mercury. Even the white had been replaced by silver, and he had a narrow, vertical pupil like a cat or dragon's eye.

"In case you hadn't noticed, my skirt is caught on the latch. It doesn't matter what direction I want to go. If I let go of the window frame to free myself, I will fall. I'm sure I'll do no damage whatsoever to those cauldrons right in the path of my imminent descent. Or, if you prefer, we can stand around here talking until my arms tire, and we'll see what happens. Shall we discuss the latest happenings in the village, or do you like to gossip about recent scandals from London?" Fern's tone became increasingly strident and annoyed.

Lord Drakeman huffed a sound that resembled something part-way between an annoyed George and an upset horse. He lowered the tongs, then strode over to the window. Reaching up, he grabbed hold of her. One leather-gloved hand slid under her thighs, his other wrapped under her arms.

"Oh." She breathed the syllable out as she found herself enfolded in a strong embrace.

While Lord Drakeman held her securely in his arms, Fern quickly tugged her skirt free of the window latch. Only then did he gently lower her to the floor, his arms staying around her body for the length of a heartbeat. Then he let her go and took a step backwards.

"Now, get out." He pointed to the heavy door, which was laced with metal strips to reinforce the wood.

Fern ignored the order. She was no timid maid to be bossed about. "I need your help, Lord Drakeman. I have a botanical problem that requires your particular expertise."

She clutched the strap of her satchel. Wrapping her fingers around the leather stopped her from tapping on the glass of a rotund jar beside her that seemed to hold a wisp of purple cloud.

"I have little interest in plants except as required by my formulas." He turned his back on her and walked to the square worktable.

"Lord Warrington has a carnivorous vine that devoured his head gardener." She followed him, sticking as close as his shadow.

"I am no gardener. Let them chop it down or burn it. I do not care." He lowered the visor of his helmet and stared into a copper pot that could have held enough soup to feed a family with a dozen children.

"There is a part to this problem that I cannot fathom. There is a small...creature bound to the vine in some way. When the vine is slashed, a similar cut appears on him." In Fern's mind, she kept seeing the imploring look on Millie's face as she asked for Squib to be saved. Her new companion alleviated a little of her loneliness, and it was evident the two cared for each other despite the short length of their friendship.

"A plant and animal are bound together?" He tilted his head to indicate his interest.

Without being invited, Fern sat on a wooden stool tucked under the table and dropped her satchel to the cluttered surface.

"Both sprang to life during the recent storm. Mrs Carlisle, she is Lord Warrington's sister, wrote a gothic tale about the ivy. Unsatisfied with her work, she turned the pages into a paper dragon. The next morning, both flesh-consuming vine and paper dragon were turned real." There. She had laid out the problem. Now he should be able to solve it.

"Obviously, the author's work binds them since they are both products of her imagination. Is she able to cast magic?" He angled his visor to rub the stubble on his chin.

"I do not believe so. I consulted with the Moray sisters. They said the recent storm was a nexus of magical energies, a rare and powerful event." Fern picked up a small stone with a sheen like copper from the table and rubbed its smooth surface between her thumb and forefinger. "They thought the storm and its magic transformed them. As alchemists seek to do."

"The air of the storm was charged in a unique way that I've not seen before and had only read of in books. It amplified the experiments I was conducting that night. A month's work was completed in a few minutes while it raged outside." He tugged the gloves up past his elbows and picked up the long tongs.

"So you will determine what binds the pixie dragon to the vine and how to sever the connection?" Fern's fingers stilled on the copper pebble, and she wondered if he would notice if she slipped it into her pocket.

"No. I am far too busy." He ignored her and fished around in the large pot with the tongs.

"Then I assume you don't want the lunanavis stamens

you requested. I will let my other buyers know that I have some stock available. The moon has waned, and there won't be any more until next month." Fern slid off the stool and settled the satchel at her side, ready to leave.

"Are they pure and undamaged by sunlight?" With his free hand, he lifted his visor. His silver eye bore through her and revealed nothing, but the brown one was lit with curiosity.

"I am a professional botanist, Lord Drakeman." A hint of indignation crept into Fern's voice. "I harvested the blooms under the full moon and removed the stamens before sunrise." She slipped her hand into her satchel and withdrew the vial.

Ensuring no shaft of sunlight reached the glass, she held the container under the shadow of the tabletop.

The alchemist leaned down to stare at the glimmering, needle-like stamens. "Extraordinary. I have wasted money buying them elsewhere only for my potions to fail due to contamination."

Ah. Now Fern had his interest, and they had only to negotiate a price. "I will give you these two free of charge. In return for a potion or way to sever the bond between flora and fauna. But the little dragon must remain unharmed. Oh, I also need access to any journals left by your family. I found a starving dragonet at Warrington Manor and need any help to nurse her back to health."

His silver eye narrowed, and dark brows pulled down as he frowned. "You have a starving dragon?"

"Yes. She was trapped under a fountain, and we only discovered her due to a storm-damaged tree. We are feeding her bone broth, but I thought some distant relative of yours might have kept books about the care of dragons." The monarch no longer kept dragons after an angry one burned a castle to the ground in the sixteenth century. Drakemans had not served the creatures for two hundred years. Did any regard for the beasts linger in his blood, or had science burned it all away?

"Three stamens. You will have one day in the library. Quint will be present at all times, and all books are to stay in Wyndham Hall." His shoulders were stiff as his gloved fingers curled and flexed.

"Very well." She accepted his terms.

He held out his hand under the table, and she pressed the vial into the leather palm. His fingers closed around it. Shielding the vial with his body, Lord Drakeman hurried into the dim recesses of the laboratory, where no daylight dared venture. A clang of heavy metal came from the gloom, then he reappeared.

"I shall inform Quint you are to have one day in the library, and he can show you where the old journals are kept. Now, to investigate this anomalous situation, I require a sample of the vine, the pen, paper, and ink used by Mrs Carlisle. And this paper creature turned real." Having rattled off his list of demands, he turned back to his current experiment and whatever lurked in the pot that required he be protected by the visor, heavy apron, and gloves.

She probably shouldn't lean over and peer within since she had no such protection. "I'll return tomorrow."

If Fern made haste, she could gather what she needed from Warrington Manor and be back in Drake's Bend by midnight. It would mean riding home in the dark, but she'd much rather catch a few hours' sleep in her own bed than spend another night under a roof that did not welcome her. It also meant putting off her day in his library until she returned. Silently, she willed Eurydice to keep improving with the care they lavished on the little dragon, even if they didn't exactly know what they were doing.

"One more thing, Miss Oakby," Lord Drakeman called out as she crossed the room.

"Yes?" What else could he need? A soil sample, or did he expect her to capture the thunder and lightning that cast their magic over the Boston ivy and origami creation?

"Use the door next time." His visor snapped back into place and obscured his unnerving silver eye.

When she unlocked the door and stepped back into the morning light, the heavy bolt slammed home behind her.

"What a charming individual. No wonder he doesn't attend the local dances," she said as she walked back across the meadow, tugging her blasted useless skirts free of a thistle. "Tomorrow, I'm wearing trousers, and I don't care if Uncle Ambrose objects." She glanced over her shoulder at the stately home, its windows catching the morning sun and winking like mocking eyes.

A tangle of emotions clung to her as ivy did to ancient stone. Relief at having secured Lord Drakeman's reluctant aid, sat alongside a flutter of excitement at unravelling the botanical mystery, and having a chance to peer inside the old home's library.

The gate came into view, and there waited George and Mrs Bentley. The cook sat on the seat of the cart. George leaned against the stone pillar, his arms crossed as he stared up the driveway. The deep lines in his forehead lessened as she rounded the curve.

As she approached, he didn't say a word. The gruff man simply raised one greying eyebrow in a silent question.

"He will help. But honestly, I think he and his butler are grumpier than you when the coffee supply runs out!" Fern huffed as she stopped to pat the horse.

"Quint let you in?" Both eyebrows shot up.

"Oh, no. The butler only muttered about Lord Drakeman not being within, but he wasn't out. So I had to search the estate, find his laboratory, and squeeze in through a window. And this silly dress got caught on the window latch," Fern said as she climbed up next to Mrs Bentley.

George's shoulders heaved in silent laughter as he climbed onto the other side of the cart and took up the reins. "Trousers tomorrow?" he asked as he urged the horse to walk on.

"Obviously," Fern replied.

Mrs Bentley placed a hand over her mouth to stifle her laughter.

"I also extracted a promise from him that I can look in his library for any journals kept by the monarch's dragon masters. There might be something that will help us with Eurydice." Fern held on to the edge of the cart as a wheel hit a rut, and she bounced on the seat. "But that will have to wait until tomorrow."

Worry about the dragon gnawed at her all the way back to Nemython House. Once there, she jumped to the ground and rushed to the stables.

"How is she, William?" she asked as she met the silvery-blue gaze of the sick creature. The juvenile dragon lay coiled amidst the blankets laid over the straw, her scales a dull grey and ribs obvious under her thin hide. She didn't seem much changed, although she breathed easier and without the shallow raggedness of when she had been freed from under the fountain. The sight tugged at Fern's heartstrings.

"She's taken a little more broth, Miss Oakby, and some water. Da and I reckon it will take some days before we see any improvement." The groom was forking fresh straw into a corner to make a clean nest for the dragon.

"I must go back to Warrington Manor. Do you and Daniel mind keeping watch again tonight?" Fern knelt beside Eurydice and reached out to rest a hand on the dragon's side. Her hide had warmed and was no longer chill. The shivers had lessened too. Did that mean she was on the road to recovery?

"Of course, Miss Oakby. Danny is ever so proud to have such an important task to do. He'll not let you down. Nor will I. We all want to see little Eurydice thrive and fly over the village when she's better." William leaned on the handle of the fork.

"Thank you." Her father had been blessed that the Bentley family, who lived in the cottage on the grounds, proved to be such loyal and hard-working people. "Could you hitch up Lord Warrington's horse to his gig, please? The sooner I get on the road, the sooner I can come home." She stroked the dragon's head, marvelling at the softness of her scales. That made her wonder if Lord Drakeman's unusual scar would be hard like leather or soft like velvet.

A snort escaped her throat at the daft idea, and little Eurydice raised her head and blinked. Fern rubbed under the dragon's chin. "Sorry, I didn't mean to startle you. I was thinking of someone else who has scales, but they are not as nice as yours."

What potion had Lord Drakeman been brewing that he ended up with a scaled scar and a silver eye? There was a tale she would have to ask Ambrose. He knew every bit of gossip that happened in Drake's Bend and further afield, all the way to London.

As much as Fern wanted to grab a book and a blanket and settle in the straw to keep watch over the dragon, she had to get moving. There was much to be done and a far smaller dragon to be saved for his anxious friend.

"Keep drinking the broth, Eurydice, and you will get your strength back and grow into a big dragon." Leaning down, Fern kissed the top of the dragon's head. Then she climbed to her feet and walked over to the house.

"I have to head back to Warrington Manor," Fern announced as she walked into the kitchen. Ambrose sat at the worn oak table, a cup of tea at his elbow and a stack of pages before him. He appeared to be editing an article he had written.

"George told me you managed to persuade Lord Drakeman to not only assist with Squib, but you can ferret out arcane knowledge in his library. I knew the gown would do the trick." He picked up the delicate cup and sipped.

Fern planted her hands on her hips. "The dress only helped if you mean he had to lift me down from the window in his lab so I didn't fall onto his experiments and turn myself purple. Or grow fur, or whatever he is working on in there."

Ambrose spluttered and stared at her. "George omitted that bit. Whatever method you employed, it has worked."

Despite the urge to grumble at her uncle about his insistence on propriety and trying to get her to dress like a lady, Fern had work to do. "I will search his library tomorrow. Right now, I have to change, and then I'm leaving for Warrington Manor to gather what Lord Drakeman needs. I'm hoping to be back late tonight. Could you keep a lantern burning for me, please?"

"Of course, Fern. We shall wait up for you." Ambrose reached out to pat her arm before picking up his pencil in one hand and striking through a line of text.

Upstairs, Fern stripped off the dress and tugged on her favourite trousers, waistcoat, and long boots. By the time she hurried back outside, William had the horse and gig belonging to Lord Warrington ready in the yard. The mare stamped a foot as the groom did up the last buckle to secure the harness.

"All set, Miss Oakby," William announced once he'd finished.

"Thank you, William." Fern climbed into the gig and settled on the leather seat. At least this one had padding, unlike George's cart. With her satchel tucked at her feet, she took up the reins and gave them a gentle flick.

"Let's not dawdle," she said, more to herself than to the horse.

# CHAPTER 18

GEORGE WAVED from where he stood at the parlour window, and Fern returned the farewell. As she guided the horse out onto the road, a cool breeze swept across her face and carried with it the fragrance of lavender from the garden. Urging the horse into a trot, her mind wandered back to Lord Drakeman's laboratory.

Did the clutter and chaos reflect a brilliant mind? His silver eye had been disconcerting at first glance, but it made her all the more curious about what had happened to him and how it had altered his sight. Did he see everything cast in the moonlit hues of night, or did it lend him the piercing sight of a dragon?

As the horse maintained a steady pace, its hooves drummed a settling rhythm for Fern's scattered thoughts. As she recalled all she knew about carnivorous plants, occasionally her mind circled back to Lord Drakeman's unnerving eye. Or the way his strong arms had held her aloft while she untangled her skirt. How long had it been since her limbs had tingled from another's touch, even through layers of clothing?

Too long.

Ambrose and George encouraged her to find someone who made her heart sing, but she didn't trust herself to be vulnerable again. Once her heart had been broken, she had encased it in layers of protective steel. She had indulged in the occasional flirtation with visitors to their village (she wasn't a nun, after all!) but avoided any romantic entanglements with locals. Fern didn't want such a complication in her life.

Shoving difficult thoughts back behind a solid door in her mind, Fern decided to give the horse a rest at the halfway point where she had found the dragon skeleton. She steered the gig off the road and over the flat clearing near the tree stump.

Jumping down, she led the horse to the water. The equine dipped its muzzle, drinking deeply with slow gulps. Leaving the mare to slake her thirst, Fern walked up to the enormous stump, as wide as her outstretched arms. Kneeling beside it, she pulled back tufts of grass to find the secret concealed by the tree. Once she had exposed some of the bleached bones, Fern rested on her heels and bowed her head for a silent minute.

From her pocket, she drew out a sprig of rosemary she'd plucked from the garden at Nemython before leaving.

"For remembrance," she whispered, placing the greenery among the ribs of the fallen creature. Then she covered it back up with earth and grass, ensuring it would not be disturbed further by any passerby or beast. As she scraped up loose soil, her fingertips brushed against something hard and round nestled in the dirt between the skeleton and stump.

Curiosity piqued, Fern dug deeper and unearthed the lump. The object was encased in soil and remnants of root fibres. She rubbed it against the dried grass to brush it off and revealed its true form. Fitting in her hand like a ball, she held a fruit that resembled a pomegranate.

Except no pomegranate tree grew to the girth of the trunk before her. Nor was a pomegranate as large or dark, even when coated in dirt. The fruit in her hand would have been a deep red when it ripened and fell to the ground. Now, it was a blackish-brown from being covered in soil. Only one tree dropped a seed pod like the one she held—the kelmsgale.

She had identified the slain ancient. Oddly, the tree had not been marked on her father's map. How had it escaped his notice? Or hers? Over the years, Fern had at other times travelled this road. And not once could she recall seeing a kelmsgale growing in the spot.

*If a tree grows by the water and no one notices it, is it really there?*

She might be mistaken, and the pod left there by another hand or claw. Fern brushed her fingertips over the stump and considered who had taken a saw to the centuries-old tree, whatever its species (although she was sure it was a kelmsgale). "What monster cut you down?"

This specimen had been healthy, with no evidence of disease in its rings. Which meant someone had cut it down for firewood, timber to make furniture, or simply because they had an axe and a spare hour or two.

Some of the rare kelmsgales had sickened and died, like

the others that once stood around the village green of Drake's Bend. Fern's father had made it his life's mission to determine what disease afflicted the trees with its magical blossoms.

She turned the seed pod over in her hand. Her father had hypothesised that there might be some connection to the decline of both dragons and kelmsgales. Sadly, he had died before discovering if flora and fauna were bound together in some way.

Like a carnivorous plant and a pixie dragon.

"Perhaps solving one mystery will provide a clue to another." Fern tucked the seed pod into her voluminous coat pocket. When she returned home, she would try to germinate the seeds. Even though all her father's attempts had failed, she wouldn't stop trying. They had tried cold stratification and heat, but there had to be another way.

Brushing dirt from her knees, Fern made her way back to where the horse now grazed on the fresh grass by the river-bank. She patted its flank, then guided the mare back to the road before climbing into the gig.

Fern picked up the reins, and with a light flick, they were moving again. An hour later, she manoeuvred the horse and gig through the open gates of Warrington Manor. The horse slowed to a walk as they approached the stables.

A groom rushed to take the reins as she hopped down. Before the lad led the horse away to be unhitched, he gestured to the main house. "I was told to tell you that his lordship wants to speak with you urgently. He said as soon as you returned, Miss Oakby."

"Thank you." Fern picked up her satchel and settled the

strap over her shoulder before striding off towards the kitchens.

She used the boot scraper by the back door to slice the worst of the mud and dirt from her boots, then she stomped on the rough mat to shake free the smaller bits.

"That will have to do," she muttered as she entered the bustling heart of the estate.

As she wove through the staff, a footman hastily swallowed a mouthful of his tea and leapt to his feet. "Miss Oakby! I will take you through to Lord Warrington."

Fern paused at the door and waited for the young man to catch up. She was quite capable of creeping along the servants' hallway, popping out the green baize door, and finding her way to Lord Warrington's study on her own. But this chap looked determined to lead the way.

The footman hurried past her and held the heavy door open. As she stepped through, he whispered, "Mrs Carlisle needs to talk to you, miss. Privately. She asked me to tell her when you were here."

"Excellent. I need to talk to her. Can you fetch her while I speak to his lordship?" Fern said.

The footman nodded and pushed the door that divided servants from family shut. They walked the short length of the hall and across the marble-tiled entrance. At the double doors, he paused and rapped softly. At the muffled, "enter", he opened the doors.

"Miss Oakby to see you, milord." The footman bowed his head as Fern walked into the study.

Lord Warrington stood at the window, gazing out at the

expanse of lawn nestled in the curve of the driveway. His attention focused on one of his groundsmen who was on his knees trimming the grass with a pair of shears, evening up the longer bits left behind by grazing sheep.

"I have enlisted the help of Lord Drakeman, Lord Warrington. I am confident he can find a way to free your sister's new friend from the vine so that the latter can be... subdued." Fern's free hand curled into a fist. The idea of chopping up the plant and burning it pained her. Perhaps after it was given a hard prune, there would be a way to move it to a secure location so it could be studied.

Lord Warrington spun around, a frown digging furrows deep enough to plant potatoes on his forehead. "Destroyed, Miss Oakby. I want the damnable thing burned to the ground. It killed my head gardener! Do you know how hard it will be to replace Corby? And the Boston ivy that used to grow there."

Fern wondered what bothered him more—that the plant had killed someone (and could a plant be charged with murder?) or that the death had inconvenienced him. She curled her hand tight into the satchel's strap until the leather bit into her palm, and she remembered to exercise patience if she wanted to be paid for the job. She was already out of pocket for the two highly expensive lunanavis stamens it took just to get Lord Drakeman to help.

"It will not be much longer, I am sure. Once I gather what Lord Drakeman requires, he can split the two, and then you can have your men deal with the vine in whatever way you see fit." As much as the words hurt, she said them anyway. She would have samples, and it might be possible to grow another from a cutting. Then she could offer them to the Botanical Society in exchange for admittance. Surely they couldn't refuse a lady member with a carnivorous plant for them to admire.

"The thing has taken over another foot of wall overnight. One of the lads saw it pluck a pigeon from the air, and it disappeared among the leaves." A shudder ran over Lord Warrington's frame, but Fern couldn't discern if it was caused by the horror marring the beauty of his rose garden or the fact she wore trousers once more.

Fern didn't think a pigeon would provide much sustenance if the plant devoured an entire man in one night. Or that might have been an extraordinary appetite triggered by its rapid growth. These were all questions that could only be answered after studying the vine. She swallowed a huff of frustration.

"Lord Drakeman has asked for samples." She had the short length tapping against the glass in her study, but if she handed that over to Lord Drakeman, she doubted the sample would survive any alchemic process. "And I must gather samples from your sister of what she used to write the story and construct the origami dragon."

Lord Warrington let out a noise that sounded distinctly like an unhappy growl. "All this to save a blasted toy of Millicent's."

"But he is a toy no longer. Just as Pinocchio was no longer a wooden puppet once made real. Besides, it is understandable that Mrs Carlisle does not wish to see her new friend harmed in any way. Surely a loving brother would not deprive his sister of a little companionship?" Fern never understood how some siblings, like the Bentley children, were the fiercest supporters of one another. Then others, particularly among the nobility, did less to help each other than they would a beggar on a street corner. It hadn't taken her long to realise there was little brotherly affection from the lord for his widowed sister.

"You have five more days, Miss Oakby, and not a moment longer. Millicent should bear the consequences of her actions." He waved a hand, and Fern was dismissed from his presence.

As she left the lord's study and retreated across the marble floor, Millie waited in the shadows by a bust of an angry-looking Roman. Squib perched on her shoulder, the little dragon peering anxiously around.

"Can you save him?" Millie rushed forwards, wringing her hands together.

"Lord Drakeman, the alchemist, has agreed to try. There is also a trio of magic casters in our village who are searching for a solution. I am here to gather samples from the vine." Fern studied the little dragon. It was odd that the vine kept growing, but Squib did not appear to have increased in size.

Millie gasped and raised one hand to cup the pixie drag-on's body. "It will hurt Squib. I know when Bertie sends his men in to attack it because poor little Squib suffers. He tried last night, but I threatened to scream the house down if he didn't call his men off."

Fern swallowed her anger. Despite his promise to give her a few days, Lord Warrington had broken his word. She rested her hand on Millie's arm. "I promise you, I do not want to cause distress to Squib. We shall find a way to gather samples with the least amount of pain to him."

Millie met her gaze, and unshed tears simmered in her eyes. "You must think me foolish. Putting you to all this effort to save a toy."

The voice was Millie's, but the words were her brother's. Having given the example of Pinocchio, Fern couldn't stop thinking about whether the old tale had another magical storm at its heart rather than a fairy (which everyone knew didn't exist).

"He is as real as you and me. What makes something worth saving? Do they have to be a certain size, or have a title, or a particular monetary value?" Fern reached up and touched Squib's chin, and the little dragon leaned into her caress just like Eurydice did. "Squib lives and he is your friend. That makes him worthy of saving in my eyes."

Millie blinked several times, and her gaze cleared. "Thank you," she rasped in a voice thick with gratitude.

"Now, I need you to gather up the pen, ink, and paper you used when writing the story and any left over from constructing Squib. I will also need him," Fern said.

Anxiety erupted across Millie's face at the mention of having to hand over her little companion. Her lower lip trembled, and her eyes glistened once more.

Before the other woman cried again, which really wouldn't solve anything, Fern continued, "I promise you, Millie, I will do everything I can to keep Squib safe. But Lord Drakeman and the Moray sisters need to understand the bond between him and the vine. Only then can he be freed of the grip the plant has over him, so your brother can destroy the vine."

Millie nodded and stood a little taller. "Very well. We will do what is necessary to save him before Bertie does something horrid. I wish I could come with you, but my brother would not allow it," she added in a quieter tone, and a little of the resolve dribbled from her straight spine.

Squib regarded Fern with a wary eye and puffed warm air over Millie's cheek, then rubbed his against hers in a reassuring fashion.

Before Fern could comment on what her brother did or didn't allow her to do, Millie started up the stairs.

"Come to my room, and I will gather my writing supplies," she called over her shoulder.

Fern trailed behind Millie, climbing the grand staircase with its plush, crimson carpets that muffled their steps. They turned down a corridor lined with portraits of stern-faced ancestors whose eyes seemed to follow their progress. At the end of the short hall, Millie pushed open a dark wooden door to reveal a room filled with sunlight. The canopied bed was draped in brocade in a soft beige with blush-pink flowers and the softest, mossy green leaves. The blankets were pulled up, and all the crinkles had been smoothed away by the staff.

The rest of the room juggled chaos and organisation. The large armoire had its doors firmly closed. A pretty lace runner on the dressing table held a brush, a mirror, and a decorative crystal pot containing something pink. Around the floor, books were piled in what, at first glance, appeared to be haphazard stacks. But when Fern noticed the desk pushed up under the window, the books seemed to make walls around it.

As though Millie had sought to enclose herself in a smaller space within the large bedroom. Parchment, ink bottles, and quills were scattered across the desk's surface like fallen soldiers.

Millie wove a path between the books and began selecting items off the desk. "This is my favourite quill. It's a goose feather, but how I long for one from a raven." She picked up the feather with its sharpened tip. The end was stained by being dipped into ink countless times. She thrust it at Fern while she shuffled around papers.

"Let me guess, Bertie doesn't approve of a raven's feather quill?" Fern said as she took the writing instrument.

Millie's eyes sparkled for a change. "It seems you have the measure of my brother already."

It wasn't particularly hard to understand a boorish, enti-tled lord who thought to dominate everyone beneath him. His sister was a far more complex character that Fern itched to know better. "What of ink?"

"I used a different one for this story. I found a little bottle hidden behind some books in the library. I thought it rather pretty and mysterious. A deep purple with a sparkle to it. But there's not much left, I am afraid." She made an *a-ha* noise as she located a small cut-glass bottle under a notebook.

Fern took the bottle. Only three inches high, the thick glass was cut in a cross-hatch pattern that nearly obscured the contents. The battered silver cap was tightly screwed on and had spots of wear and discolouration. When she held it up to the light, a teaspoon of dark-purple liquid that shimmered rolled up one side.

"Is there any paper left?" Fern tilted her head to read the

hurried words scrawled across one loose page on the corner of the desk. It described a woman trying in vain to escape the dark tower where she was being kept prisoner.

It seemed there was a theme to Millie's work—damsels in distress in need of rescue from the heartless villain.

# CHAPTER 19

MILLIE STARED at the scattered pages. It appeared she scribbled her tales and then tossed them to one side. "Let me think...I found an old dusty ledger near the ink. The binding had come apart, but the pages were unused. I cut them free and used them to write my unimaginative tale..."

"I wouldn't call it unimaginative. What came to life out there is the botanical discovery of the century. I'm assuming Lord Warrington often says that about your stories?" Fern asked. The more time she spent with Millie, the less she liked her older brother.

Millie glanced over her shoulder, and her lips thinned. "Yes. If he spots my scribblings, he is quick to dismiss them as a waste of time. Apparently, I should be embroidering decorative throw pillows instead."

Fern thought there was some merit in being able to use a needle and scissors with precision. "Men. They are the first to complain about too many pillows. Keep writing your stories, Millie; you have an amazing gift. All you lack is an appreciative audience."

Another idea sprouted in Fern's mind. They were just the sort of stories that could be serialised in the *Midnight Chronicle*. She would ask Ambrose if the editor would consider giving the woman a chance.

A shy smile crept over Millie's face at the words of praise. "I remember now! After our talk in the library, I went back and retrieved the last few unused pages. The paper had such a lovely feel, and I thought to make a companion for Squib." She pulled open a drawer and picked up a few loose sheets.

Fern tucked paper, ink, and quill inside her satchel. "Now, let's see if we can gather a sample from the vine without hurting Squib. I wondered if snipping a leaf might be like losing a scale. Or the end of a tendril, like clipping a toenail. Do you think he could endure that?"

The little dragon made a low keening noise and huddled closer to Millie's face. Millie stroked his papery hide, where his scales were created by loops of lettering. "He will be brave and try. But promise you will stop if, if..."

"I promise we will stop if it hurts him too much." *Or slices him into pieces*, Fern added to herself. If the little dragon was diced up like a carrot, would he heal or stay that way? Perhaps they could glue him back together if he didn't repair himself.

She didn't know why she was focusing on saving Squib rather than finding a way to preserve the rare botanical specimen. *Because Squib didn't eat anyone*, she thought.

Or perhaps it was the deep loneliness in the other woman's eyes that tugged at a similar hollow inside her.

The two women hurried outside and through the grounds to the enclosed space that protected the harmonious blend of roses. The stone wall on one side was almost entirely engulfed by the carnivorous plant, and it now stretched for over twenty feet. The groundsmen had strung up a rope barrier in front of it so that no one could venture closer than six feet.

As they approached the rippling wall of leaves, Squib became agitated. Millie crooned to him and patted his small body. The pixie dragon retreated further under her hair, pulling strands loose with his mouth and front paws to create a curtain to shield him.

Moyles stood watch over the vine and touched the brim of his cap as they approached. "Mrs Carlisle, Miss Oakby. How is little Eurydice?" he asked.

"She is taking broth, but no better, sadly. It may take some days for her to show signs of improvement." Fern appreciated that his first concern was for the starved dragonet. "Whereas this fellow has grown bigger overnight." She stood by the rope and studied the undulating mass.

The thick, glossy leaves formed a solid, impenetrable mat. At least two dozen hand-shaped flowers jutted out with their lips pursed as though waiting for a tender morsel to come closer. Two appeared to have set and now resembled tightly curled fists. Bright-green tendrils poked through the leaves and waved in the air like hands sticking above water.

"Lord Warrington said it plucked a bird from the air." Fern pointed to a delicate tendril, not quite believing what she had heard.

"Yes, it did, miss. Right horrid it was to watch too. One of those shot out and wrapped around it like a rope, then curled in, and it disappeared behind those leaves. One startled coo was the only sound the poor pigeon made." He gestured to the wall of deep green with its dark-red blotches.

The vine rustled as though it whispered among itself and knew it was the subject of discussion.

"Fascinating." If Fern used a rake to knock open a flower where the groundsman gestured, would she find the bird's skeleton wrapped in woody limbs, or had it been fed whole into the gaping mouth of a flower?

"This is monstrous and isn't what I wrote at all!" Millie exclaimed. "The ivy in my story holds the heroine safe and unharmed until she is rescued."

"Sadly, this is an unfaithful adaptation of your work. Your words were taken and transformed into something else." Fern thought this version was more exciting, but she would keep that opinion to herself.

Millie glared at the plant. "I suppose this is what happens when a writer loses control of their work."

Fern turned her attention to Moyles while keeping one eye on the seeking whiskers of the plant. "I need samples, Moyles. Is there anything left from when the men first tried to cut it back? I have a small cutting, but Lord Drakeman requires more."

"There were only a couple of small pieces, miss. You took one, and his lordship ordered the others burned. This thing is right dangerous." Moyles picked up long leather gloves from a nearby wheelbarrow that contained implements more often used for cutting firewood. A variety of axes and a long-handled saw that required two men sat alongside shears and what appeared to be a fishing net.

"But Squib is not burned, is he?" Fern asked Millie. The pixie dragon hid under the fall of hair. But from what she remembered from earlier, he didn't appear to have any burn or scorch marks.

"No, thank goodness." Millie touched a lock, the stylish up-do now hopelessly ruined by the frightened dragon.

Once Moyles had the gloves pulled on, he picked up a pair of long-handled shears. "You tell me what you want, Miss Oakby, and I'll be quick about it."

Fern assessed the death ivy and made a swift decision. She would use her sample to spare Squib and add another leaf and the tip of a tendril. That way, she hoped, there would be no risk of accidentally cutting off a limb on the diminutive dragon. "A leaf and the tip from one of those waving tendrils, please."

"Use the rake to drag them near, miss. Whatever you do, don't step close to get them, or it will take a hold of you. One of the lads got close last night, and it took three of us to wrestle him free," Moyles warned her as he stepped over the rope.

"That might be what affected Squib last night, Millie, and not your brother secretly trying to pull it down. It seems he only feels what happens to the vine when it is intact, not what happens to bits once removed from it." That reassured Fern that the origami creation hadn't felt it when she sliced into the cutting. She grabbed the rake with both hands and stood ready.

Moyles stepped forwards and tracked a waving length of greenery as it arched towards him. As the string-like growth reached out as though it intended to tap on his nose, the groundsman lunged upwards with the shears and snapped the blades together. An eight-inch length fell to the ground and writhed while a shrill cry came from Squib.

Fern used the rake to draw the tendril closer to the rope. Then, after tugging on a leather glove, she picked it up between thumb and forefinger and dropped it into a nearby jar that was of a size to hold preserved peaches. The length curled up in the bottom like a slumbering serpent. Thick purple sap oozed from the open wound at one end.

Millie lifted Squib from her shoulder and cradled him against her chest. "Hurry! Be quick about it."

Fern nodded to Moyles. "A leaf, please."

Moyles used the shears like a divining rod, moving them back and forth as he tried to find where to cut next. Having made a decision, he reached out and snipped a thick leaf from the stem. The moment the blades bit through the vine, Squib emitted another high-pitched screech that turned into a mournful whine interspersed with sobs.

Moyles hurried back over the rope as tendrils plaited themselves together into a thick rope and tried to lasso him. He jumped as a loop touched the top of his head, but it slid down his shoulder.

"It's done," Fern called out as she used the rake to catch the fallen leaf while the groundsman hurried beyond the reach of the hungry vine.

Then, on impulse, she struck out with the rake and knocked one of the seed pods free. Squib gave a short, sharp yelp, and she whispered an apology to the little creature. With care, Fern raked the fallen pod towards her. The leaf and pod were added to the jar, although she had to shove to get the fist-sized pod through the glass mouth, then she screwed the lid on firmly. The container barely fitted in her satchel with the writing supplies, but she managed to secure the straps to stop it from falling out.

"It's all right, my brave little Squib. It's all over now." Millie's voice was laced with distress as she whispered to the paper dragon.

"How is he?" Fern tried to see between Millie's fingers if the dragon was intact. It appeared that Moyles hadn't inadvertently clipped a wing, nor had the pod removed his head or ears.

"He lost a claw for the tendril, and a scale for the leaf and the pod." Millie lifted her hand and gestured to two spots on the dragon's side where the words had been erased and the paper hide was grazed. Squib balanced on three feet to hold up a hind leg with the missing claw, the empty sheath darkened by a drop of purple blood.

"I am sorry, Squib." Fern apologised for the injuries. Although she thought the little dragon as prone to dramatic excesses as his owner. He certainly hadn't suffered a fatal injury. "Let us hope Lord Drakeman can break the bond you share with the vine, so that Lord Warrington can destroy it without affecting you."

"He simply has to, Fern. I could not bear to see Squib cut into tiny pieces or burned alive." Millie raised the dragon and kissed the top of his head. "Now, you must be very brave, my dear friend, and go with Fern. She will look after you and return you to me as soon as she can." She raised wide, worried eyes to Fern. Something else lurked in their depths— a wistful yearning.

"Are you sure you can't come with us?" Fern asked.

The woman was a widow, not a prisoner. Or was she?

Millie closed her eyes and drew in a deep breath. "Bertie wouldn't approve. How I conduct myself reflects on him and Annabelle. A noble widow shouldn't be roaming the countryside like some deranged woman who needs to be confined in Bedlam." Her voice tapered to a whisper at the end of what sounded like a well-rehearsed speech. No doubt having heard it a million times as her brother castigated her for seeking the freedom of the surrounding meadows and hills.

Another worrying thought wriggled into Fern's mind. Bedlam. That was a place of nightmares made real by those who ran it. That one word was whispered to scare young ladies in the same way parents told children of a monster under their bed when they were naughty. Did Lord Warrington threaten to have his sister incarcerated if she didn't do as she was told?

Fern stared at the sky while she formulated a plan. Then she smiled at Millie. "Drake's Bend is a lovely place to live. The villagers welcome all kinds of people, and while they gossip, they know never to pry into secrets best left undisturbed. It's the sort of place a widow who loves books and tales might find a new life for herself...and new friends."

Millie breathed out a sigh. "It sounds lovely. Does it have a bookstore?"

"No, sadly. It is the one thing we lack." Fern's books came

from when George and Ambrose ventured further afield. Or she traded them for seed and cuttings with other botanists.

"Well, that is a story I shall craft while I wait for you to return. I will write a story about a lonely widow who opens a bookstore and finally finds the peaceful place where she belongs." Millie cast her eyes downwards as she shared what sounded like a very personal dream.

"I had better get going. The sooner I can deliver everything to Lord Drakeman, the sooner we will have a solution." Fern held out her hand to Squib.

The kitten-sized dragon rubbed his muzzle against Millie's cheek, and then, with an exaggerated limp, he hopped along her arm to Fern.

"I am riding back, Squib, and I fear you would fall off my shoulder. Would you like to nestle in my satchel?" Fern tapped the bulging bag at her side. It was rather crowded.

Squib huffed warm air at her and narrowed his eyes into slits. He might not speak, but he had a way of expressing himself. "Not the bag, then. How about tucked inside my coat? Then you can tell me if you need out?" He could burrow in there and be held securely by the buttons at the same time.

The little dragon limped further up her arm, which she took as agreement. Holding her elbow high so as not to toss him to the ground, Fern buttoned her coat, then held the woollen fabric away from her body.

Squib trilled at Millie, then leapt into the space. He wriggled to make himself comfortable and soon settled with his head above the top button.

The two women walked to the stables where the groom

had readied Fern's mare. She placed a foot in the stirrup and swung up into the saddle.

"I'll be back as soon as I can, I promise. Most likely either tomorrow or the day after," she said to Millie.

Fern touched the mare's side. Once free of the yard, they picked up a canter. Squib, ensconced within the folds of her coat, shifted now and then as though he sought to remind her he was there. This time, she didn't stop to water the horse, only slowing to acknowledge the fallen tree and creature as they passed.

Dusk fell over the countryside as they made their way into Drake's Bend. On riding through the village, a sense of homecoming washed over Fern. Others might relish the lights and sounds of life in London, but she preferred the serenity found in the countryside. The quaint thatched roofs and packed earth roads comforted her like the pages of a well-thumbed novel and reminded her of Millie's dream to open a bookstore.

She mulled over how to make that possible as she trotted up the drive between Nemython House and the Bentley family cottage. Fern swung her leg over the pommel of the saddle to dismount so she didn't have to lean forwards and risk flattening Squib.

Her Uncle Ambrose must have been watching from the kitchen, as he hurried out. George followed at a much slower pace, holding a lantern.

"Do you have him?" Ambrose asked, a look of childlike anticipation lighting up his eyes.

Fern unbuttoned her coat and carefully lifted Squib out. She placed him into Ambrose's outstretched palms. He cradled the little dragon as though he held a delicate porcelain figurine rather than a living creature made from paper and ink.

"Oh, my stars! He truly does live. And what a magnificent wee specimen you are at that," Ambrose cooed as he inspected Squib, and the dragon basked in the warm praise. Ambrose ran a fingertip from the dragon's head along his spine, and Squib made a soft, trilling purr of contentment. "Just marvellous. George, explain this incredible creature if you can," he challenged his partner.

George made a noise in the back of his throat and leaned in closer to study the origami dragon. "I admit this creature's animation is...perplexing. One theory could be the electromagnetic energy from the storm. Lightning and thunderstorms generate tremendous energy. It's possible, albeit remotely, that it could have activated some latent properties in the paper or ink."

Ambrose raised an eyebrow and chuckled. "Latent magical properties, you mean?"

George sighed. "That is a possibility, however remote, regardless of what the three witches say. Having given the matter some consideration, I am inclined to think the answer lies in the ink. If it contained certain minerals or elements responsive to...let's say, unusual environmental conditions, that might explain the—"

"Magic, George," Ambrose cut the other man off. "It's all right to admit it was magic. It does, after all, exist in our world. Even if it quietly fades away."

George met his partner's gaze, and the argument drained from him. "I believed in magic once, on the day I first met you. I think I am flexible enough to admit that it also played a part in creating this little fellow."

He patted Squib's head with a bit too much pressure, and the dragon's head bobbed up and down, creating a new wrinkle in his neck.

"I knew I loved you for a reason," Ambrose murmured.

# CHAPTER 20

"What of Eurydice? Is there any change?" Fern asked, her focus switching from the little dragon to his larger cousin.

George shook his head. "She has slept most of the day and only taken a few spoonfuls of broth."

Worry knotted itself in Fern's stomach, and the two types of dragon intertwined in her mind to form one large problem. "If there is nothing I can do to help her at the moment, I shall take what Lord Drakeman needs out to him."

She hurried through the house and fetched the smaller jar with the cutting from the lockbox. When she held the jar up to the candle, the piece inside barely moved. The dark sap was smeared over the glass from where she had sliced it open. Next, she found the vial with the droplets of sap she had gathered and crammed everything into her already stuffed satchel.

Returning to her horse, she found Ambrose still fussing over Squib. George watched from a respectful distance as if he held himself apart from magic.

She took the reins, and Ambrose finally looked up and frowned. "You're not riding to Wyndham Hall now, are you? It is dark. You should wait until morning."

"I can't afford to wait. Lord Warrington is most insistent that I have only a few days before he burns the vine, which will destroy Squib. I only hope Lord Drakeman can find a way to sever their bond in time." Fern climbed back into the saddle and patted the tolerant horse. At least their next journey was not as far. They only went to where Wyndham Hall nudged up against the northern tip of the village.

"Take good care of our magical friend." Ambrose handed Squib up to Fern, and she nestled him into the warm sanctuary of her coat.

"Let us hope Lord Drakeman is as good an alchemist as they say. Otherwise, it will be up to the Moray sisters to save him." Fern loved the trio of old women, but their magic waned like a moon long past its full potency.

She nudged her horse, and the mare popped into an easy canter. The road through the village was quiet. The shops were shut, and people had hurried home for dinner. Silhouettes moved behind curtains, and light through the windows cast golden shafts into gardens. It didn't take long before they squeezed through the partially open gate and trotted up the curved road to Wyndham Hall.

The shape of the building was etched into the star-filled sky at its back. Despite her issues with conservatories, a pang of sadness washed over Fern as she stared at the dark expanse of glass on one end. Both of them had been discarded.

Fern dismounted when she reached the last tree before the house. With no signs of life inside, she needed somewhere to hitch her horse. She looped the reins around a branch and promised the mare she wouldn't be too long.

Checking that Squib was still in place, she strode towards the double doors and grabbed the knocker. She rapped three times and waited. Tonight, the butler answered in under a minute. Perhaps he was a nocturnal creature and more alert after dark.

Quint pulled the door open, his features as rigid as the stone facade of the house. "You." He arched an eyebrow, while his voice held a note of resignation, as if her presence was both expected and unwelcome. "Lord Drakeman mentioned you might call."

Fern met his gaze with a wide smile. If her presence annoyed him, she would go out of her way to be sweet. "Did Lord Drakeman also mention we will be spending an entire day together in the library?"

The frown on the butler's face deepened. Did that mean he didn't know or did and hoped she'd forget about it?

"I trust I am not intruding at too late an hour or interrupting Lord Drakeman's supper?" she continued.

Quint's lips twitched in something that might have been a smirk or a grimace; with him, it was hard to tell. "He's still in his laboratory. I'm told you know the way."

Then he slammed the door in her face.

"Thank you for your help!" Fern yelled at the solid oak, the only thing that stared back at her. Lord Drakeman's butler was ruder than George with a hangover during a coffee shortage.

Fern headed along the path and around the side of the house. She walked faster across the meadow as the last edges of dusk surrendered to night. Dark had settled over the meadow by the time she reached the stout stone building.

Yet again, Fern rapped on a thick door and waited for any sign of life.

"What?" came a shout from inside. Obviously, master and servant shared the same disdain for social niceties. Not that Fern was any stickler for rules, but at least she could be marginally polite.

"It's Miss Oakby. I've gathered what you require." Fern glanced sideways. The narrow window was firmly closed. Unless she broke the glass with a rock, she would have to go in through the door.

After what seemed like hours but was likely only minutes, bolts were drawn back with a series of metallic snaps and clanks.

Lord Drakeman appeared in the doorway, his face half-illuminated by the flickering lantern light from within. His expression was inscrutable, and his silver gaze had the eerie reflectiveness of a cat's eye at night.

His broad body blocked her way. "You have everything I asked for?"

Fern tugged the edge of her coat down to reveal Squib's head. "Yes."

He arched one eyebrow at the tiny dragon. Then, with a slow step, he moved aside to allow her entry.

Lord Drakeman hadn't tidied up from her previous visit. The same chaos reigned over the shelves and benches. She picked her way to the square table under the skylight and deposited her satchel. Opening her coat, she allowed Squib to hop out. The little dragon reared up on his hind legs, flapped his wings, and shook all over to shake free any wrinkles from his travels.

Fern reached into the satchel and wrestled free the large jar containing the samples of the vine. The seed pod was now absent from the container. That had gone into a secure metal cupboard in her workroom. The pod was something she intended to examine for herself.

Next, she set out Millie's writing supplies—the quill, paper, and cut-crystal ink pot.

Lord Drakeman stepped forwards to examine Squib first. "Fascinating," he said as the little fellow stretched up his neck to stare back in a display of either trust or bravado—Fern wasn't sure which.

The alchemist's silver eye flashed with a scientific hunger that Fern recognised. It was the same look she'd seen in her father's eyes whenever he'd discovered a rare plant species. The same gleam she had when she first regarded the transformed Boston ivy, or what she now knew was *Helix mortifera*, or death ivy.

"His name is Squib," Fern said.

On hearing his name, the dragon fanned out his wings to display his delicate folds and calligraphy sentences.

Lord Drakeman grabbed a pair of goggles and tugged them over his face. The left eyepiece was blackened, and the right one magnified his eerie mercury gaze. He leaned closer to examine Squib, studying the words turned into ink-drawn scales.

"Remarkable." His voice was roughened by years of solitude (and probably yelling at his butler), and it sent an unexpected shiver down Fern's spine. "Explain to me again how this paper construction came to life."

"Mrs Carlisle, that is Lord Warrington's sister, wrote a story about a ravenous vine. She wasn't satisfied with her literary creation, so used the pages to craft Squib." Fern sat on a stool and leaned her elbows on the table.

The alchemist made a noise in the back of his throat, which Fern assumed meant she should continue. The dragon rustled under his scrutiny, lifting his head and puffing a small gust of warm air towards the goggles that misted one lens.

"Mrs Carlisle discovered Squib was connected to the vine when Lord Warrington ordered the plant be cut down. As his men hacked into it, slashes appeared in Squib's hindquarters." As Fern narrated events, Squib spun and nipped at the scar lines on his papery side. Remarkably, the wounds had healed and now gave the appearance of deep creases highlighted with silver ink. "He lost two scales and the tip of a toe when we took these samples for you."

As Fern mentioned each injury, the little dragon spun to the affected area and then held up his foot. He made little squeaks as though he complained about how much it had hurt.

Lord Drakeman picked up a scalpel and a two-inch slide of glass. When he reached out towards Squib, the little dragon growled and jumped back to Fern's protective hands. "Don't hurt him!" Fern reached for the little creature and cupped his shivering body in her hands.

He held the scalpel aloft. "I need a sample, but I'll not cut him."

"Sorry, Squib. You will have to be brave once more," Fern said to the indignant-looking creature.

With a huff, he waddled a few steps across the table and plonked himself down on his hind end. Squib made a high-pitched whine as the alchemist scraped the scalpel over a patch of hide. When Lord Drakeman had a tiny amount of fibres and writing on the slide, he placed another small piece of glass on top to stop the sample from fluttering away when the air was stirred.

Squib whimpered and licked his hide. A spot the size of Fern's fingernail was now bare of words or drawn scales, but true to his word, there was no slice to the papery skin. He had been grazed only.

Silence fell. Lord Drakeman's silver gaze lingered over the mark he had made, and the tiny healed slashes in the dragon's hind leg. Then, without warning, he stood upright and pushed the goggles up onto his head as he walked over to one of his worktables. There, he scribbled notes.

Fern stroked Squib and reassured the little creature that he still looked marvellous, even with the bald patch. They both watched the alchemist, whose broad back was turned to them. He wore a rough linen shirt of a deep blue under his leather apron, with the sleeves rolled up to his elbows. His intense focus on his notes seemed to fill the room, seeping into every nook and cranny.

After several quiet minutes, Lord Drakeman set down his quill and returned to the table to turn his attention to the samples of vine. Without any gloves on, Fern noticed that one finger had a long, silvered scar as he used the tongs to extract the tendril. She wondered what he had done or if it had been caused by the same explosion that altered his eye and face.

"I have a small vial of its sap too. It resembles ink more than any sap I have seen." Fern reached into her satchel and fished out the finger-sized vial.

Squib peered at it and snorted before hurrying into the crook of Fern's elbow.

"I will examine the plant first." He placed the tendril in an unusual vice. Square and made of clear glass, he eased the sample between the sheets. The sides were framed by brass rods that had knobs, and he turned them to flatten the piece of vine. As the glass sheets joined and the sides interlocked, they made a sort of vase with an opening at the very top.

"That looks similar to the press George made me for preserving flowers and leaves." Although Fern's press allowed moisture in the flora to escape and let it dry out. She couldn't see that happening with organic material trapped between glass.

Next, the alchemist retrieved a bottle from one of his shelves. Glass of a thick brown obscured the contents. Using a dropper, he sucked up some of the liquid within and dribbled it through the neck of the glass press. A rich-blue fluid slid down the side of the glass in rivulets, pooling around the length of vine.

The leaf began to shimmer, reflecting an array of autumnal colours. The tendril uncoiled awkwardly, bashing itself against the confines of its prison. It, too, cycled from a fresh bright green to a forest green, then from blood red, it lightened to an orange-scarlet. Once both leaf and tendril were the same hue of copper, an odd blueish vapour swirled in the vase and sought to escape.

Lord Drakeman grabbed a cork and plugged the neck. Picking up the sheets of glass, he held them to the light.

"The enchantment is deep," he said finally. "This is no shape-shifting spell. The plant has been fundamentally altered in ways I've not seen before."

Fern picked up the vial of purple-black fluid that had bled from her sample and shook it. "Down to its very sap?"

"You said it was like ink?" Lord Drakeman abruptly placed the vase on the table and reached for the vial. His fingers brushed against Fern's. His skin cool to the touch.

"Yes. Here's the bottle of ink." Fern found the small cut-glass bottle, which had been nudged under a sheet of paper.

He took the bottle, then held both small containers to the light.

Squib growled and puffed heated air as his mistress's writing tools were scrutinised. Fern stroked the dragon's spine and murmured reassurances.

"The secret must reside in the ink," Lord Drakeman muttered to himself.

Fern held in a sigh. George would be insufferable if the alchemist supported his theory that it was ink plus lightning, instead of magic, responsible.

Lord Drakeman placed both bottles on the tabletop to fetch a dropper and two finger-like glass tubes. One tube had a white line running down one side, and Fern wondered if it was to tell the two samples apart.

With care, he first extracted a few drops of the purple, shimmering ink that Millie used to write her story and let them slide to the bottom of the tube. Then, he did the same with the thick sap that bled from the plant.

Fern leaned on the table, Squib nestled between her bent arms and chest, as she watched the alchemist conduct his experiments. It was all a bit boring, and she'd rather watch dandelions grow between cobblestones.

The laboratory was a stark contrast to her usual environment, surrounded by lush greenery and flowers, with its vials, tubes, and arcane instruments scattered haphazardly across worn wooden tables. Lord Drakeman worked methodically, with an air of single-minded focus. He seemed oblivious to both Fern and the almost sentient nature of his experiments. Around them, beakers popped and fizzed or occasionally emitted puffs of smoke.

To alleviate the boredom, and since the alchemist seemed to prefer muttering to himself rather than engaging in conversation, Fern decided to explore. She picked up Squib and placed him on her shoulder, and she drifted towards the enticing darkened area that extended into the hillside.

"Don't touch anything!" Lord Drakeman barked.

In a deliberate move while she smiled at him, Fern reached out and picked up a lantern from a nearby bench. *Oh, no, I touched something,* she cackled to herself. If he didn't want her bumping into things in the dark, she had to take a light with her.

The room narrowed like a funnel, and stone walls turned into packed earth. The walls were covered in shelves laden with books. Their spines were inscribed with titles in languages Fern didn't recognise. Odd-shaped tools made from materials she couldn't identify sat on another table, their purpose unknown.

As she ventured deeper, she came across a cabinet filled with what appeared to be physical specimens. A mummified snake curled upon itself in a corner. Frogs' legs were crammed into a jar. Another held what appeared to be (but she hoped it wasn't) human fingers floating in oil. But surely he didn't keep bits from people? That made her wonder where he got them from and where the rest of the unfortunate person was.

Her attention was drawn back to Lord Drakeman as a particularly loud pop echoed through the room, followed by an audible curse. Squib groaned, and his wings rustled against Fern's cheek.

Lord Drakeman held three small glass slides and took them to a bench holding a peculiar-looking brass device. Fern recognised it as a Schmalcalder microscope. She had always wanted one for examining plant samples, but they were ridiculously expensive and beyond the reach of her family.

The alchemist hunched over the microscope, the dragon-scaled side of his face illuminated by the nearby lantern. At times he tilted his head, peering with first his normal eye and then his silver one.

Fern crept back along the dirt floor while he worked. Lord Drakeman stiffened, his back ramrod straight. He leapt from his stool and rushed along the dim hall to the book-shelves. Talking to himself, his hand hovered over the books, seeking something. Then he plucked one free. He flipped the pages until his hand stilled, and he tapped a section.

"Stormborne Serum! That the three samples are identical

confirms it," he announced triumphantly. His voice resonated in the cramped space of the laboratory like a bell chime at midnight. "Ink, sap, and scrapings from the paper creature are indistinguishable from each other."

"Stormborne Serum? You mean the ink?" Fern looked from the scattered writing supplies and samples of vine to where he stood in the shadows.

"It's an ancient and potent brew. This ink wasn't concocted by any ordinary magic caster or alchemist. It's a relic of an older world. A forgotten arcane recipe from a time when magic casters had motes simmering in their veins." He carried the book to the table and set it down.

Fern's mind bloomed with the implications. "The vine has ink for sap. Just as I thought."

# CHAPTER 21

Lord Drakeman's unsettling silver gaze fixed on Fern. "Precisely. The liquids match in every way. There is a slight magical signature to the fluid I remembered seeing before." He tapped the page, which showed swirling symbols and runes and what looked like constellations. "The tempestuous energy from the storm was the catalyst needed for the enchantment within the ink to activate. As a boy, I imagined what I would write if I had such a bottle of ink. But I always thought it a myth. Until now."

"Squib's hide is covered in the words Mrs Carlisle wrote with that ink." Fern plucked Squib from her shoulder and held him in her hands to stare at his papery skin. "Now that you know the ink connects everything, how do we disconnect Squib and the vine so Lord Warrington can destroy it?"

"The only way to sever the bond between the two is to erase the ink," Lord Drakeman said.

"If we remove the ink from Squib's body, what will happen to him?" On instinct, she drew the little dragon closer to her body. She promised Millie she would protect him and return him unharmed.

Lord Drakeman shrugged. "Without the Stormborne Serum, the paper will lose the magic that animates it. The transformation will be undone."

Fern's throat tightened. Squib was far more than a few pieces of cleverly folded paper. The tiny creature had come to life through the accidental discovery of the old bottle of ink, combined with Millie's vivid imagination and a magical storm. Even more magical was how the dragon had eased the other woman's loneliness. They couldn't repay such kindness by *erasing* him.

"He will die," she rasped.

"It's paper." He crossed his arms and glared at her. "You asked for my help. This is my solution."

"He is no more paper than Pinocchio was a piece of wood. Squib lives. Bleeds. Feels." Fern couldn't continue as anger flared through her limbs. She drew a breath and tried again. "I sought you out so you could find a way to disconnect Squib from the vine to *save* him. Your solution will destroy him!" She had half a mind to demand the lunanavis stamens back. Drawing her anger into a ball, Fern turned on him and lobbed her building vitriol. "Your family were renowned for their care of the monarch's dragons for hundreds of years. Would a drake man have condemned *any* dragon, no matter his size, to death in such a cruel and callous manner?"

He crossed his arms and narrowed his gaze. Glaring at her through half-closed lids. Silence sat heavy between them, neither of them calling back their words.

Squib nuzzled against Fern's palms, and he emitted little worried chirps.

At last, Lord Drakeman huffed and dropped one hand to the book. "There is a chance he could be reanimated again, afterwards, in the same circumstances. Or you can. let Warrington proceed, and you will be left with a handful of ashes."

She stared at him. Squib's heated breath brushed her skin in gentle puffs. She stroked him, marvelling at the silken feel of his scales under her fingertips. "You have no regard for the feelings of either Mrs Carlisle or Squib. This little pixie dragon has more compassion in his tiny body than you have in all of yours. You're a monster!"

Lord Drakeman's features hardened, and he ground his teeth.

In hindsight, that possibly wasn't the best thing to blurt out. Fern swallowed. She didn't mean he was a monster because of the eye and scar, but due to his actions. "Oh, honestly, it has nothing to do with how you look and everything to do with your callous dismissal of Squib's life."

She grappled with the weight of an impossible, and unfair, choice. The potion to erase the ink would undo the magical transformation that enabled Squib to exist. Fern's heart clenched at the thought, her fingers instinctively tightening around the little dragon. Ten years ago, she had broken a promise to a pixie dragon that lived in Kew Gardens, and the small creature had died. Was she doomed to repeat a past mistake and likewise condemn Squib?

Squib sensed her distress and nestled closer, his body rustling softly. Fern gazed into his ink-drawn eyes. A concoction of characters and prose had sparked life in this unique creature. How could she consign him to oblivion?

Size was irrelevant. Squib was as deserving of being saved as Eurydice. A man born into a family that had long served dragonkind should know that. Unless he had scoured away any such emotions through his experiments.

"There has to be another way. Can you not brew something that will neutralise what binds them without turning him back into an origami figure?" She would visit the Moray sisters. The magic casters might know of a way.

"Perhaps. If given enough time. The enchantment is ancient. It is easier to erase it than to try to alter it. It would take months, if not years, to find a way to keep him animated but separate from the plant."

"Blast! Lord Warrington only gave me a few days." Fern's thoughts turned to Millie.

To the other woman, Squib was not just an extraordinary occurrence or a specimen to be studied. He was company who relieved her solitude. He was proof of the creativity and magic that existed in their world. The prospect of telling Millie that Squib had to be sacrificed for the greater good twisted in Fern's gut like a knife.

*Millie trusted me. I promised to save Squib.*

A part of her had hoped the seed of friendship had been planted between them. Destroying Squib would poison the roots of that tentative relationship before it even sprouted a single leaf.

"If you only have a few days, you need to make a decision. It will take me two days to brew the necessary potion if you wish me to proceed," Lord Drakeman spoke in a clipped tone.

Fern swallowed hard. "Is there truly no other way? No method by which we can preserve Squib?"

Lord Drakeman leaned back against his workbench, his hands resting on the cool surface of the wood. "You can consult with the Moray sisters, but I doubt they will have any remedy for magic this ancient and powerful. You need a solution that combines science and magic. Even then, alchemy may have answers for many things, but life—true life—is a riddle that even the most skilled practitioners struggle to solve. There is a possibility—slim though it may be—that the creature can be restored once the vine has been dealt with."

"A possibility is not a certainty," Fern said, the words catching in her throat.

"No," Lord Drakeman admitted. "It is not. But the chance remains, however slender. There is also the possibility that severing the bond may have an effect on the vine."

"What sort of effect?" Her evening was getting worse.

He shrugged. "For every action, there is a reaction. What that might be, I cannot say. The safest course of action is to destroy both."

Fern turned away from him, closed her eyes, and let out a shuddering breath. Why did life only ever offer her hard choices? Why must she walk a rough and lonely path when others were wrapped in comfort and softness? She either gave up and allowed both Squib and the vine to be cut up and burned or grasped the slim hope of re-animating the pixie dragon...while potentially causing some unknown effect on the death ivy.

Was a sliver of hope worth the risk?

She had only known Millie for a few days. It wasn't like they were lifelong friends, and she was trying to save a loyal companion. Yet her family had rallied to nurse Eurydice back to health the moment they laid eyes on the sickly dragon. Size, species, or length of time of an association didn't make a creature worthy of care or saving. How did you quantify or measure how you *felt* about another living being?

Fern glanced down at Squib, who nestled close to her, and she recalled the pain in Millie's eyes as she begged her to save him. She blew out a huff.

Consequences be damned. She would grab hold of hope with both hands and do all she could to save Squib.

"Brew the potion. Tell me what you need. But I'll not make the final decision about this. Mrs Carlisle must be told of the effects and given a choice. And Squib." Fern looked down at the pixie dragon. His warmth seeped through her fingers like sunlight through leaves—a gentle reminder of life's delicate nature.

Lord Drakeman turned to the shelves with the bottles, vials, and little wooden casks. "I have most of the ingredients I require here. But there are some that you can assist me with. It will use one of the lunanavis stamens you gave me. I am missing flowers from a pearl-lace vine and tips from the spiralling tendrilstem." He grabbed a fresh sheet of paper and scribbled notes.

Fern took the note that specified a few other uncommon herbs and quantities. "I have all of these."

"The sooner you get them to me, the better. I will start

with the other required elements from my stores." He gestured to the dark recesses of the tapered room.

"You don't want to sleep and start fresh in the morning?" Only now did it strike her what a lonely existence he had, shut away in the laboratory with only his butler for company. At least Millie had Squib. Or she did until they returned him to his origami state.

"I prefer to work at night." He turned away from her and started gathering equipment. "Once you fetch what is on that list, I will need two days. Possibly less if the lunanavis stamen is as pure as you say."

She bit her tongue and ignored that slight. "I'll call on the Moray sisters. They may yet be able to help. You also said I can spend time in your library to find any journals left by your ancestors." There was so much Fern had to do. It pained her that she neglected Eurydice, even though she knew the sick hatchling was well cared for by her family.

"Quint will not admit you after dark, and I have asked him to find my great-grandfather's diaries. That will reduce the amount of time you have to spend inside Wyndham Hall." He picked up a clean beaker from the shelf.

"I will wait until the sun is up, then. Assuming he opens the door to me." Locking the doors and windows so she couldn't get in seemed to be a trait shared by residents of Wyndham Hall.

Fern wouldn't be able to sleep knowing that she would have to tell Millie they needed to *erase* her friend. But there was much to do during the quiet night hours, starting with fetching the supplies for the alchemist. Then she would pay a call to the trio of witches.

Fern tucked Squib into her jacket before hurrying from the laboratory and stepping into the inky night. Heedless of the danger, she ran across the meadow, trusting her memory of the path to avoid any rough areas or holes.

Wyndham Hall sat shrouded in dark, except for one pale light in a downstairs window that threw a narrow shaft of illumination. Fern's patient horse snoozed by the tree and startled awake as her rider's boots crunched on the gravel of the drive.

Gathering up the reins, Fern swung up into the saddle. "Come on, girl, we have things to do before you can rest in your stall."

They trotted along the treelined drive, the way ahead swallowed by the dense shadows thrown by the ancient oaks and elms. As they emerged through the gates, the waning moon peaked out from behind a cloud. The shimmering light reflected off the river and guided Fern's way home.

When she rode past Nemython House, Ambrose and George rushed from the kitchen and across the yard.

"Well?" Ambrose asked, holding a lantern aloft as George took the reins to the horse.

"Lord Drakeman will brew a potion to disconnect Squib from the vine. I need to fetch some ingredients that I grow here and return to his laboratory." She withdrew Squib from his spot nestled against her and handed him over to Ambrose. "Could you care for Squib, please? I'd rather not take him back to Wyndham Hall." Frankly, she didn't trust the alchemist not to test his potion by erasing the ornate words etched into the little dragon's hide. If she returned in the morning to find a motionless origami dragon...well...it wasn't worth contemplating just yet.

"Of course. I am delighted to host the wee fellow." Ambrose swapped the lantern for the dragon and placed Squib on his shoulder. Somehow, he managed to resemble a rather dashing pirate.

"I will be back for him. Once I deliver the cuttings to Lord Drakeman, I will take Squib to see the trio." While the alchemist might have dismissed the abilities of the old witches, Fern knew better. They might discern something about the magic that animated the dragon.

"Not before you have some dinner, you won't. Those old hags will wait until after you have eaten." George took the reins of the horse.

Fern didn't bother to argue. Her stomach rumbled, and she couldn't remember when she last ate. The Moray sisters were often awake all night when the moon was high, so she didn't worry about banging on their door when they were all abed.

Leaving her uncles to tend to both dragon and horse, Fern headed for her greenhouse. Inside, the air hung heavy with the scent of damp earth and living greenery. She breathed in deeply, finding solace in the aroma that reminded her of her father's presence.

The lantern cast long shadows amongst the rows of plants as Fern moved between them, searching for the specific ingredients. This late-night visit to her greenhouse felt more like a communion with the past than a simple foray for supplies. Each plant she touched whispered stories of her childhood.

Every rustle of leaves echoed with her father's voice, guiding her through the intricacies of botany.

Her father had been a man wholly devoted to his plants and research. He had inspired and nurtured Fern's love for botany. The greenhouse had been their sanctuary, a place where societal judgements held no sway over them—a scholar and his keen apprentice.

She approached a swath of vines resembling clustered pearls, draping over their trellis like gossamer curtains in the night breeze. Its clumps of small, pale-cream flowers glowed faintly under the starlight. It was one of her father's prized cultivations, a plant that required both skill and patience to nurture.

Surrounded by the lush plantings that were as much part of her as any limb, memories of her father flitted through her mind.

Fern reached out to caress an oval-shaped bloom. "How you used to love a challenge."

Her father had taken great pride in his ability to coax a response from even the most stubborn seeds—an attribute Fern had inherited. But there was one that failed their many attempts. The kelmsgale. Both cuttings and seed had failed to embrace life.

She snipped a bract holding the creamy flowers and dropped it into a basket. Next, she wandered to the beds filled with vibrant mallowdrops and spiralling tendrilstem. As she selected leaves from the tendrilstem, careful not to disturb its delicate spiral growth pattern, Fern reflected on how her father had balanced his pursuit of knowledge with an almost childlike delight in each new discovery.

He would have revelled in this challenge. Untangling the mystery of Squib's existence and its link to that menacing vine at Warrington Manor. His scientific curiosity would have ignited at such an enigma, pushing him into frenzied studies until he found an answer. Fern's father lingered all around her, in every plant that grew from his teachings and every success born from his guidance.

As she placed one last sprig into her basket, something caught her eye. A tiny sprout emerging from soil recently turned and enriched. A sign of new life pushing through despite the darkness surrounding it.

Fern straightened up and clutched the handle of her basket. She had much to do this evening, and she hurried from the greenhouse back to the stables. George stood out in the yard with the horse and took the basket as she climbed back into the saddle. Then he handed up the cuttings.

Fern looped the handle of the basket over her arm and settled it before her, resting on the pommel of the saddle. "I'll not be longer than an hour. I only need to hand these over to Lord Drakeman, and I'll come straight back."

"I'll have a meal ready for when you do." George patted the horse's neck.

"Thank you, George." Fern waved and then turned the horse back towards the road.

Once more, they rode through the slumbering village, with only the murmur of the river for company. Leaves rustled, and an owl hooted as they approached Wyndham Hall. This time, she guided the horse around the house and across the meadow.

When she jumped to the ground, the opportunistic mare

dropped her head to graze. Fern looped the reins into a knot so the horse wouldn't stand on them. Then she rattled the handle of the laboratory door, surprised to find it locked. She was starting to think she wasn't welcome at the estate.

# CHAPTER 22

FERN CURLED her hand into a fist and thumped on the solid wood.

A few heartbeats later, the door was flung open. Without a word of greeting, Lord Drakeman strode back to his workbench, where he had set out flasks, a mortar and pestle, and a beaker suspended over an eerie purple flame.

Fern pushed the door shut behind her. At the table, she cleared a spot to set down her basket. "Your cuttings," she said, resisting the urge to match his coldness with her own.

"Leave them. Come back tomorrow night," he replied tersely, his attention on a bottle of some bronze-coloured powder. He scooped a small amount out with a flattened piece of metal and dropped it into the mortar.

Fern's grip tightened on the edge of the workbench. His dismissive tone chafed, but she swallowed her retort and retreated from the laboratory. She could ill afford to engage in a battle to demand a certain level of civility when she needed his assistance.

The journey back to Nemython House seemed to take no time at all. Lost in her thoughts, Fern let the horse find her way home. As she approached the stables, she dismounted and walked alongside the mare. Woman and equine matched their stride, and Fern's inner turmoil settled, soothed by the regular pulse of the horse's large heart.

At the stables, she unsaddled the horse and removed the bridle before rubbing the mare down with handfuls of straw. Once the equine was settled and happily tucking into her dinner, Fern turned her attention to the opposite stall, where the too-thin Eurydice lay. Her head was tucked under her wing, and it took a long moment before Fern spotted the slight rise and fall of the dragon's chest.

Just inside the doorway waited a bowl of stew. Steam curled from the rich gravy. George must have timed placing it there with her return. Love for her uncles rippled through her as she picked it up.

Fern sat next to the dragon and gently stroked her flank with her free hand. Eurydice lifted her head and blinked. Slits of silver were visible under her half-closed lids.

The dragon's piercing gaze reminded her of another. "Lord Drakeman has a silver eye just like yours."

She scooped up a spoonful of stew and chewed, all the while wondering how the scarred man saw the world with a dragon eye. Would he find it disconcerting with two different types of vision? That would explain the goggles with the lens over his human eye blacked out. She decided to ask him how he saw things from the silver eye. It wasn't like his demeanour could get any worse for an impertinent question, and she had already called him a monster.

Fern ate her dinner with a heavy heart, noting there had been no real improvement in the dragon's condition. Eurydice drew shallow breaths that made her scales pull tight over her ribs. While she took water and broth, she didn't gain any weight and continued to be lethargic.

Fern tried to temper her expectations. "It hasn't even been two full days yet, girl. Rest and care will soon see you improve."

After cleaning out the bowl, and managing to entice the dragon to eat a chunk of meat, Fern tucked the blanket in around the creature and placed a kiss on the top of her head. William would take the night watch while she was away.

"I will be back. Tomorrow, I will see what books Quint found in the Wyndham Hall library. There is sure to be something to help you get better, perhaps a tonic of some kind." Hope simmered inside Fern. The knowledge they needed to make Eurydice healthy again would be there. The king's drake men had to have written of such things in their personal journals.

Heading back across the yard, Fern slipped in the back door to find a quiet kitchen. She left her bowl by the sink and went in search of her uncles and Squib. She found them in the parlour. Squib sat in the middle of the chessboard as though he commanded a personal army.

"Thank you for dinner, George." Fern rested one hand on the large man's shoulder.

George reached up and patted her hand without taking his focus off the game in play.

"I need to steal away your general." Careful so as not to disturb any pieces, Fern leaned in and lifted up Squib.

"When I come back, I'll sleep in the stall. Tomorrow, I am heading out to Wyndham Hall to see what I can find in its library."

Guilt gnawed at her that she wasn't spending as much time with the sick dragon as the one who had once been cleverly folded paper.

"I shall await with interest what the trio have to say on the matter. Poor old George is grumpy that his belief in the rational sciences is being challenged by Squib's existence." Ambrose advanced a pawn.

George huffed. "Science will yet explain what you call magic. I expect Galvanism has activated the creature."

"You weren't too far from the answer, George. Lord Drakeman found that something called Stormborne Serum had a part to play. Although that is an ancient sort of magical ink, so we are back to magic being at the core of things. Perhaps you two can discuss the role of alchemy and lightning over your game. In the morning, during breakfast, I will tell you all the trio have to say." Fern kissed each gentleman on the cheek, then left with her precious passenger.

It wasn't far to the trio's cottages. Since Fern could find the way in the dark and with her eyes closed, she walked. The waning moon provided enough silvery light if she needed it to avoid puddles and holes. As she strode along the road, Fern grappled with the moral quandary that ensnared her thoughts like brambles. Could she truly sacrifice Squib in order to destroy the vine?

The carnivorous ivy had to be razed to the ground. Its very presence at Warrington Manor posed a threat to all manners of animals, birds, and people who might venture into the rose garden. But how could she weigh one life against another? Squib hadn't asked to be created any more than Eurydice had sought to be trapped under the fountain. Yet both had been caught by circumstances at Warrington Manor.

Was Squib's life of a lesser value because he was a small pixie dragon? But diamonds were also small, and yet people regarded them as more precious than a pile of boulders. So size did not of itself denote value.

Another worry gnawed at Fern. How could she expect Millie to relinquish her accidental creation with only the slightest hope of resurrecting him afterwards? But surely a shaft of hope, no matter how narrow and tenuous, was better than no hope at all?

"Let us see if the trio can light a path forwards for us, Squib," Fern said as she approached the cottages.

Soft orange light flickered in the windows, signalling that the Moray sisters were awake and probably up to something. Fern had only raised her hand to knock when the door swung open.

Decima grinned at Fern. "Morda said you were at the door with a treat for us. Come inside and out of that chill night air."

Fern murmured a greeting and entered the cosy cottage. The interior was as eccentric as its inhabitants. The furnishing a mismatch in construction, size, and colour. Small lilac pillows sat on a hard wooden bench next to an over-stuffed armchair of russet brocade. Squib, perhaps sensing the magic in the air, peeked out from his hiding place in her coat. His paper-thin wings fluttered against Fern's chest.

She eased him free. "I have brought a special visitor. Nona, Morda, Decima, I would like to introduce Squib. Squib, these sisters are all magic casters, and they may help us understand what happened to you better than Lord Drakeman's explanation."

Morda cackled, and Nona rolled her eyes to the ceiling. "She said you would tangle with the alchemist."

"Morda also claimed he wouldn't let you in his front door," Decima added.

"Morda was correct in both things. He didn't let me in the door. I had to climb in through a window." Fern sat on her favourite large yellow pillow before the fire and let Squib hop to Decima's outstretched hand while Morda continued to cackle in glee.

Decima ignored her sister, and Nona slipped her a coin. Apparently, she had lost a bet. Which was her own fault—the sisters should have learned long ago not to bet against a seer.

The middle Moray sister leaned closer to examine Squib. "Ah, the energy of the storm and the ink that flows within him are old...very old. This is no ordinary magic, but some-thing ancient."

"That's what Lord Drakeman said. He said the ink was called Stormborne Serum and that it's a relic of an ancient world." Fern tested what the alchemist told her against the combined wisdom of the old women.

Decima passed Squib to her younger sister, holding Morda's hand flat as she eased the pixie dragon onto her palm.

Morda's fingers were as nimble as they were wrinkled. She used touch to learn what she could from the little dragon, stroking his sides and causing him to trill softly. Her nostrils flared as she inhaled, breathing in his aroma that reminded Fern of an old book. "Well, little friend. You are a wondrous thing. Bound by desire and loneliness, entwined with the heart of the one who created you."

"Can you sense what binds him to the *Helix mortifera?* Squib feels every slash and cut made in the vine, and I need to separate them. Lord Drakeman says it is the ink that is the lifeblood of both of them." Worry climbed up her gullet, and Fern's breath became shallow as she contemplated the fate that awaited the diminutive creature.

To be...erased.

A shiver ran over her body, and she rubbed it away with her hands. She wouldn't think about what might happen. Instead, she chose to focus on what she could do.

Nona took the little dragon from her sister and held him at eye level. She puffed a warm breath over him, and Squib reared up, squeaked, and blew one back. After a silent minute, Nona lowered Squib and placed him in her lap. "This is more than mere ink. Vine and dragon are but parts of a whole. One is the soul, the other the body. To disconnect them will have consequences."

Bother. That was what Lord Drakeman said. Much to Fern's consternation, it seemed he was actually right about a number of things. She swallowed a snort. Not that she'd ever tell the insufferable man that.

"Could you do it, though? Could you release Squib from its hold so the vine can be destroyed without hurting him?" She held her breath, waiting while the three women conferred.

It was Decima who spoke, with sadness in her eyes. "Even combined, our magic would not be potent enough to undo what was created by the storm and the ancient power in the ink."

Fern let out a disappointed sigh. A teeny part of her had hoped that the sisters would craft a solution and she wouldn't need to rely on the alchemist.

"Find the true desire of the heart that called them into being. Then you will know how to subdue the body once separated from the soul," Morda crooned to the fire.

"The heart that called them into being. That's Mrs Carlisle." Fern mulled over the cryptic words, piecing them together with what Morda had said the previous day. "You said I had to understand the true essence of the story that she created."

What had Millie told her about the story written over Squib? The vine was supposed to hold the heroine safe and unharmed until she could be rescued from the villain of the story. The nub of an idea formed in Fern's mind.

Morda nodded and turned her milky gaze on Fern. "Everything happens for a reason. As much as you chafe against the hands of Fate, sometimes she nudges you in the direction you are meant to take."

What was that supposed to mean? Had Mr Corby been destined to be consumed by the carnivorous ivy, and Fate had pushed him into its grasp? Or, more likely, the three women were meddling in her life in other ways. Fern harboured a suspicion that they had been talking to Ambrose.

"Thank you, ladies. I shall leave you to your evening." She rose and reclaimed Squib. The little dragon chose to sit on her shoulder, where he nestled against the collar of her coat.

She walked quickly back to Nemython House. The night wrapped tight around the trees, and drifting clouds obscured the moon. A soft orb of light glowed in the parlour window, but the rest of the house was clad in dark. Her uncles must have gone to bed already.

Fern made her way to the stables and crept into Eurydice's stall. William was curled in a corner, and she bent down and touched his shoulder.

"Go home, Will. I'm going to stay with her," Fern whispered when the man stirred.

"She's had a little water not so long ago and then went back to sleep." William climbed to his feet and shook out the blanket.

"Thank you, Will." Fern approached the slumbering dragon, and she knelt in the straw beside her. She laid one hand on Eurydice's side to reassure herself the dragon's heart continued to beat.

Squib cooed at the much larger dragon. He fluttered from Fern's shoulder to the blanket and stood on Eurydice's back. Then he turned around three times and padded at the wool before curling himself up in a ball in the hollow made where her shoulder met her neck.

The hatchling stirred but didn't wake, Squib weighing no more than a kitten. Leaving them to sleep, Fern returned to the corner and settled on the pile of hay. She wrapped herself in the blanket. As she watched the two very different drag-ons, resolve solidified within her. She didn't care what anyone thought. Both lives were precious to her, and she would find a way to save them.

Sleep came in snatches that night. Fern roused a few times to check on Eurydice, offer water if the dragon was awake, and then she returned to her corner for another hour or two of restless slumber. The next morning, the soft chorus of birdsong in the surrounding trees made her eyelids flutter open. The light that spilt into the stable was pale and weak as she uncurled from her makeshift bed. Her muscles protested the hours spent propped up in the corner, although she had keeled face-first into the straw at some point.

Spitting out bits of bedding stuck to her dry lips, Fern stretched her arms over her head. Squib lifted his gaze and emitted a soft coo. Eurydice's breathing remained shallow but steady.

"Come on, Squib, let's get some breakfast ready for when she wakes." Fern held out her arm, and the pixie dragon flapped his wings to fly to her like an origami hawk returning from a hunt.

She crept from the stall and stomped her feet to alleviate the pins and needles in her legs. The morning chill had pervaded the stables through the open doors. On her way past the chocolate-coloured mare, Fern caressed her velvety muzzle. The horse hung over the half-door in anticipation of her breakfast while her stable mates continued to doze.

Out in the yard, William walked towards the stables. "Morning, Miss Oakby," he called out.

"Good morning, Will. I'll need my mare saddled in about an hour, please. I'm going to change and have some breakfast, then I am heading out to Wyndham Hall," she said.

"I'll have her ready for you." He continued into the stables.

Mrs Bentley was tying her apron on as Fern snuck into the kitchen. A critical eye swept over her appearance. "I'll have coffee ready by the time you have changed clothes, washed, and brushed the hay out of your hair."

Hay?

Fern patted her head, and when she pulled her hand away, she clutched a strand of straw. There was no point in wasting time arguing with the housekeeper. She would lose anyway. "Yes, ma'am."

# CHAPTER 23

FERN PASSED through the kitchen and up the stairs with their familiar creaks and whispers. In her room, she shed her soiled clothes and left them in a pile on the wooden floor. Pouring water from the jug into a basin, she briskly washed herself with cold water that stole her breath and brought a flush to her cheeks. A quick pat dry with a rough towel left her skin tingling and awake.

Slipping into fresh garments—a clean blouse and trousers—she brushed her short hair to remove any trace of straw from her night with Eurydice. By the time she picked up Squib (who had been investigating the items on her dresser) and returned to the kitchen, delicious aromas were wafting from the range.

"Hot coffee, as promised." Mrs Bentley used the wooden spoon in her hand to point to the silver pot on the worn table. "Breakfast won't be long."

"Thank you, Mrs Bentley." Fern sat at her usual spot, and

Squib hopped to the table. She pulled the coffee pot towards her and poured into a large mug, leaving room for a splash of cream, and then stirred the brew. Taking a sip, she let out an exhale and waited for the drink to revive her senses.

George appeared next. He always rose earlier than his partner. He silently dropped to a chair and poured coffee into a beer tankard. Squib waddled over to stand before him and reared up on his hind legs, letting out a trill. Then he continued along the table to scratch his head against the salt pot.

"Morning, George." Fern nursed her coffee and took only occasional sips.

The hot temperature of the drink didn't seem to deter George, who had an iron gullet. "You'll want porridge today to stick to your ribs and keep you going." He lowered his mug and poured more coffee into it.

Mrs Bentley dropped a bowl in front of Fern. "Lucky, that is exactly what I made this morning."

Fern spooned a little honey over the porridge and then created a moat with cream. She didn't know how the Scots could eat their porridge salted. Squib flopped over onto his back and began preening his scales in a similar manner to how a cat cleaned itself.

She ate slowly, despite parts of her brain urging her to hurry up so she could gallop off to Warrington Manor. It wouldn't do to give herself an upset stomach. "I'm riding out to Wyndham Hall this morning. Lord Drakeman promised I could have a full day in his library, reading the old journals of the king's drake men."

George grunted. "I hope you find something." Then he nodded a thanks to Mrs Bentley as she placed a bowl of porridge in front of him. His was accompanied by another plate with bacon, toast, and eggs.

"If only I could find the answer to why Eurydice doesn't seem to be improving. She's certainly better than when I first found her, but she won't take any solids and seems so tired." Fern scraped her bowl to gather up the last spoonful of porridge.

George huffed. "It's only been a few days. You're like your mother and want results immediately. Sometimes, you just have to wait."

At times, she wished she had inherited her father's patience.

"I will try to wait, even though it is not a trait of mine. The old journals are sure to contain some guidance. I know how to nurture an ailing plant, but dragons are beyond my expertise." Fern finished the last of her cooling coffee.

George swallowed a mouthful. "I'm searching my periodicals. A few months back, I read an article by a scholar who specialises in dragon physiology. He might have more recent knowledge."

"I'll take any help you can find. Thank you." Fern took her dishes over to the bench. Then she collected Squib, who was still grooming himself and emitted a squawk when she scooped him up. She placed a kiss on George's cheek. "I'll be back for dinner—hopefully with some answers."

She rode at a canter back to Wyndham Hall, waving to the local residents she passed who were out on early morning errands. Across from the grand house, she tethered the mare to a tree and approached the front door. Grasping the knocker, Fern rapped several times and waited.

At length, the heavy oak door creaked open to reveal Quint, his stony gaze as uninviting as the chill morning air.

"Good morning, Quint. I assume from the excited expression on your face that Lord Drakeman told you we'd be spending the day together," she said in a breezy tone.

His scowl deepened, and the butler didn't move.

Fern slipped through the half-open door and under his arm into the vestibule. "Do you want to show me the way, or shall we make a game of me finding the library by myself?" she added when he still hadn't moved.

With an audible groan, he slammed the door and stalked towards her.

As they passed through the vestibule's doors with stained glass panels at the side, Fern stopped and gasped. From the forlorn state of the long-neglected gardens and the sad appearance of the exterior of the house, she had expected to find the inside a ruin. She thought leaves would be piling up along the skirting boards, wallpaper torn and hanging in strips like birch bark, and holes in the ceiling where bats roosted.

Except...it wasn't.

The newel posts and rails of the grand double staircase were polished, with the scent of beeswax in the air. The floor was swept and mopped, and side tables dusted. High above her head, a light well flooded the interior with morning sun.

"When you're done gawking. It's this way," Quint muttered as he walked across the open space that could have hosted a party for dozens of people.

He stopped at a pair of panelled doors high enough to admit an eight-foot giant and slid them apart.

This time, Fern swallowed her gasp in case the butler thought her some country yokel who had never seen a library before. But it was an awe-inspiring spectacle that left her momentarily breathless. It was a vast room stretching two storeys high, lined from floor to ceiling with shelves groaning under the weight of countless leather-bound volumes. In one corner, an ironwork spiral staircase wound its way up to a gallery where even more books awaited discovery and allowed access along a metal walkway to the upper level. On one side was a mezzanine, where people could look down on those below, and Fern could just see glimpses of arched doors to something else beyond.

"Lord Drakeman says the journals are to stay here. You have today to read them and then at dusk, I get to throw you out." For the first time in their acquaintance, he grinned at her. It was such a sinister thing that Fern wished he'd go back to scowling.

"Then let us hope I can find what I need in the journals before then." She made her way to a desk the size of a single bed, set with its back to the shelves so that the light from the window came over the right shoulder of a person seated at it.

Two piles of dusty old journals sat at the edge of the green leather inlay, waiting for her. Fern placed her satchel on the desk and dropped her bottom onto the leather chair. Reaching into the satchel, she pulled out her notebook, quill, and a bottle of ink. She came prepared to make notes.

Picking up the first journal on the nearest pile, she smiled sweetly at Quint. "A pot of coffee would be wonderful and help me work faster. Also, should it come to it, you'll not find me as easy to evict as you think."

He stared at her, then made a noise that *almost* sounded like a huff of laughter. "You're to stay put while I fetch madam's coffee. Wouldn't want you getting lost or trapped somewhere no one ever goes, now would we?"

His words were sound advice in a house the size of Wyndham Hall, but they had the tinge of a threat to them. Fern could see the foul-tempered man shoving her into a closet and locking the door so he wouldn't have to deal with her anymore.

"I shall be right here when you return. I certainly wouldn't want to inconvenience you by having you waste hours of your busy day searching for me." The more he scowled, the more she grinned. The naughty idea to hide while he was gone crossed her mind, but finding a remedy for Eurydice was more important. Perhaps she could needle the up-tight butler on another visit to the Hall.

She opened the journal. On the front page, in faded text, was the date 1578.

"Tudor times," she whispered as she turned to the first page. The last drake man had served under Queen Elizabeth. When she died, the distraught dragons had set fire to their wyvernry and a nearby palace in London. King James had declared that the creatures shouldn't be kept like horses in stables and were to live freely. Even over two hundred years ago, there had been fewer of the beasts than in previous centuries.

It took her a few attempts to become accustomed to the rhythm of the old English. Soon, Fern lost herself in a world where dragons were kept as companions for a monarch. No wonder everyone remembered Queen Elizabeth as such a formidable character when she had a dragon lounging on either side of her throne.

True to his word, Quint returned with a coffee pot and a cup, placing the tray away from the old journals with the same care George used around Fern's drawings. Then he disappeared, only to return with another tray carrying knives, a stone, oil, and a cloth. Taking a seat across from the desk where he could watch Fern, the odd man proceeded to sharpen a deadly collection of knives.

Fern poured coffee and took a sip. The brew was surprisingly good. Emboldened by the drink, she asked a question of the grim man. "I thought butlers were supposed to polish silver, not play with knives?"

"I'm not just a butler," he replied without pausing in his work. Before she could enquire as to the finer details of his employment with Lord Drakeman, he pointed to the ornate grandfather clock with a blade. "Tick tock, Miss Oakby. Do you want to chat about our personal lives or find something that might help your dragon?"

Now it was Fern's turn to scowl, even though he had a point. It took time to decipher the old writing. "Maybe another time?" she said, then returned to the journal before her.

The coffee pot was empty, and the clock had struck twelve when Fern finally found what she had hoped for.

"I've found it!" She looked up, excited to share the discovery with anyone—even Quint. "A young, feeble dragon is much improved by the feeding of fish. Especially those taken from rivers where the kelmsgale grow as opposed to the ocean."

Dipping her quill in ink, she made notes in her notebook. She had gleaned many snippets pertaining to the general health and care of dragons, but this was the first mention of anything specific for a sickly one. She scanned the text. The long-ago drake man said either a broth made with the bones or the cooked flesh would improve the condition of an undeveloped hatchling. "As they grow in strength and size, the dragonet should be allowed to fish for themselves in the river."

She leaned back in the chair, satisfied with the knowledge she had learned from the old books. George could catch a few fish that afternoon, and Mrs Bentley could make fish broth for Eurydice. The dragon's condition should improve over the next few days.

Quint rose to his feet and placed her empty coffee cup on the tray. "You'll be leaving then." The way he said it, it wasn't a question.

Fern glanced at the unopened journals. There was much to learn, but the minutes were slipping by, and she had spent most of the day hunched over the desk. As amusing as it might be, she didn't want to learn if Quint would actually toss her out the front door like a cat with the approach of dusk.

"Yes. Thank you for your assistance." Fern tightened the lid on her ink pot and blotted her quill on a cloth. Then she placed everything back in her satchel.

Once Fern returned home, she shared what she learned with her uncles. Then, with what remained of the afternoon, she and George set off for his favourite fishing spot just south of the village. Only when they had caught three fish did they return, and Mrs Bentley took over the next stage. Before she sat down to her own dinner, Fern knelt by the little dragon and fed her spoonfuls of fish broth.

"That's it, Eurydice. I have it on the best authority that this will help," she murmured as the dragon lapped the nourishing soup from the spoon.

The following morning, Fern examined the dragon and contained her disappointment that she hadn't put on weight and grown several feet all from one bowl of fish broth. "Patience, Fern," she muttered to herself. Eurydice had drunk the soup; that was a good first step.

William appeared and took over watching the slumbering dragon. Inside the house, George was already brewing coffee.

"I'm heading out to Wyndham Hall this morning and, hopefully, onwards to Warrington Manor after that. I am running out of time to save our little friend." She watched Squib use the milk jug as a backrest while he groomed his belly.

"Take the cart. You'll probably want to haul most of the vine behind it," George said.

Fern considered arguing with him, but he was right. It would be far easier to load up the cart with cuttings and samples than being limited to what her satchel could hold.

"Brilliant idea," she agreed and took an offered coffee from George's hands.

When the clock in the hall gently chimed six times, Fern gulped down the last of her drink and swept Squib off the table. As she walked from the house back to the stables, she settled the pixie dragon into her waistcoat.

Back at Wyndham Hall, she ignored the grand house with its long-neglected conservatory and guided the steady cob and cart across the meadow to the laboratory. This time, the door was unlocked, or perhaps Lord Drakeman had failed to re-latch it behind him. Fern slipped inside and immediately wrinkled her nose. An unpleasant odour rather like sweaty boots permeated the room.

Squib hunkered down lower inside her clothing as though he didn't want to have his scales scraped again by the alchemist.

Lord Drakeman leaned over the table, his hands curled around the edge as he stared at a flask before him. Inside, an inky liquid shimmered as though he had captured the stars from a night sky and mixed them into the potion.

"Is it morning already?" he rasped. When he looked up, she saw tired lines radiating from his human eye, and dark stubble erupted along his chin. He washed his hands over his face and tugged at dark locks.

"Yes. It's after six. Have you slept since I was last here?" Surely he hadn't worked for two nights and a solid day.

"A few hours, no more. Did the witches have a solution more to your liking?" His silver eye scrutinised her.

Fern shuffled her feet. "Not directly. They said that what the storm created is arcane magic and beyond their abilities. They said that Squib and the vine are parts of a whole—one the soul, the other the body—and that I need to understand the desires of the heart."

"That's poetic but not practical. You are fortunate that I

am done." He turned to the shelves and selected a bottle. From the tabletop, he found a funnel and wedged it into the neck of the bottle. Then he poured the midnight brew from the flask.

A niggle at the back of Fern's mind whispered that there was still something in what the Moray sisters had said, and she'd carry their words with her.

# CHAPTER 24

EMOTIONS TRICKLED through Fern as the potion filled the bottle. A restlessness fuelled by fear as to what might happen made her jiggle from foot to foot. "How will the potion erase the ink? It looks much darker than what Mrs Carlisle used to write the story."

"This has powerful alchemic properties that, when combined with the enchanted ink, will react and dissolve it." He finished filling the bottle and pushed the cork into it. "You must rub it over the creature."

She would paint it over the top of the writer's words, removing the sentences that animated the dragon. That thought gave rise to another. "Will it dissolve Squib?" The potion was supposed to remove the words, not the paper they were written on.

"No. It will be similar to the process of evaporation. Remember that eradicating the ink from the creature may also impact the vine, and I do not know the extent of any such effect. I tested the samples here, and it became agitated when I applied a few drops." He gestured to the length of woody limb that Fern had provided. It tapped repeatedly at the glass prison as though it sought to break out. "You can also dilute the potion with water and spray it over the vine. One part potion to fifteen parts water will be effective, as long as it has contact with the sap."

Fern took the bottle and placed it in her satchel. "Thank you, Lord Drakeman. And many thanks for letting me read the journals in your library. I found something that I hope will help the dragonet." It seemed polite to thank him for his work, even if his solution would erase the spark of life from Squib.

Now, all she had to do was return to Warrington Manor and tell Millie what the potion would do to her friend. Then she hoped they could destroy the vine before it did anything...unexpected.

Returning to the solid horse who dozed in his harness, Fern once more set off along the familiar path away from Drake's Bend and towards the Warrington estate. At the halfway point, she stopped to water the horse and set Squib down on the kelmsgale stump. The little dragon sniffed at the wood and then followed a ring around the entire circumference.

Fern perched on the edge of the remaining trunk and traced a thicker line with her finger. "My father tried for years to get both cuttings and seed to grow and failed. Perhaps George is right, and magic will slowly fade from our world as science explains everything."

That reminded her of the seed pod she had found. What had she done with it? She thought she had shoved it in her satchel but couldn't recall seeing it. Perhaps it went into a pocket instead. Patting herself down, Fern found the ball-sized lump in her coat pocket.

"You are my next puzzle," she told the seeds that lay dormant within the hard outer casing.

Once the horse had drunk his fill, they continued on their way. The yard at Warrington Manor bustled with people, and a young lad took the reins of the horse as Fern jumped from the seat of the cart. Stomping dirt from her boots as she walked, Fern headed for the kitchen door, propped open to catch the breeze.

She strode through the bustling heart of the house, the air thick with the delicious aromas of fresh bread and bacon from the recently prepared breakfast. Maids scurried about. The clatter of pans was punctuated by barked orders. A footman caught sight of her and rushed forwards.

"Miss Oakby," he huffed, slipping in front of her. "Lord Warrington is at his breakfast."

Fern had hers hours ago. Some nobles didn't break their fast until closer to noon. Although, when you had nothing to do, why rush to get out of bed and have more empty hours to fill?

"Is Mrs Carlisle with him?" Fern paused as a maid danced between them with an armload of laundry.

"Yes, miss," the footman said.

"Excellent. Take me to them, please." She wondered what her chances were of a second breakfast. Her meals had been irregular due to recent events, and there was always space inside her for a bit of bacon and a cup of coffee.

The footman blanched. Mortified at the idea of interrupting the family at breakfast. "You cannot, miss."

Fern winked. "I rather think I can. But I don't want you to get in trouble, so point me in the direction of the dining room, and I'll announce myself."

The footman's mouth opened and closed. Then he drew himself up. "I would be in far more trouble if I let you do that, Miss Oakby. Please, follow me."

He led her out of the servants' area. In the main part of the house, he turned along a much wider and carpeted hall. A short distance down, he stopped at double doors and opened one side.

"Lord Warrington," the footman said with a half bow. "Miss Fern Oakby to see you."

His lordship sat in a sun-dappled breakfast room; silverware glinted amidst the white linen and fine china. At the head of the table, he was engrossed in the newspaper. Millie sat to one side, her eyes downcast as she stabbed at a piece of toast that appeared to bleed from the jam pooling in one spot.

Lord Warrington glanced up from his newspaper with a raised eyebrow. The gesture conveyed both irritation at the interruption and an expectation that she would deliver a solution to his gardening problem. "About time. Can I get rid of the abominable plant now?"

Millie's gaze snapped up. "Oh, Miss Oakby! Do tell us you have good news, and Squib can be saved!"

On hearing his mistress's voice, Squib squirmed up from inside Fern's coat and glided down to the table. Then he waddled over to her, flapping his wings and cooing like a contented dove.

Millie scooped him up and nuzzled her cheek against him. Their obvious devotion to each other, despite the short length of time of their relationship, made a pang shoot through all the hollows inside Fern.

She had once considered getting a dog for the companionship but didn't want to risk one digging in the garden. It seemed cruel to her to present a canine with such an expanse of rich earth and then tell them they weren't allowed in it.

Lord Warrington narrowed his gaze at his sister and huffed. Then he glared at Fern. "I don't usually have to ask twice."

Fern tightened her fingers on the strap of her satchel and tried to remember what he had asked before the reunion of Millie and Squib distracted her. She didn't like Lord Warrington, and her first impression of him hadn't changed. Oh, that's right. He asked about the exceedingly rare death ivy that he wanted to destroy. "Lord Drakeman was able to brew a potion that will sever the bond between Squib and the vine, allowing it to be...removed."

Millie glanced up and beamed. "That is excellent news. Is it not, Bertie? Squib can remain with me, and the horrid plant will be gone from the rose garden in time for your garden party."

Fern stared at the toes of her boots while she considered how to deliver her next bit of news. "There is more. Lord Drakeman advised that there might be...consequences from breaking the bond." The Moray sisters had issued a similar warning. Hearing a similar thing from two different sources made Fern cautious in her next step.

Millie frowned, the skin of her forehead puckering as she glanced from Squib to Fern.

Lord Warrington folded his newspaper with precise movements, his breakfast forgotten. "Speak plainly, Miss Oakby. What are these consequences you mention?"

The room held its breath as Fern weighed her words.

"Lord Drakeman discovered that the ink Mrs Carlisle used was a very old and rare type of enchanted fluid called Stormborne Serum. The storm combined with the ink on the pages to bring Squib to life. It is his blood. It also flows within the vine as sap and is what binds them." She paused, struggling to find the words to tell her new friend what would happen next.

"We had rare enchanted ink, and you used it up on a silly story? Honestly, Millicent, I have reached my tolerance for your behaviour. As if getting your husband killed wasn't bad enough," he grumbled.

Millie sucked in a breath, and her shoulders slumped. "How was I to know the ink was rare? It was shoved in the back of a shelf in the library and was long forgotten." Her voice was little and faint as she shrank into herself.

Fern clenched her teeth before she gave his lordship a piece of her mind. "Given your plan is to immediately destroy the vine, I'm sure that goal will be accomplished before anything untoward happens." Fern didn't know that at all, but she wasn't above sliding a little blame in Lord Drakeman's direction.

"Get it done, then. Lady Warrington will be returning from London tomorrow, and I'll not risk her being grabbed by that monstrosity." He picked up his teacup and returned his attention to the plate before him.

Fern fidgeted and glanced at Millie, who had placed Squib on her shoulder to free up her hands to eat her toast as though everything was settled.

Except it wasn't.

She had to tell the other woman the full extent of what would happen. The next words rushed from her. "There will be consequences for Squib too. He will no longer be as he is now." In her mind, Fern heard Lord Drakeman say it was possible the origami dragon could be re-animated the next time there was a rare storm swirling with magic. As slim as that hope was, she had to cling to it.

The toast dropped from Millie's finger, and it landed jam-side down on her plate. "What do you mean? Is he going to die?"

"That wasn't the word Lord Drakeman used. He said he will no longer be animate." Dead people weren't animate either, so Fern wasn't clear on the difference.

"No! You promised you would find a way to save him." Millie stood abruptly, and her chair fell to the rug. She snatched Squib from her shoulder and cradled him to her chest.

A footman rushed from his spot by the buffet and quickly righted the chair.

"You lied! You promised he would be unhurt." Tears formed in Millie's eyes as she curled her body around the pixie dragon to shield him from view.

"I have had enough!" Lord Warrington boomed. "Give the damn paper toy to Miss Oakby and have done with this nonsense." He gestured to the footman. Then he rose from his chair and yanked on the bell pull by the door.

"He is not paper! He is real!" Millie cried to her brother. Then she turned pain-filled eyes to Fern. "You promised."

The footman reached out a hand but hesitated to seize either the noblewoman or the little creature in case Squib gave him a vicious paper cut.

Fern stepped towards her and spoke in a soft tone. "Lord Drakeman said we can re-animate Squib once the vine is destroyed and the danger to him has passed. What we have to do can be undone."

"Truly?" Millie whispered the word, laced with hope and fear.

She couldn't lie to the woman who, in a few short days, she had come to view as a friend. "The tendril of hope is better than no hope at all. However tenuous."

Millie's shoulders heaved as she sobbed. "Will he feel anything?"

Fern's chest tightened at the question. "I don't believe so. The potion will erase the words, and Squib will simply... cease in this form."

Tears spilt down Millie's cheeks, and one dropped onto Squib. He arched his neck and puffed warm air to dry her tears.

Lord Warrington cleared his throat with an awkward cough that showed a hint of discomfort at his sister's distress. "Have done with it, Miss Oakby. Either way, I am ordering my men to burn the monstrosity," his voice was softer than before.

The door opened a fraction to admit someone summoned

by the bell. His lordship spoke to whoever stood on the other side, and then the door was pulled shut once more.

Fern reached into her satchel and extracted the bottle and a cloth. "I need to wipe this over Squib."

Millie sniffled and wiped her eyes with the back of her hand, leaving a smudge of jam near her temple. She nodded mutely, cradling Squib even closer. She placed a kiss on the top of his head and then gently set him down on the table. "You must be very brave, my friend. I shall see you again in a little time."

*Or thirty years*, Fern thought. Since that was how long it had been since the last magical storm.

She dropped her satchel to the table and pulled out a chair.

"How will it work?" Millie sat in a chair close by and stroked Squib's head with a trembling hand.

"As I wipe the potion over the words, the ink will fade, and with it, his connection to the vine," Fern explained as she readied what she needed.

Millie bit her lip, and another tear joined the trail, spilling down her cheek to drip off her chin. "And then?"

"Then Lord Warrington's men may safely destroy the vine before anyone else is harmed or killed." Fern offered Millie a reassuring smile that didn't quite reach her eyes. Or her heart.

Millie would lose her little companion. Fern would lose her chance to study the death ivy.

Taking a deep breath as if gathering every ounce of courage within her, Millie nodded. "Do it, then."

Fern uncorked the bottle and held the cloth over the neck

to moisten the fabric. Her hand hesitated as her mind raced. She struggled to save Eurydice yet was about to destroy Squib. How could she let the little dragon die by her hand?

*Every life has value*, she thought, as tears burned in her eyes.

Blinking them away, she drew a breath through her nose and made a silent apology to the pixie dragon. Then, with utmost care, she dabbed at Squib's ink-written scales. The magical creature looked up at them both with curious eyes. Then he craned his neck to see what Fern was doing to his body.

As she worked, the once-vibrant purple ink began to fade from Squib's hide like mist dissolving under sunlight. The little dragon's movements slowed until they ceased altogether. As Fern wiped the last part of his wing, Squib let out a sigh and...deflated. His empty hide shrivelled up until only a flat, origami shape rested on the crisp linen where there had once stood an alert, warm air-breathing pixie dragon.

Millie's fingers shook as her hands hovered over the lifeless form of Squib, her chest heaving with each laboured breath. Her gaze was a mix of disbelief and anguish as it lingered on the little creature, now flattened and inanimate on the tablecloth. Fern watched. Helpless, as her new friend's world crumbled into fragments too delicate to piece back together.

"Oh, Squib," Millie whimpered, the name barely escaping her lips before she collapsed into sobs. She gathered the origami toy to her chest as though she could breathe life back into its creased wings.

At that moment, the breakfast room door swung open to

admit a stern-looking woman dressed in a plain grey gown with a starched white apron over the top. She nodded her head to Lord Warrington.

"Excellent. Connor, take my sister to her room." He gestured to Millie, curled upon herself as she sobbed.

"Come, Mrs Carlisle. This behaviour is unseemly," the woman's voice sliced through the air like a hot knife through butter.

Millie didn't notice as she keened for the dragon in her hands.

The forbidding woman advanced on Millie with determined strides. Fern jumped to intercept her. "Leave her alone to grieve! It's normal to be upset when someone we care about dies."

Fern had to look up at the woman, who must have been at least six feet tall and as wide as a beer keg. She suspected even George would think twice before tackling her.

"Who is this...personage?" Connor's lip twitched in a sneer as she took in Fern's short hair, trousers, and dirty fingernails.

"A gardener who shouldn't be interfering in family business," Lord Warrington said.

Connor pushed past Fern and took hold of Millie's upper arm, hoisting her from the chair. The footman scuttled forwards to assist, his features twisted at the task he had to perform. Briefly, Fern wondered who he feared most—Lord Warrington or the formidable nurse.

"Come along," Connor said in a tone that brooked no argument. She prised Squib's lifeless body from Millie's fingers and tossed him to the floor.

Millie screamed and would have thrown herself upon the delicate, folded paper if not for the nurse and footman who practically dragged her from the room.

Fern swooped on Squib before he was trampled underfoot.

"You can't treat her like this!" she called out, tucking Squib inside her waistcoat.

The nurse paused at the threshold and narrowed her gaze at Fern. "I hardly think one such as *you* is in any position to tell me what I can or cannot do."

Before Fern could argue with the woman, Lord Warrington walked around the table. "You will let Connor do her job, Miss Oakby. As I expect you to do yours. You are required to oversee the vine's removal from my rose garden. Or you will, if you want any payment for the job," he snapped out.

# CHAPTER 25

ANGER BUBBLED through Fern's limbs as she teetered on the verge of telling Lord Warrington where he could shove his payment...then she decided it might be better to allow Millie time to grieve. Once Fern had dispatched the plant, she could take Squib up to the other woman's room, and they could formulate a plan for re-animating him.

Fern's attention darted between Lord Warrington and Millie, who was dragged away, leaving behind an echo of stifled sobs and a heavy silence that settled like dust after an upheaval.

"I will gather your men immediately, Lord Warrington. But before I go, who was that woman?" The figure had made icy fingers stroke down Fern's spine.

Lord Warrington brushed an invisible piece of lint from his sleeve. "That is Nurse Connor. I hired her recently to deal with Millicent's histrionics."

"Histrionics? Your sister is grieving the loss of a beloved friend." She really didn't like this man, and would find a way to thwart him. At the very least, she might be able to persuade him to let Millie visit her at Nemython House while he hosted his house party. Ambrose would certainly delight in having the woman to spoil rotten. And Fern might be able to repair the ruptures in their fledgling friendship.

"The matter is none of your concern," Lord Warrington's voice held an edge that warned against further inquiry.

Fern could, on occasion, curb her tongue. Though it took some effort. Her hands balled into fists at her sides as frustration coursed through her veins like fire. How could Lord Warrington be so callous? But arguing would not change his mind. Nor would it help Millie when Fern had another pressing task to attend to.

Instead, she turned and strode out of the breakfast room without another word. The corridor outside seemed colder. All the morning's warmth had been siphoned away by that one heartless act within the breakfast room's walls. Fern could still hear faint traces of Millie's cries echoing down the stairs.

As she emerged from the house into the yard that stretched to the stables, she stared up at the grand building, and a shudder raced over her. However luxurious its furnishing might be, if there was no comfort to be found within its walls, it was a prison for Millie.

"The heart of the story. A woman held safe by the monstrous vine until rescued from the villain," Fern whispered as she regarded the house. Pieces fell into place in her mind.

She made a silent promise to see Millie as soon as the vine was destroyed. If the other woman wrote a new story—

preferably one without a man-eating plant—on Squib using the remaining ink, the little dragon would be re-animated during the next storm. If nature could helpfully provide another that was bursting with old magic in their lifetime.

Fern marched across the yard, around the stables, and headed for the greenhouses and smaller outbuilding used by the gardeners. Moyles sat on a weathered bench, oiling a collection of shovels and shears.

The groundsman jumped to his feet as she approached. "Miss Oakby, I hope you have good news about that little dragon."

For a moment, her brain stuttered as she tried to decide which one he meant. In the end, she addressed both creatures. "Not yet. But I am hopeful that fish broth will see Eurydice on the mend. Mrs Carlisle's little friend has been returned to his origami state. Which means we can now destroy the vine without inflicting any damage upon him."

She eyed up the gardening tools laid out by the groundsman and selected a pair of long-handled shears.

"I shall rustle up the men." He walked towards the assorted sheds and yelled, "Right you lot, grab something sharp!"

Men emerged from the sheds, greenhouses, and one even popped up from behind a hedge. In total, there were seven of them, each clutching a favourite tool with a well-maintained and sharp edge. Two large wheelbarrows would be used to transport the offcuts to where the vine would be burned.

"Do you have a sprayer? We can use the remaining potion on the plant." Fern pulled the bottle from her satchel.

Moyles rubbed his chin. "That's a small container for an awfully big vine."

"We don't spray all of it, only the cut edges. This needs to come into contact with its sap. Lord Drakeman said that if we dilute it with fifteen parts of water, it will still be effective. Who among your men is quick and can spray the cuts we make?" She passed over the container.

"Turner." Moyles pointed to a young man with a wiry build. "Mix that up and bring it to the rose garden." He pressed the bottle into the man's dirty hands, and Turner strode towards one of the sheds to do as instructed.

With Moyles at her side, Fern and the assembled men marched through the manicured gardens to where the head gardener-eating plant had staked its claim on the rose garden. They were a motley crew armed with an arsenal of gardening weaponry.

As they approached the rose garden, shouts wafted over the hedges.

"That's the chaps left to guard the ivy." Moyles gripped the axe in his hands and set off at a trot.

Fern broke into a run as the shouts became more urgent, and one tapered to a scream.

As they pushed through the arch in the yew hedge that should have opened to a peaceful and beautiful garden, Fern was met by chaos. The two men tasked with guarding the vine were being driven back by an onslaught of tendrils.

The vine had become more aggressive than it had ever been. The main body writhed and thrashed. Long, thin tendrils snapped through the air like whips as they sought to reach the men leaping away from the assault. Offshoots sprouted and raced away from the wall like serpents.

"Good grief!" Moyles skidded to a halt, and the men behind nearly collided with him. "What has set it off?"

"I broke its connection to Squib. Lord Drakeman warned that there might be consequences. It appears my actions have rather upset it." Their task had just become harder, and the alchemist's words drifted through Fern's mind—that it might have been better to let Squib be destroyed alongside the monstrous ivy rather than risk disconnecting the two.

As Fern watched in horrified amazement, new growth extended from the main vine at an alarming rate. With the rapacious habit of ivy, it sought to root itself wherever it could find purchase; in the rich soil between rose bushes, digging into stone pavers, and climbing up the trellises that had once supported vibrant blooms.

"We need to dig up the off-shoots before they can take root!" Fern shouted over the commotion.

Excitement surged through her and overwhelmed the fear. Never had she dreamed that pursuing botany would one day see her leading men into battle against a sentient plant.

*Father would have been as giddy as a schoolboy, despite the danger*, Fern thought.

Moyles hefted his axe and hacked at lashing tendrils as the two men who had been guarding the ivy fought their way free. The rest of the staff spread out, each tackling a different area.

Fern charged forwards, shears extended. She snipped at a wriggling runner and severed it from the parent stem. The purple-black sap oozed from the wound. Using the closed blades, she scooped up the runner and tossed it into a wheel-barrow as another tendril lunged for her boot.

She dodged and weaved between the whip-like appendages as the groundsmen sliced and hacked through the tender stems. Woody limbs cracked as they gave way, and the wheelbarrows began to pile high with severed lengths of plant.

Yet for every runner they cut down, two more seemed to sprout up. An unending tide of green threatened to over-whelm them like a rogue wave at the beach.

Fern wondered if a better course of action would be to toss oil over the ivy and set fire to it. But that would destroy the rose garden. She could well imagine Lord Warrington's ire if she wrecked the crowning jewel of the estate just a few weeks before his planned event.

"Careful! Don't let it trap you!" Fern shouted as some offshoots retreated, shrinking back and closer to the main vine. One man nearly fell into the wall of leaves in his pursuit of the green enemy.

A strangled cry came from Fern's left. Spinning around, another groundsman fell to the stone path. A tendril wrapped around his ankle like a grasping hand. Slowly, it drew him backwards towards the vine-covered wall. A flower erupted through the dense leaves, and the petals opened and closed like the hungry mouths of baby birds waiting to be fed.

Fern's heart hammered. This was much more dangerous than deadheading a wickedly thorny rose. She darted forwards. Severed tendrils waved in the air like the tentacles of an octopus, and where the exposed ends grazed her cloth-ing, they left damp streaks of inky sap in their wake.

"Hang on!" she cried out to the ensnared man being dragged backwards.

He struggled against the sinewy grip, his face contorted with panic. He flailed around, smacking at the woody arm holding him with a shovel.

Moyles jumped forwards and brought his axe down on the thickening limb. Fern used the shears to snip off another waving bract that tried to grab the man's other ankle. The tendril recoiled, dragging its severed length.

The freed man rolled away, panting heavily as Moyles helped him to his feet.

"Are you hurt?" Fern asked.

"No." He brushed himself down, and Fern noted the fine cut to his waistcoat. The item far better than a gardener could afford, even with its mismatched patch on one side.

The rescued man retrieved his shovel, a slight tremble running through his hands and his gaze wary.

Mentally, Fern thought they were lucky that no one had been eaten or stripped of their flesh, as the wiry growth dragged their prey closer to the fat flowers. Poor Mr Corby, for all his gruff and unpleasant manner, wouldn't have had a chance as he stood alone before the ivy as he examined it during the early hours of that fateful morning.

Another shout came from behind them. Turning, Fern's gaze fell on the wheelbarrows. The offcuts were twining their bodies together to form thicker lengths.

"We need to burn it, or we will find ourselves surrounded." As much as it pained Fern to admit it, Lord Drakeman had been right about the *unintended consequences* of freeing Squib. Not that she would ever tell the rude man that.

Moyles pointed to one of his men. "Light the bonfire. Once it is going, come back for a wheelbarrow. But don't take one on your own. I want you men working in pairs at all times. Look out for one another."

The gardener, who had nearly been claimed by the vine, brushed dirt from his trousers, gave a grateful nod to Moyles, and then resumed his task.

They continued to cut, slash, and hack. The men stayed in a tight group, making sure no one was singled out by the grasping tendrils. The man who had been sent off to start the fire soon returned and tapped another fellow on the shoulder. The two of them wheeled away one barrow. One man gripping the handles, the other smacking at the writhing mass that tried to wrap around his wrists or crawl over the sides.

Fern paused momentarily to catch her breath and watched the men working in unison to contain the malicious plant life. A plume of smoke rose in the distance from the bonfire as the men threw green offcuts onto the flames.

"I'd like to see you escape that," Fern muttered under her breath.

Before her, the mass of foliage covering the wall gave a violent shudder. A low groan emanated from within the tangled mass as it pulled away from the wall. Stones clattered to the ground where its fibrous tentacles had burrowed deep into the mortar. Small skeletons of birds and rabbits littered the grass close to the base of the wall.

"What...?" Fern gasped, open-mouthed. Objectively, it really was an utterly fascinating specimen.

The once-static vine morphed before their eyes into a mobile, monstrous form. Its central trunk thickened, pushing out roots that now functioned as grotesque legs. Tendrils became nimble appendages, each one writhing with an eerie semblance of purpose.

"That's not fair and surely against the rules of nature." Suddenly, the shears in her hands didn't seem big enough when the plant was not just defending itself but attacking.

The lumbering plant flowed along the path, waving its tentacles. In size, it was enormous and larger than an elephant...one with multiple trunks all over its body and a trailing tail that whipped back and forth. It resembled an elephant-octopus hybrid with a dose of dragon and was made entirely of plant material.

"Fall back!" she called out.

Moyles blanched at the sight of the newly ambulatory vine. "Retreat! Behind the hedge!" he bellowed to his men, walking backwards with his axe raised.

Fern doubted the yew hedge would prove much of an impediment to the carnivorous plant. As the mobile *Helix mortifera* ignored a groundsman who had fallen over in his haste to get out of its way, her mind sparked with an idea. It was heading towards the house with an almost single-minded determination.

Like it had a purpose.

Or a target.

Spinning around, Fern spotted the man whom the plant had tried to drag back to the wall. "You! Where did you get that waistcoat?"

A confused look crossed his face as he stared down at the tweed item of clothing. Frowning, he met her gaze. "From his lordship. It was torn, but my Ma patched it up."

"With all respect, Miss Oakby, this isn't the time to discuss what the men are wearing," Moyles called as he waved for men to hurry through the hedge.

"When we found Mr Corby, you recognised him by his coat. A rather well-cut great coat that I believe was another cast-off from Lord Warrington." Fern struck out at a sneaky runner that tried to lay a snare for her to step into.

"Yes. Old clothes are distributed among the staff," Moyles huffed with effort.

"Don't you see? It thought they were his lordship. It's trying to rescue Mrs Carlisle from the villain." She grabbed a confused-looking Moyles by the arm. "It's after Lord Warrington. It must be able to scent him, somehow, which is why it devoured Mr Corby and then latched onto that man. They are wearing his old clothing." It was unprecedented proof of an olfactory ability in a plant if the sentient ivy could smell its intended victim. She also recalled how agitated the plant had become when his lordship was nearby. Further proof that he was the object of its desires.

Fern resisted a strong urge to stamp her foot in frustration. If only she could study the plant—under rigidly controlled circumstances, of course. Perhaps if she grew one in a pot it would be confined in size rather like Japanese bonsai. However, given how it now rolled over the rose garden like an ocean wave, Ambrose would not be impressed if it escaped and took over the house.

She jumped as a root whipped against her knee. Now wasn't the best time to get distracted with thoughts of the scholarly paper she wanted to write. "Send someone to fetch Lord Warrington urgently."

"You want to feed his lordship to...that?" Moyles let out a gasp as he glanced from the lumbering monstrosity to the stately home.

"No." Well, a little nibble might teach him a lesson, but...no. "I believe it is fixated on Lord Warrington and can somehow sense him or his clothing. Since it has so kindly detached itself from the wall, we can ask his lordship to lure it closer to the bonfire. We don't want it harming the staff if it decides to lumber through the house to reach him."

"Finch! Fetch his lordship urgently." Moyles shouted at the young man, who took off at a run, needing no encouragement to get far away from the rampaging plant.

The rest of the men had retreated as the elephant-giant octopus-ivy hybrid creature continued along the path. In its new form, it needed a much better name than *Helix mortifera*. Perhaps *Helix mortifera x elephantidae* or *helix mortifera x architeuthis*, in reference to the giant squid. The perfect scientific label for the new hybrid was something she could ponder much later when she wrote up her battle debrief.

Fern and the men set up a blockade in the archway, standing two abreast with their axes raised. The invading plant stopped when it reached the hedge and reared back. Green tentacles waved in the air (perhaps that was how it scented his lordship?) and then tapped on the dense greenery of the yew.

Tendrils pushed through the foliage of the other plant as the rampaging vine merged with the clipped hedge and passed through it to emerge on the other side.

"That really does feel like cheating," Fern said as they all leapt out of its way and retreated through the perennial beds.

"What is the delay, Miss Oakby? You said you would cut the plant down," Lord Warrington shouted as he wove his way along the gravelled paths.

"Excellent news, Lord Warrington! The vine has decided to relocate from the rose garden." Fern gestured to the mass that had coalesced on the other side of the hedge and resumed its elephant-octopus-ivy form, with numerous centipede feet formed from stubby roots.

"What the blazes?!" Lord Warrington stopped and raised one arm to point. In case Fern hadn't noticed the monstrous growth undulating through the garden. The colour drained from his face. "It's ruining my azaleas!"

# CHAPTER 26

Lord Warrington's accusatory finger swung to Fern. "This is all your fault, Miss Oakby. Sentiment for my sister and her *toy* has allowed this thing to run amok."

The limbs on the plant stilled, and then, as one, they swung in the direction of Lord Warrington's form. Leaves and petals swirled in the air as it deviated course and reached for him. The gardeners fell in around him, forming a protective guard. They wielded axes, shears, and rakes, fending off the hungry plant with desperate determination.

"It is after you, Lord Warrington. As...um...master of this estate." Fern's brain raced as fast as her feet to come up with an explanation. It might not bode well for Millie if Fern told her brother that the monstrous creation sought to eat him to end his oppressive reign. Men could be blind to their own failings and not take kindly to having them pointed out.

The vine surged forwards, its trunk-like body pulsing with an eerie, unnatural life. The groundsmen hacked at the seeking tendrils, their blades slicing through the fibrous flesh.

Inky sap oozed from the wounds, staining the ground a sickly purple-black.

"We need to lure it to the bonfire," Fern said, pointing towards the rising plume of smoke in the distance.

Lord Warrington hesitated for a moment, his pride warring with an instinct for self-preservation. Then, with a grunt of fear as a whip-like length skimmed his head, he turned and ran towards the bonfire, his coattails flapping behind him.

As they closed ranks behind his fleeing form, Fern caught sight of Turner with a metal container hung over his shoulder and a long metal pipe in his hands.

"Spray the wounds. It has to make contact with the sap." Fern pointed to where tendrils had been severed.

He nodded and darted under a flailing branch as he squirted the concoction at the open wounds. The alchemic brew sizzled as it made contact with the lifeblood of the plant.

A strangled scream came from up ahead as Lord Warrington fell to the ground.

"Oh...bollocks." Fern ran, jumping over a cluster of dahlias.

His lordship struggled with what appeared to be ropes wrapped tight around his ankles. The cunning ivy had sent runners under the ground in an attempt to cut off its prey. It was at that point Fern decided the plant might be a little too clever to try to keep in a pot for her to study. Acclaim from the horticultural society wasn't worth risking anyone in Drake's Bend being harmed. She made a mental note to burn the seedpod when she returned home.

"Turner!" she yelled as she hacked at a length of greenery. Fortunately, it had the soft consistency of fresh growth, and the shears sliced through it easily.

Turner sprayed the exposed ends, and the tendrils recoiled as though in pain. Shudders now ran over the vine creature, and its movements became erratic and sluggish as the potion seeped into open gashes.

"It's working! Keep cutting at it and applying the spray," she ordered.

Moyles swung his axe and severed the last grasping limb, trying to tighten around Lord Warrington's leg. Fern helped him to his feet. His cravat was pulled to one side, and the sleeve of his jacket ripped, although she wondered if any of the staff would wear his discarded clothing after this.

"Keep going, Lord Warrington, across the yard. It won't be able to sprout up through the cobbles." Fern shoved him in the direction of the stables and the hardened surface.

A groundsman ran on either side of the fleeing noble, lashing out with axes to lob off any greenery that got too close. A daphne that was minding its own business got an impromptu prune when Lord Warrington stumbled into it.

The monstrous vine lumbered behind them in near silence. The buds opened and closed like screaming mouths, but no sound came from them. The only noise was the slither of roots over grass or the crunch as it navigated the lime chip paths. Once they reached the yard, the going was easier, but the floral predator also found it a smoother path.

Fern noticed its movements became jerky, and at times, it paused as though disorientated. Leaves waving to locate its prey. New growth stopped sprouting, and the edges of its leaves turned a dark brown as though they died for winter. But still it continued its pursuit.

Around the side of the stables, they neared the bonfire. Heat from the flames washed over Fern's face. Turner had continued spraying the alchemical potion, but now only a dribble came from the end of the metal wand. He pushed the lever up and down with one hand, but nothing came out. The brew had been exhausted.

Lord Warrington reached the edge of the bonfire and spun around, facing the approaching monstrosity, his hands clenched into fists at his sides.

"Come on, you vile thing!" he taunted, his voice trembling slightly. "I will show you who is master here!"

The seething mass of leaves and tendrils answered his challenge and surged forwards on its woody feet. Now, the men surrounded it and redoubled their efforts. As one, the gardeners surged forwards, hacking and slicing at whatever they could reach.

Each piece they severed was tossed onto the growing fire, and bit by bit, the plant diminished before them.

"Let's give it a push." Fern gestured as Lord Warrington darted out of the way.

Rather than finally grasping its intended target, the plant found itself trapped between the fire and the groundsmen.

The men dropped their tools and yelled with the effort as they shoved with all their might. With a final, desperate creak, the vine toppled forwards like a felled oak, and its writhing body crashed into the heart of the bonfire. Flames licked along its limbs. The sap caught fire, bursting apart as purple jets shot high into the air.

They jumped back as the bonfire consumed the plant. A flaming tendril reached out, trying to escape, but then it slowly fell back into the pyre. As the mass broke apart and surrendered to the fire, the odour of rotten meat wafted in the air.

Fern held her sleeve over her mouth. That was one foul-smelling plant.

Lord Warrington drew a ragged breath and glared at Fern. "I want every part of this thing destroyed."

"Of course," she rasped, not wanting to draw too deep a breath of the smokey stench.

He huffed and strode away. No doubt to bathe, change into clean clothing, and have a stiff drink. Or given how quickly he walked, his lordship would probably reach for the brandy decanter while his bath was filling. Fern heaved a sigh at the idea of steaming hot water scented with lavender. That would have to wait until she returned home.

Methodically, they raked up every part of the vine and threw it onto the pyre. More men scraped off what remained stuck to the stone wall and wheeled it to the fire. Fern oversaw the work, and sadly, nothing remained of the Boston ivy that had once graced the rose garden.

"A complete metamorphose from one form to another, like Squib." She observed as she ran a hand over the cleared stone.

After two hours, when there was little more to do but watch the bonfire, Fern headed for the main house.

"I'm not done here yet. The heroine still needs to be rescued." She refused to leave without Millie—the heart of the story.

Closing her eyes, she recalled the route she had taken to get to Millie's room and what she had seen from the windows. The other woman resided on the first floor. Not at the front of the house with its view over the sweep of the drive and the expanse of green. Fern had glimpsed the roof of the stable and the garden beyond. She had a rough idea, but which window exactly?

Moyles had walked with her, and before they said their goodbyes, she leaned closer and spoke in a quiet tone so they weren't overheard. "Do you know which window is Mrs Carlisle's room?"

A frown pulled on his forehead as he stared at the manor. "I can't help you there, Miss Oakby. I know the grounds like the back of my hand, but I'd get lost in there beyond the servants' hall."

Blast. She needed someone who knew the house as intimately as the groundsman knew the gardens. Like a footman. One who might be sympathetic to Millie's situation.

"Thank you, Moyles. It has certainly been a memorable experience battling alongside you." She patted his shoulder.

"I'll not forget today, even if I live to be a hundred. I am certain that little dragon will thrive under your care, miss." He tugged on the brim of his hat and took his leave.

Fern walked with a slow, measured step as she approached the kitchen door while she wondered how to find her friend. She had planned to climb up the stone and lever the window open—assuming she could find the right one.

As she stood by the door, she ran a hand over the side of the house. There was no ivy to climb (not that she wanted to tangle with one for some time!), and the mortar grooves didn't offer a sufficient finger hold.

Inside, she kept out of the way while scanning the busy workers. After a few minutes, a footman entered carrying an empty tray. The same man who had alerted Millie to Fern's presence on a previous visit.

She caught his eye and gestured him over.

"Can I help you, Miss Oakby?" he asked.

"Yes. I need to see Mrs Carlisle." Fern kept her voice low in case anyone alerted Lord Warrington to her escape plan.

"That won't be possible, miss. Mrs Carlisle is unwell, and his lordship says she's not to be disturbed." He glanced around as he spoke and then looked at Fern and gave a tiny shake of his head.

*Ah! I have found an accomplice*, Fern thought.

Aloud she said, "That is a shame, as I wished to say good-bye. Perhaps you would be so kind as to show me through to Lord Warrington?"

"Of course, miss. If you'd follow me." He swept towards the dim hallway and the solid door that denoted the line between servants and family.

Fern fell into step behind him. When he held the felt-covered door open, he whispered to her, "I can take you there, but Connor is guarding her like an angry dog."

"If you can guide me to her door, I'll figure out what to do from there. I'll not have you lose your position because of me," she murmured.

Up the stairs and along a corridor, they walked in near silence. Their footsteps muffled by the thick, plush carpets. As they turned a corner, the footman halted.

"Second door on the right," he whispered before retracing his steps.

Fern proceeded alone and stopped at the door in question. She could grab the handle and try her luck, but given how Millie had been removed from the breakfast room, she strongly suspected the door would be locked. She also recalled the whispered warning that the nurse guarded the other woman.

How could she discover what was happening on the other side of the door? Fern pressed her ear against the wood, but not so much as a muffled sob or whisper leaked through.

Now what?

Glancing at the ornate brass door plate, she found her answer. Kneeling, she peered through the keyhole. Fortunately, the door was roughly in the middle of the room and not to one side. From her narrow viewpoint, Fern could just see the bed and Millie's stocking-clad feet. She was still and possibly asleep.

Movement caught her attention, and there, at the very edge of what she could see through the keyhole, was the formidable nurse sitting in a chair not far from the bed.

Blast. How to rescue a sleeping Millie out from under the nose of her guard dog?

Glancing around, Fern spied a vase of flowers on a side table down the hall. An idea struck. Moving quietly, she grabbed a few stems and stripped off the blooms. Creeping back to Millie's door, she folded the stems into thirds and then crammed them into the keyhole to jam the lock.

Standing, she rapped sharply on the door. "Nurse Connor?" she called in a timid voice, mimicking the maid who had once brought a tray to her room. "I am sorry to bother you, but his lordship is asking for you."

From inside came the scrape of a chair and footsteps. Then the rasp of metal as a key was shoved into the lock.

"Just a moment, the key won't turn," came the muffled voice accompanied by jiggling of the key.

"He said it was urgent, ma'am." Fern added a touch of panic to her voice.

"Tell him I will be there shortly," came a brisk order.

Hoping that the nurse would be busy for a few minutes, Fern hurried to the window at the end of the hall and threw it open. She uttered a quick prayer of thanks that she was wearing trousers and had climbed dozens of trees as a child. Then she clambered out the window onto the decorative ledge that ran underneath. Step by cautious step, she moved along the narrow and precarious length of stone to Millie's window.

Hoping that the Fates were on her side for once, Fern grabbed the window frame and exerted a little pressure. The sash slid upwards. With a sigh of relief, Fern pushed the window open and climbed over the sill and into the safety of the room.

The nurse had her back turned as she jiggled the key in the lock. Millie appeared to be asleep. Fern made a quick decision after spying a brass vase on the dresser. Grabbing it, she crept up behind the nurse, who still struggled with the jammed door. Raising the vase in both hands, Fern brought it down hard on the back of the woman's bent head. The nurse crumpled to the ground with only a thud as her body hit the floorboards.

Fern stared at the prone figure, then at the vase. "Well, that was surprisingly easy."

Putting the vase on the ground, she grabbed hold of the nurse's arms and dragged her limp form closer to the bed. Casting around, Fern pulled the tie from a silk robe hanging on a nearby chair. Using the soft length of fabric, she bound the nurse's hands together around one of the sturdy wooden legs of the large four-poster bed.

Once satisfied the woman was securely restrained, Fern straightened and turned to the occupant of the bed. Millie lay oblivious to what had just transpired in her room. Fern hurried over and gently shook her friend's shoulder. "Millie, I need you to wake up. We don't have much time."

Millie's eyes fluttered open. She stared up at Fern in confusion. "Wha...what is...happening?" The words were awkwardly formed as if her tongue was too thick for her mouth.

"I'm going to take you away from here. But we must go now before your guard wakes up." Fern pointed to the uncon-scious woman propped up by the corner of the bed.

Millie rolled over and waved her away. "No. Want...to sleep."

Bother.

Fern tried to think of another plan. That was when her gaze caught on the small blue bottle that had rolled from the nurse's apron pocket when she had dragged her from the door.

Snatching it up, she read the label. "Laudanum."

No wonder Millie wanted to sleep. The *tonic* her brother insisted the nurse administer was a potent sleeping draft. She tucked the bottle into her pocket and shook Millie's shoulder again. "Millie, I know you're sleepy, but you must get up. Your story hasn't reached its end. The heroine has to escape."

Millie blinked up at Fern, eyes glazed. "Escape? Where to?"

"Somewhere safe, where your brother can't control you anymore. A place where you will be able to write as many stories as you want. But we must go *now*." Fern eased Millie upright.

Millie leaned heavily against Fern, head lolling. "Oh, Fern. I don't think I can walk. Connor made me drink that horrid tonic, and my limbs feel leaden."

Fern wrapped an arm around Millie's waist and helped her to sit upright. "You don't have to do this alone. We'll do it together."

Fortunately, Millie's soft shoes were by the bed, and Fern slid them onto her feet as though she dressed a large child. Next, Fern selected a shawl and wrapped it around the other woman.

"One last thing to do." Grabbing a hatpin from the dresser, Fern removed the key from the lock. With the long and sharp pin, she poked the bits of stems out so she could unlock the door.

With her arm around Millie's middle and Millie's arm over her shoulders, Fern lifted the other woman to her feet. Step by agonising step, they made their way to the door. Fern eased it open and peered out. The hallway was empty. She manoeuvred Millie through the door and closed it softly behind them.

Fern locked the door and tossed the key into a vase. That

would slow down the nurse if she managed to untie herself. Slowly, the two women made their way along the corridor and down the stairs. Fern couldn't risk the servants' stairs as they were too narrow and steep, and she worried about Millie falling. But the main stairs ran the chance of discovery.

They had almost reached the bottom step, and Fern was about to congratulate herself on a job well done when a booted heel rang out on the tiles.

Lord Warrington strode from his study and stood at the bottom of the stairs with his arms crossed. "Just where do you think you are taking my sister, Miss Oakby?"

# CHAPTER 27

Lord Warrington glared at Fern. "Millicent is ill, and you will return her to her bedroom at once."

Fern eased Millie down the last step and draped her arms around the newel post. Then she faced Lord Warrington. "She is not sick! Your horrid nurse has forced laudanum down her throat to render her senseless."

The lord huffed and crossed his arms. "Millicent was hysterical. It was for her own good."

"Hysterical?" Fern took a step closer and curled her hands into fists. "All she did was speak up for herself about your horrendous treatment of her. Men label women hysterical when we dare speak our minds and refuse to be treated like chattels...or cattle."

"Why look. You're the one being hysterical now, Miss Oakby." A smug smile sat on his lips, and Fern longed to wipe it away.

Why exactly did she save him from the rampaging vine?

She drew a deep breath through her nostrils to control her rising temper. "The greatest lie perpetrated in history is by men telling women we are the hysterical ones. Men lash out in anger. Men have no ability to moderate their emotions. Men conduct wars. Why, I have seen *hysterical* men start brawls over a spilt beer. Yet you stand together and call such behaviour manly. But if a woman dares venture a differing opinion, she is hysterical and whisked off to Bedlam."

"Yes, well, as enlightening as this all is, my sister will be taken back to her room. Now, be off with you and don't come back. Frankly, I am reconsidering if I shall even pay you since this entire debacle has been your fault." He gestured to the footmen standing by the door.

Not pay her? Cold fury rolled through her veins.

Then, Fern smiled. A wicked grin of someone holding the trump card.

"You will pay me and let me leave here with your sister. Two days ago, I took a seedpod from the death ivy when we collected the samples. As I strolled your grounds, I buried the seeds on your estate."

Lord Warrington rocked back on his heels, and his eyes widened. "You will remove every last trace of that heinous plant at once, or I'll have you arrested!"

"Arrested for what? Gardening? That seed pod contained twenty seeds. Even now, they are soaking up the warmth of the sun and the overnight dew. Who knows when they will erupt from the soil throughout your garden. It probably won't even need a storm. They could be anywhere. Even right under your study window. Quietly germinating. Waiting." Fern locked gazes with him and refused to be intimidated.

The lord's face flushed red and white as he alternated between rage and sickening fear. No doubt imagining the horror that would be unleashed upon his estate and his person. "You will dig them up. Now," he hissed between clenched teeth.

"No." She enunciated the word slowly and clearly. Enjoying the look of shock at being refused that flashed over his features. "Not only will you allow me to leave with Mrs Carlisle, but you will instruct a maid to pack her things into a trunk. When we are both in the cart, and I have my fee, I will tell Mr Moyles where I planted the seeds. One word of botanical advice: make sure you throw the seeds in the fire, should your men find them."

"You're bluffing." He blocked her way when she sought to return to Millie, now being held up by a footman.

Without looking away from his furious gaze, Fern reached into her pocket. Her fingers found the kelmsgale seedpod, which looked a little like the one sprouted by the carnivorous plant. Not that the noble would know the difference anyway. It had been squashed during the battle and spurted out the seeds all over the lining of her pocket.

Fern pulled out the empty casing and held it up. "Look for yourself. The seeds are gone. Ask Moyles if you do not believe me. He saw me knock the pod free with a rake and take it with me."

Lord Warrington blanched and ground his jaw. He addressed one footman while staring at Fern. "Find a maid. Have her collect a few things for Mrs Carlisle, and be quick about it, man."

Fern skirted around the angry lord and took Millie's arm.

"I'll take Mrs Carlisle. You make sure she has a few changes of clothes, please," she said to the footman. "Oh, and you'll need a spare key for the door."

Then she grinned at Lord Warrington. "Send a man out with my payment. It's been a pleasure doing business with you, your lordship. I'm sure you'll understand that I will never return to this estate."

Slowly, the two women made their way through the house and out to the stables. The cart that George had insisted Fern take sat to one side. The solid cob stood in the tracts, waiting to take her home. With the help of a groom, they lifted Millie onto the seat. The drugged woman slumped, and Fern worried she would tumble to the ground.

Before too long, a maid hurried out the kitchen door carrying a carpetbag. Behind her, the young footman dragged a trunk. The luggage went into the back of the cart.

"I squeezed in as much as I could," the maid said in a breathless tone. The poor thing had obviously worked as fast as she could.

Fern laid a hand on the footman's sleeve. "Thank you."

He nodded. "I wish Mrs Carlisle well. She is much liked by the staff." Then he reached into his pocket, withdrew a folded sheet of paper, and pressed it into Fern's hand. Peeking inside, she saw sufficient bank notes to ensure she wouldn't ever return.

Fern climbed onto the seat beside Millie. Her friend leaned against her. From a parlour window, Lord Warrington watched.

"Moyles!" Fern yelled out, hoping he was nearby.

The groundsman hurried from around the side of the stables. "Yes, Miss Oakby?"

When he was close enough for a whispered conversation, Fern told him of the slight deception she had played upon his lordship in order to free his sister. "After I am gone, could you take a handful of lemon pips or pomegranate seeds and make a show of digging them up, please? You will need twenty in all. Lord Warrington thinks I planted seeds from the carnivorous vine around the estate and that I am telling you where to find them."

The groundsman rubbed his chin and chuckled. "I can do that for you, miss."

"I would suggest you throw them into the fire before he can ask for them or examine them too closely. Oh, and if you could find one under his study window while he can see you, that would be much appreciated." She was grateful for the assistance of the staff like Moyles and the footman. Without them, Millie's story might have had quite a different ending.

He tugged his cap, and Fern took up the reins and clucked her tongue at the horse. They made the return trip as fast as possible with the rotund horse and cart, worrying that Millie would bounce off the side. By the time Fern turned the cob into their drive, Millie was asleep in her lap.

George and Ambrose rushed out to greet her.

"Another house guest?" Ambrose said on seeing the woman collapsed over Fern.

"Yes. This is Mrs Carlisle, and I have helped her escape her horrid brother. She's been dosed up with laudanum." Fern gently eased herself out from under Millie and let the woman recline on the seat.

"The yellow guest room, if you wouldn't mind, please, George." Ambrose pointed from the slumbering woman to the house.

Wordlessly. George scooped Millie up into his arms.

"I'll be in shortly. I need to check on Eurydice first." Fern led the horse towards the stables, where William rushed out to take over and unharness the cart.

Fern shoved her hands into the deep pockets of her coat as she walked the wide aisle to the end stall.

"Ew." She had forgotten about the squashed seed pod. She pulled her hand out, and the black seeds were stuck to her fingers.

The little dragon was tucked up in a blanket, and Fern knelt beside her in the hay as she pulled a seed from her finger.

Eurydice's nostrils flared, and she lifted her head. Before Fern could scrape the seed off, a silver-blue tongue flicked out and caught it. The dragon cracked open her eyes and licked all of Fern's hand and palm with a vigour she had not seen in the creature before.

"I'm not sure that's good for you," Fern said.

She had never heard of dragons eating kelmsgale seeds. Certainly, people didn't eat them. The seeds were as hard as metal shot, and many a person had broken a tooth by biting on one. "But I am glad to see you are much revived."

It must have been the fish broth. Then, following a whispered instinct, Fern stuck her hand back in the coat pocket and used her nails to gather up spilt seeds mixed with lint from the lining. The dragon gobbled the horrid mix up, and she nearly lost a finger. "You are hungry. I shall see if any fish is left over for you."

Back inside, Fern left her coat in the kitchen and climbed the stairs. George had laid Millie out on the bed in a room decorated with a pale yellow-and-cream wallpaper. Ambrose fussed and draped a blanket over their guest. Fern pulled a crumpled origami figure from inside her waistcoat.

Approaching the bed, she lifted one of Millie's hands and tucked Squib underneath. "I'm sorry. Truly I am," she whispered as she placed the other woman's hand over the flattened body.

"I'll leave her trunk in the kitchen and bring it up when she is awake," George said when they were out in the hall.

"I'm going to pay a quick visit to the trio and tell them what happened. I'll be back for dinner." Fern trotted down the stairs and out the front door.

Across the river, Decima opened the door after the first knock. "You look a complete fright. Come in and tell us everything."

Fern hugged each old woman before dropping to the cushion with a sigh. Nona poured a fragrant cup of tea, and clutching it between her hands, Fern told her story.

"Mrs Carlisle wanted to escape her brother," she explained. "The vine was seeking him out so she could be free."

"You found the heart of the story." Morda nodded in satisfaction. "We have a gift for Mrs Carlisle. Decima, could you find it, please?" She gestured to her older sister.

Decima approached a shelf and searched among the

many strange objects. "Ah. Here it is." She held aloft a long feather. While at first it appeared black, it shimmered with deep green-and-purple hues.

Fern rose and took the feather. "It's from a raven?"

"Yes," Morda said from her chair. "Tell your friend she must write a new tale if you wish to resurrect her paper friend. A storm will come within the next sennight."

"But you said that storm was an incredibly rare event, and it's been decades since the last one. How can there possibly be another so soon?" Fern twirled the feather between her fingers.

Morda chuckled. "Sometimes, two rare things are found close together. Or perhaps nature wishes to address an imbalance."

Later that night, after they had a quiet dinner, Millie roused and joined them in the parlour. She curled up on the sofa by the fire and seemed lost in her thoughts as she held Squib. Fern fetched the little cut-crystal bottle from her study. When she returned, Millie had risen from the sofa and knelt before the fire, holding out the origami figure like an offering.

"Don't!" Fern called out.

"Bertie was right. It is just a silly toy." Her eyes were red from crying.

"No. Squib was an amazing and magical creature brought to life by your imagination. You can't give up. I promised you that we had the hope of restoring him." Fern sat on the rug beside Millie.

Millie let out a sad sigh. "What is the point? You said that a storm such as the one that brought him to life might not reoccur for decades."

"Or, there might be one within the next few days." Fern stroked Squib, now made of blank pages.

Millie frowned. "If that happened, then it wouldn't be rare."

"Two rare things might be found close together." Fern repeated what Morda had said to her. "There might not be another for thirty years, or there might be one soon. I think we should be prepared for when it does happen, don't you?" Fern produced the raven feather quill from behind her back and the remains of the Stormborne Serum. "There isn't much ink left, so you will have to make every word count. And please, no stories about overprotective vines."

Millie's face transformed as she grabbed the tendril of hope and wiped away the traces of her tears. She reached for the feather and twirled it before the light. "This is a beauty. What stories I could tell with such a quill."

"Let's make a space for the author to work." Ambrose cleared off the table.

George fetched a tray with hot chocolate. Then Millie laid out the paper dragon and unscrewed the ink. She stared at the wrinkled paper with a bowed head. After a silent minute or two, she tilted the bottle and dipped the quill into the little bit of ink that pooled in a corner. Then she began to write.

They left her to craft a story that would unfold over Squib's surfaces. Fern watched her uncles play backgammon, pointing out moves to Ambrose and making George scowl.

When Millie had finished, she held Squib behind her back. "I am going to place him by my bed and pray to whatever fates control the weather that you are right."

THREE NIGHTS LATER, just as Morda foretold, there was a fierce storm.

IF YOU ARE curious about Fern's disastrous debut in London, you can find that tale in the exclusive novella THE MIDNIGHT VIOLETS available when you subscribe to my newsletter.

https://BookHip.com/FAZQVBS

Fᴇʀɴ ᴡɪʟʟ ʙᴇ ʙᴀᴄᴋ with another botanical mystery in book 2, THE TATTLING WHISPERWOODS.

## *Words have power, and secrets can kill...*

The village of Drake's Bend has long been guardian of a sacred grove where ancient trees offer gentle counsel to those who dare share their secrets. For centuries, this delicate balance between confession and wisdom has been maintained.

Until now.

The whisperwoods have turned venomous. The trees sharpen sacred confidences into devastating weapons of betrayal, threatening to tear the local community apart. Old friendships are being torn apart, and villagers fall ill with a mysterious sickness. But the whisperwoods hold still darker secrets that are twisted and spread to the highest reaches of London society. The old sentinels could be lost forever as the call to silence them grows louder.

Fern must uncover the truth behind what poisons both trees and people before time runs out and lives are ruined. The ancient sentinels are the last of their kind, and their loss would forever silence a magic as old as Britain itself. But in the race to save both grove and villagers, Fern discovers that some secrets were meant to stay buried—and awakening them could destroy everything she holds dear.

Hᴛᴛᴘꜱ://ᴛɪʟʟʏᴡᴀʟʟᴀᴄᴇ.ᴄᴏᴍ/ʙᴏᴏᴋꜱ/ʟᴇᴀꜰ-ᴀɴᴅ-ꜱᴄᴀʟᴇ/
ᴛʜᴇ-ᴛᴀᴛᴛʟɪɴɢ-ᴡʜɪꜱᴘᴇʀᴡᴏᴏᴅꜱ/

# ALSO BY TILLY WALLACE

For the most complete and up to date list of books, please visit the
website: https://tillywallace.com/books/

Available series:

**Tournament of Shadows**

**Manner and Monsters**

**Highland Wolves**

**Grace Designs Mysteries**

**Magic of Wyldefen**

**Leaf and Scale**

# ABOUT THE AUTHOR

Tilly drinks entirely too much coffee and is obsessed with hats. In her spare time she writes whimsical historical fantasy novels, set in a bygone time where magic is real. If you love found family and comfort reads, come and escape reality in her tales.

**Email:** tilly@tillywallace.com
**Web:** https://www.tillywallace.com
**STORE:** https://www.tillywallacebooks.com

If you would like to support Tilly for as little as a coffee a month, her *Caffeination Crew* read early chapters of her current work, vote on story ideas, and read exclusive short stories and novellas. You can find more information at: https://www.patreon.com/TillyWallace

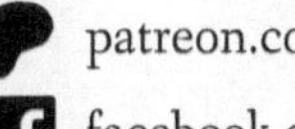 patreon.com/TillyWallace
 facebook.com/tillywallaceauthor
 instagram.com/tillywallaceauthor

www.ingramcontent.com/pod-product-compliance
Lightning Source LLC
Chambersburg PA
CBHW031250120726
47906CB00003B/677